SHARK'S *Rise*

SHARK'S EDGE: BOOK THREE

ANGEL PAYNE & VICTORIA BLUE

This book is an original publication of Waterhouse Press.

This is a work of fiction. Names, characters, places, and incidents either are the product of the author's imagination or are used fictitiously, and any resemblance to actual persons, living or dead, business establishments, events, or locales is entirely coincidental. The publisher does not assume any responsibility for third-party websites or their content.

Cover Design by Waterhouse Press
Cover Photographs: Shutterstock

Paperback ISBN: 978-1-64263-153-1

SHARK'S *Rise*

SHARK'S EDGE: BOOK THREE

ANGEL PAYNE & VICTORIA BLUE

David—after 25 years—still just another lover,
the Shark attack! (get back, don't fight it)

Thank you for the support,
encouragement, and enduring love.

—Victoria

For the two dolphins in my world
who keep showing me the magic of it all:

Tom and Jessica, you are the stuff
that makes my heart beat and my hope rise.

—Angel

CHAPTER ONE

ABBIGAIL

"This is medium rare, but I'd be happy to put it back on the grill if you'd like it ruined." Elijah grinned while placing a plate in front of me. A luscious tri-tip steak held pride of placement between a baked potato and roasted Brussels sprouts. I stared at the food petulantly, then transferred the look to him.

"Not even a thank you?" He raised a dark brow while looking at me with disappointment. "I'm surprised Sebastian tolerates such ill-mannered behavior."

I grimaced. For a second. He wasn't wrong. I had been terribly rude to the guy since we'd arrived at the safe house four days and three nights ago. But nothing had changed about my truth. I didn't want to be here in the first place. I didn't care how many cool bells and whistles this complex had or how thoroughly Sebastian believed he was doing the right thing in sending me here.

Because in the end, this whole stunt only felt like one thing.

Banishment.

An opinion I'd made abundantly clear as Elijah dragged me from Sebastian's office.

And yes, intellectually, I knew their plan made sense.

Understood it was for my own safety. But it didn't mean I had to like it. Didn't mean I had to be pleasant about it. And if Elijah thought we would spend this time getting to know one another better and becoming friends, he could think again. I had no plans of changing my attitude or becoming more agreeable or more cooperative anytime soon.

I pushed my plate toward the center of the table. "I'm not hungry. I'll be in my room." I pushed back, stood, and turned toward the large living room. Through the sprawling space with its leather couches and inviting décor, I could access the wide hallway that led to the bedrooms.

While I hadn't done much exploring, I knew the house was an open-concept ranch-style estate. The bedroom I was using was located at the end of a hallway with at least six other doors along the corridor before mine on the right. The hall concluded at a set of French doors that opened to a stunning backyard with a waterfall-fed pool. Other elements I'd seen but not explored were a koi pond, a rose garden, a shuffleboard court, and a poolside villa with an awning-covered ping-pong table. A small staff bustled around the home at all hours but gave me plenty of privacy, though one of them always seemed to emerge precisely when I needed something.

"Abbigail." Elijah's commanding tone of voice stopped me in my tracks, although I didn't turn to face him. "You need to eat. Come back to the table. Now."

"No," I replied through gritted teeth. "I said I'm not hungry. Thank you, though."

I was sure if he were standing closer to me, he would hear how my fury had my heart thudding in my chest.

"Don't turn this into a battle of wills," the man warned. "You won't win."

Slowly, I turned to face him. I tilted my head. "Do you really think I see this as a game?"

He relaxed his stiff posture. "Frankly, I don't know what to think. It's been the better part of a week, and you haven't had more than a bowl of cereal. I gave my best friend my word that I would take care of his woman. Right now, I'm not doing a very good job."

Lifting my chin in realization, I said, "Now it's making more sense. This is actually about you. I'll tell you what, Mr. Banks. I hereby release you of your duties and your misplaced heroism."

"My God, you're a handful," he said, rubbing his forehead. "I'd have spanked your ass red by now."

The last part was more to himself, but I still heard the comment. Great! Now all I could think of was Sebastian doing those exact carnal things. My lonely imagination—and pussy—were taking over rational thought. Now I was hungry, still not for food, so I pulled my cell phone out of my back pocket to check my messages as a distraction. My *lack* of messages would be a more accurate statement. I'd averaged about five texts back and forth with Sebastian each day since I'd arrived at the safe house. And, despite his promises that he'd visit a day or two after Elijah moved me in here, I still hadn't seen him. My understanding and patience were wearing dangerously thin.

My stomach ached from my jangled nerves as I pushed through the door to my sanctuary. Quickly, I closed and locked it behind me. The space was apparently the master bedroom suite. It was decorated as beautifully as the rest of the home and at least provided a peaceful, calming place in which to hide out. The color scheme was dominated by the darkest navy blue I'd ever seen. At times, I couldn't tell if it was blue or black. Cream and khaki accented the dark shade and lent a casual vibe to the regal blue. I'd instantly fallen in love with the hideout—if there was anything to "love" about this place at all.

The room even had a window seat, and it was large enough for two people to snuggle up in. A thick upholstered cushion ran beneath the abundant pillows and cozy throw blanket. It was a perfect book-lover's escape.

According to my phone's GPS, we were in Twentynine Palms, California. After the emotional turmoil in Sebastian's office the day I left—correction: the day I was extracted from—Los Angeles, Bas's driver, Joel, brought Elijah and me to this estate in the Mohave Desert. I had exhausted myself with a tear-filled breakdown, followed by a fit of rage, wrapped up by shamelessly pleading for my freedom. My dramatics ended with Elijah handing me a monogrammed handkerchief from his suit's inside breast pocket before eyeing me like a grenade with its pin pulled.

In the end, I'd fallen asleep against the limo's window, lulled by the mindlessness of counting red cars as they passed by on the far side of the freeway. It was a silly game my brothers and I had played as kids during family road trips. It made the long hours pass a bit quicker while confined with my rambunctious siblings. At that moment, when everything else felt like it was turning upside down, the game gave me some familiarity and safety.

Neither of which I felt anymore. Not by a long shot.

Maybe if I asked nicely, Elijah would let me call Rio. I was worried sick that things were falling apart at Abstract. If I could check in on the business, it would help settle my nerves.

I hurried back out into the hall. Once there, I spotted my

jailer out by the pool. I took a chance that the French doors were unlocked. To my surprise, the handle turned freely. I hadn't been outdoors since I'd gotten here, and the warmth of the sun on my skin brought tears to my eyes. It was a melodramatic reaction, but my emotions were like a swollen river after a storm. I was the damn Rio Grande, ready to crest over every situational bank and shoreline.

But this bullshit had to stop. Soon. Something already told me that my tears wouldn't carry the same weight with Elijah as they did with his friend, the MIA Mr. Shark.

I stepped in front of the lounge chair he lazed on, blocking the sun from his face and ensuring I had his attention. As soon as he looked up, I asked without preamble, "May I use the phone?" Through gritted teeth, I added, "Please."

"Not until you eat something," he answered without opening his eyes. "It's a fair trade."

"I told you I'm not hungry." My stomach actually pitched at the thought of eating.

"And I told you, I'm responsible for your well-being. You need to eat something."

"Let me make the call first."

"No."

"Elijah! Damn it!" I shifted from one foot to the other, deciding how far to go with an explanation. "I'm not feeling well," I began. "I'm assuming it's stress, and I think if I talk to my business partner, some of that will be alleviated. Then maybe I will feel more like eating. I would like to make the phone call first." I explained it with barely veiled frustration—and then dawning recognition. "And why do you have cell service here while I don't?"

"Your carrier must not service this area." He shrugged as

if the answer was obvious.

"That's not true. I looked online"—I *was* able to do that, thanks to the Wi-Fi in the house—"and I should have a cell signal here. Something's wrong with my phone. I need to go to a store and have it looked at. Can you take me? Or loan me a car so I can do it myself?"

"You can use my phone to call Grant. We'll worry about the rest when Sebastian gets here."

I frowned. Deeply. For some reason, I sensed he wasn't being honest about this. About all of it or some of it, I had no idea—but my bullshit meter, honed by years of dealing with every crooked food-supplier in Los Angeles, was crackling like an out-of-control Geiger counter.

"I don't want to talk to Grant," I told him. "I want to talk to Rio Gibson, my business partner."

"Grant is with Rio," he explained while already dialing. "He can put her on the line."

I took his actions as progress—until, as the call connected, he stood and walked away from me a few feet. Despite how I tried to linger close by, he continued the conversation at a volume next to a whisper, ensuring I couldn't make out a word of the conversation. Finally, Elijah turned back to me. With a couple of efficient steps, he closed the space between us.

"Is she there now?" he asked his friend with a grin. "Oh, I can just imagine. If it's anything like what I'm dealing with . . ."

He cut in on himself with a long laugh. The full, hearty sound had me imagining all the mischief my sister-in-law was probably committing upon Sebastian's best friend, the equally bossy Grant, as he hung around our Inglewood prep kitchen.

"Let me talk to her." I held my hand out expectantly, and Elijah gave me a reproachful look. Clearly these three men had all attended the same "Dominants Do It Better" correspondence course. I rolled my eyes just to piss him off and gesticulated more aggressively for the phone.

Finally—thank God—he gave in. As soon as Elijah gave me his phone, I began walking away from him.

"Stay. Here."

"I'd like some privacy," I snapped back.

"This is the only place there is a signal. You'll drop the call if you wander too far."

"Then would you mind?"

"Not at all," he said with that grin he always wore. He settled back into the lounge chair, clearly having no intention of relocating.

"Asshole," I mumbled before catching Rio's groan on the other end of the phone line.

"So I'm not the only one having my patience tried? I guess there's some comfort in that, at least," she muttered from her end of the call.

Despite her grousing, I relaxed immediately when hearing her voice. "Hey, sister. What's going on?"

"I think I should be asking you that, no? How much longer am I going to have to put up with this one here? I want you to be safe, Abs, more than anything, but this guy is pushing every single button I have and others I didn't even know I had, too." She laughed, but there was still a bit of tension underneath the sound. Okay, maybe more than a bit.

"At least he's not hard on the eyes, right?" I offered in the way of consolation.

"Mmmph." Her sound wasn't an opinion either way. "That wasn't exactly answering my question."

"I know," I soothed. "And I wish I had a better answer for

you, but I haven't even seen Bas since I've been here." I dared to take a few tiny steps away from Elijah. The signal strength on the call remained strong. I almost glowered at the back of his head but decided not to waste the time. I wouldn't put it past the guy to feed me a line just to keep me within earshot so he could monitor the call.

Asshole.

I managed to keep the insult to myself this time. Rio's comforting croon helped with the effort. "I'm so sorry, Abs," she said. "I know that has to be tough on you. Is the place nice at least?"

I laughed. "What do you think?" Barely waiting two seconds before going on. "I don't think Bas knows how to anything but over-the-top extravagant."

"Well, if one must be held against their will . . ."

When spoken out loud, those words sounded so much worse than they should have, prompting me to respond. "I know I shouldn't be complaining. In my head, I understand all this is for my own good . . ."

"But?" Rio filled in the word I'd already intimated.

"I . . . well, I just haven't been feeling well."

"Gee, not like you haven't been under juuust a bit of stress lately or anything."

"Tell me what's going on there. I think it will help ease my mind. How are the orders going? Is the website still busy? You got everything handled? Not too overwhelmed?"

Her reply was accompanied by background noises from the kitchen, which were more soothing than I expected. "Strangely, everything has been running smoothly," she filled in. "Although this guy is annoying as hell, he's a very hard worker and actually knows his way around a kitchen. I guess that's why they sent him here." Her pause was thick with a contemplative subtext. "And likely why Elijah's with you, yes?"

"I doubt that." I felt comfortable muttering it, having carefully stepped my way at least ten feet away from him now.

"What do you mean?"

"Well, Elijah is the security guy. The private investigator. Right now, and right here, the concern is more about my safety than about Abstract."

"And you're not feeling good about that."

I shrugged. It was a good substitute for losing my shit altogether. "I can't 'feel' one way or the other about it, Rio," I admitted with sincerity. "All I know is that Sebastian isn't leaving any stone unturned—and because I love him and trust him, that means going along with this plan. It also means that the main thrust of the focus is here, on me. Although I know for a fact that he's also ordered eyes on you, Sean, my dad, and the rest of the guys."

"The . . . guys?" Rio prodded. "Your brothers?"

"Are there other 'guys' I don't know about?" My snark was probably unnecessary, but dear God, it felt good to have someone who actually understood it—and me. "Anyhow, just in case Grant hasn't filled you in on all that already, I wanted you to know. You're not in danger. Sebastian won't let anything happen to anyone in the family. He's promised me. And I truly believe him."

At least I did about that part of things.

His promise to come here and actually see me, on the other hand . . .

Rio's chuckle broke me out of my sulk. "Ohhh, sister. Do you think I've ever felt in peril with your brother around?"

"No," I laughed out. "I guess not. But you've never had

Sebastian Shark in your life before now, either." I cleared my throat while pacing a little faster. "So how are you handling the lunch orders? You're making the deliveries, I'm guessing?"

"Yep. No worries, Abs. I got this. I promise."

I bit my lower lip. "So... what's happened when you've delivered to Viktor? Has he asked where I am?"

"Oh, you know he has. Now that I know more about him, he totally creeps me out. But I told him exactly what Grant told me to say. That you're visiting a sick family member back east. He said to let you know he was sending his well wishes and if he can help you in any way, do not hesitate to reach out. Blah, blah, blah." She laughed, and I could picture her rolling her eyes while saying it, making me snicker too.

It felt so good. Damn good. To finally relax a bit... if only for a few minutes...

"Times up," said a deep voice right behind me, making me yip as I whirled around on Elijah. He held out his hand for me to give the phone back. "Tell Grant to get back on the line."

"I'm not finished talking yet. I'll let you know when I am." I turned my back to him and gritted my teeth instead of punching him in the face.

"Holy shit. All of them have this bossy bullshit down to a science, don't they?" Rio asked me with a giggle.

"Oh, shit, you don't even know. I think they must jerk each other off with it."

And just like that, the phone was plucked from my hand. I was left gaping at my empty palm. Elijah only raised his eyebrow while I spluttered to say something.

"Mrs. Gibson? Please put Mr. Twombley back on the line. Yes, thank you." More of the silky-smooth voice. Crap, he was even being kind and considerate with Rio. I narrowed my eyes as he waited for a moment, presumably while Grant came to the phone. There was a slight-yet-annoying smirk on his lips.

"Hey, man," he murmured, presumably to Grant. "Give me one second." He covered the phone with his broad palm. "If you'll excuse me, Abbigail, I have to take this call." He gestured to the phone with his chin.

I'd been dismissed.

And was furious about it.

While my follow-up action wouldn't be considered my most mature moment, I'd had all I could take of his smug attitude. I decided to hit the bastard where it hurt. Without giving my moves a ton of thought, I detoured right to the lounge chair he had been occupying and scooped up his book, shirt, and shoes. Yes, the shoes he'd likely spent a few thousand dollars on. I didn't know everything about Elijah, but the man's high-end shoe habit was damn near legend. I'd heard Bas and Grant tease him about it on more than one occasion.

I swung around and threw the whole bundle into the pool with so much force, they splashed like cannonballs.

"Abbigail!"

I kept on walking as though he hadn't bellowed my name like calling a hit on me from the hounds of hell. If that was the case, let the dogs come. I was over his bullshit, and if Sebastian didn't come here or call soon, I was packing my lone suitcase and leaving.

Safety be damned.

Though my belly seemed determined to have the last laugh tonight.

Talking to Rio didn't do much for my stress level or my nauseated stomach, especially after the altercation with Elijah. I took a long bath in the opulent bathroom attached to my bedroom, and that worked better than anything else had. I found some lavender bath salts in a jar on the countertop, and I refilled the tub with more hot water twice, not wanting to get out and face reality.

I'd kept my bedroom door locked, and a handwritten note had been slipped underneath the portal while I was in the tub.

You owe me a meal.

Well, shit.

He was right.

And I wouldn't go back on my word, supplying him with that ammunition too. Besides, my stomach was finally settled for the first time since I'd arrived. I was just happy the lavender aromatherapy had worked its magic in more ways than just calming my nerves.

I pulled on a pair of burgundy pajamas and headed out to the kitchen. The house was quieter than usual, if that was possible. I would typically encounter a staff member in a hallway or in the kitchen, at the very least.

I found a note from Elijah on the enormous commercial-grade refrigerator.

There are two different options for you. One is in the warming drawer of the oven, and one is in the refrigerator. I wasn't sure what you would be hungry for and knew your stomach has been bothering you. Whatever you choose, eat everything on your plate.

"Jesus Christ," I muttered. Even his notes were bossy. I rolled my eyes and went for the refrigerator option first, realizing I was smiling. Elijah was an asshole, but he had taken the time to make sure I had some menu choices. I would give him props on this one; he was really trying to take care of me.

For Sebastian.

I knew their relationship went back a long way, nearly as along as Bas had known Grant. But there was something more intrinsic about the dynamics my man shared with Elijah Banks. Something more complicated. Something . . . heavier.

Whatever the reasoning was, I was starting to recognize the truth. Elijah didn't want to piss off or disappoint Sebastian. Whatever the motivation was, he had definitely gone the extra step with the meal offerings.

In the refrigerator, I found a fruit and yogurt parfait. Beside the cut glass bowl of mixed fruit was a smaller matching bowl filled with granola to mix in when I was ready to eat. That way the topping stayed crunchy. So thoughtful, Mr. Banks . . .

Curiosity had me checking the warming drawer, though the parfait sounded perfect. In the oven, I found a small, one-serving casserole dish filled with baked ziti. The cheesy pasta was perfectly golden brown and crusty on the top. A piece of French bread, drizzled with butter and garlic perfection, sat on the tray beside it.

There was an oven mitt waiting to be used on the countertop beside the appliance, so I pulled the tray from the oven and rested it on the stovetop. After studying the knobs for a moment, I figured out how to turn off the warming drawer. That led me to the dilemma of glancing back and forth between my two options. If I had to finish the whole thing, I stood a better chance with the yogurt. All the carbs in the pasta would have me sleeping halfway through the meal. While it looked delicious, someone else was going to have to enjoy that Italian feast.

About two-thirds of the way through the yogurt and fruit, I had to tap out. I was so full, I felt like I was going to explode. Because I hadn't had a proper meal in so many days, I just couldn't handle more in one sitting. Of course, my keeper chose that exact moment to saunter into the kitchen. Elijah was fresh from a workout, judging by his clothing and sweaty condition.

"Thank you for this." I motioned to the food in front of me and then over to the counter where the pasta sat. "Are you hungry? I can heat that up for you." I made the offer in heartfelt kindness, seeking to repay his gesture.

He waved a dismissive hand. "I can do it. Don't want to interrupt your meal. After all, I see you haven't finished yet." He raised a brow, looking at what was still left in my bowl. "I'll warm this up while you keep working."

"Elijah." I dropped my spoon, making a loud clatter. "I can't eat another bite."

"Abbigail." He extended the last syllable like a reproaching teacher. "We had a deal."

"And I'm not reneging. I'm just so full. I'm finally feeling better than I have in days, and I don't want to get sick from forcing more down." At his hard stare, I just resorted to begging. "Please."

He didn't surrender an inch of his scowl. His veiny biceps contracted as he stared at me.

Jesus H. Christ.

But I didn't lift my spoon again.

Maybe changing the subject would be a better tactic. "Have you heard from Sebastian since this afternoon?" I asked. "Has he said when he will be here?"

"No." He pushed a few buttons, and the microwave

whirled to life.

"No, you haven't heard from him, or no, he hasn't said when he's coming to Twentynine Palms?"

He whipped his head around. His scowl was still in place, only now it had at least twenty-two more stern angles to it. His gaze was just as incisive, a double-edged sword forged of copper and jade. "What has you thinking we are in Twentynine Palms?"

"Uhhh... my cell phone?" I picked up the device and waggled it. It was never far from me these days, just in case Bas texted again. "Location services in just about every app? This is a pretty remote place, though. I have to give you guys that much. I did notice there is a bit of shopping not too far away. Maybe that's where we can go to have my phone looked at regarding the cell situation. I should definitely have better phone reception here."

"Bas can deal with that when he gets here." He mumbled—okay, growled—it around his first bite of ziti. "Damn, this is good. Sure you don't want some?" He pushed the casserole dish toward me on the island.

"No," I all but snapped. I slid off the stool and grabbed my bowls. As I turned with them, a petite woman seemed to materialize from thin air. With a gentle smile, she took them from my hands.

"I can get this, Miss Gibson," she offered. "Please, just relax."

How could I deny her sweet, serviceable manner? "Thank you," I murmured while giving up the bowls without hesitation. "And thank you for the food, as well. It was delicious."

She smiled again. "Well, that was all Mr. Banks." She motioned to Elijah with her chin since her hands were full.

My turn for the stunned double-take—but my quizzical stare met the top of the man's head. Surprise, surprise; Elijah was suddenly laser-focused on his own food.

"You made the parfait?" I pressed anyway. Not surprisingly, he stayed hunched over his plate like a street urchin with a fast-food cheeseburger. "I would've eaten the pasta the chef made, like everyone else."

At last, Elijah raised his head and said, "It was no trouble, really. And I thought that having a choice between a couple of things would make you more likely to eat something." He rolled his shoulders. "Gives me hives to see people go without eating."

"Seriously?" I flung a teasing gawk. "I had no idea. You hide that so well."

Fortunately, my jibe earned me a smirk this time. The man's hazels actually twinkled in the kitchen's overhead light.

"So . . . is this some kind of childhood trauma thing?" At least I knew how to push gently. "I know you knew Bas growing up, and I know the kind of childhood he had. It stands to reason you and Grant have stories of your own to tell too."

He blinked at me. Then again. "Doesn't everyone?" He finished chewing. "Have a story to tell, I mean. You don't have to have a fucked-up childhood to have a cause you feel passionately about."

"Point well made." And now that I felt like a total idiot, it was as good a time as any to leave the man to his meal and escape back to my hideout. "I'll leave you to your meal. I . . . have one last thing, though, if you don't mind?"

He set his fork down, seeming annoyed. Whether it was because I was keeping him from his meal or he simply found me bothersome, I wasn't sure. Regardless, I pressed on. At this point, I didn't have a choice. This frustrating, confusing man was my only real conduit to the outside world. A world that contained Sebastian.

"Would you call Sebastian for me, the way you called Rio today?" I forced my chin to stay firm and my gaze to stay dry. "I . . . I need to speak to him."

He rewarded my honesty with a giant chunk of silence. At last, one word. "Why?"

"Because I miss him. And I need more than just a text exchange here and there."

He sat silently for another long moment. But at least he seemed to be thinking over my request. Until he jabbed a big pin into the balloon of my hopes by picking up his fork and eating again.

In seconds, I was at his side. Then grabbing his wrist, halting him just before the pasta reached his mouth. His lethal hazel glare sliced through me, but I didn't back down.

"No. Stop this. Why am I having to beg to use the phone? This is ridiculous. I'm not a fucking prisoner here. Am I? You're making me crazy!"

He looked down at where I was clutching his arm. "Yes, I see that."

At last, I let go of him. I wasn't getting anywhere with the man tonight, if the terse line of his jaw could be believed. And yes, here came my holding-back-the-tears headache. Like my effort had done me any good.

With a resigned sigh, I stepped back from the island. "I'll be in my cell . . . my room. Whatever. It's all starting to feel like the same thing," I mumbled, swiping my cheeks as I walked away.

"Okay," he mumbled back.

With every passing hour, my supposed "safe" house really was feeling more like a prison. I knew with absolute certainty, if I didn't see or speak to Sebastian soon, I wouldn't be staying here much longer. I would find a way out of this house, out of this desert town, and my own way back to Los Angeles.

Elijah Banks be damned.

CHAPTER TWO

SEBASTIAN

Slowly but surely, I was losing my mind. I went from having Abbigail beneath me every night and within arm's reach every day to nothing but a few sparse text messages—if I was lucky—per twenty-four-hour period. And forget about any voice contact. Christ, I never realized how her musical laughter, throaty sighs, and sweet sarcasm had become the balm for my soul—until they were no longer resonating on the same air I breathed.

Each time I picked up the phone and dialed her number, it rang straight to her voicemail. And every time, I sat and greedily listened to her sultry voice through the greeting. I'd close my eyes and picture her here in my office with me. Maybe she was sitting on my lap in my chair. Better yet, she was propped on my desk in front of me, her legs spread just wide enough to let me peek at the wet treasure between them.

A stiff ache brought my attention back to the present. To my lonely reality.

"Goddammit," I muttered. This sucked, and in no small way. I needed to talk to Elijah and hear his daily reassurance that she was well. And yes, probably to hear about her mounting fury about my avoidance of talking to her directly. Yeah, it was a dick move. And yeah, I was the first to admit it.

Didn't change anything. I couldn't bring myself to do it. I'd figured that one out the hard way just two days into this ordeal, when we'd talked for less than five minutes. The conversation had consisted mostly of her weeping pleas for me to bring her home. For hours afterward, I'd pretended to be a functioning member of society. Inside, every synapse in my senses was fried.

Enough was enough.

We were now closing our sixth day apart, and I planned on being with her by nightfall.

She didn't know I'd made plans to leave the office early and make the drive out to the safe house. Elijah and I agreed it would be best to stay quiet about my intention, in case something—more like one of a thousand things—fell through. He said she had been increasingly disagreeable and sad, and I didn't want to add to her misery if this wasn't going to happen.

That was my newly found heroic side speaking.

On the other hand, there was something pulse-quickening about hearing what a hard time she'd been giving him. Her spirit hadn't dwindled with our separation, though if anyone could handle her spunky personality, it was Elijah Banks. The bastard was probably routinely looking for ways to egg her on, just to keep the days interesting during their forced sequestration in Twentynine Palms.

And damn it, I had no news about when it would be coming to an end either. We—meaning Grant, me, and the sizable investigation team Elijah had assembled from across the globe—weren't getting anywhere with discovering who was harassing me. We had feelers out into every dark and creepy corner of the city I could think of, and none of the efforts were yielding results. Nothing beyond more frustration. I was finding it harder and harder to focus on the work piling up on my desk as each day passed.

I was shaken from my musings by Terryn's easily identifiable knock on my office door.

"In!" I didn't bother with other words or niceties for this one.

"Do you have a minute, Mr. Shark?" she asked sheepishly while closing the door behind her.

"Not really." I stood and walked around from behind my desk, not comfortable in a relaxed position when this woman was around me. "Is there a problem?"

"I won't take up too much of your time. I know how busy you are. I mean, of course I would, right? I organize your schedule, after all." She laughed brightly—too brightly—at the dumb comment but sobered when I just stared in return. She needed to get to the damn point. I wouldn't want to make small talk with Terryn Ramsey if she were the last person on the planet.

I stepped forward and squared off with my assistant. "What can I do for you, Terryn?"

"Well, I . . . I hope this doesn't seem presumptuous of me, but I've noticed Ms. Gibson hasn't been delivering your lunches this week. She also hasn't been calling multiple times a day like she usually does." She nervously twisted her fingers in and out of the delicate necklace she wore. If she yanked any harder, the thin chain would snap—much like my patience.

"Terryn."

"Hmmm?"

"Focus, damn it."

"Oh, yes! Of course, of course. Well, I just wanted to tell you that if you needed someone to . . . well . . . talk to . . ."

I glowered. "About what?"

"About . . . well . . . anything. You know, if you two are having a lovers' quarrel, or . . . or . . . you know, whatever, I'd be happy to lend an ear." She quickly put her flat palm up to interrupt herself. "Just as friends, of course! I don't want to give you the wrong idea or anything, okay? Seriously. Just as your friend."

She narrowed her eyes as if trying to gauge my reaction and then smiled slyly, as if she were pulling one over on me. It was one of the strangest interactions with another human I'd ever had in my entire life. And I'd met some characters in my time.

"So, anyway . . . yeah. I just wanted to say that."

I stepped back. "Very well." They were the only two words that came to mind—but they were far from the right ones.

"Oh! Wait! And I also wanted to give you this!"

She dug into the pocket of her boxy blazer. I would've thought the pockets on the ill-fitting jacket-skirt combo were just for show, but she popped the flap open at the hip and fished out a small parcel. She handed it to me with a beaming smile, like a schoolgirl giving her secret crush a bracelet she'd made during study hall.

"I hope you like it." She clasped her hands together under her chin and waited for me to open the tissue paper bundle. The wad looked like something Vela would leave under her pillow for the Tooth Fairy.

I was genuinely concerned to discover what was inside. "I . . . umm . . . don't think I can accept this, Terryn." Again, the only words I could muster. Again, feeling like a thousand kinds of weird. "It seems inappropriate, given our professional relationship. I don't want there to be—"

"Open it."

She cut me off so abruptly, and in such a different—and alarming—tone of voice, my own gaze started doing strange things. I shot it from the insane woman in front of me to the door and then back again. How many steps would it take for me to get the fuck away from this crazy train and then call security? I was rarely caught off guard by another person—but this nutcase had done the job with her two-word sentence. Or command, as the case had been.

I fumbled with the tissue wrapping, attempting to distract my gaze anywhere but her avid face. Not a wise choice. When had Terryn gotten so thin? She was looking particularly boney today—but I made a habit of not noticing her most days, so it could've been something that had been happening over the last month or longer. Was she sick beyond her obvious mental instability?

"I guess I got a little crazy." She snorted. "With the tape, I mean."

Good thing she cleared that up.

"I like to make people work for it, you know?" She snorted again. It was nearly an inhuman sound. I did my best to ignore it while fighting through the layers upon layers of tape and tissue.

Finally, I began unrolling what was inside. Once I got to the center, I tried making sense of what I was looking at.

"What the hell?"

I darted my glare to my mousey assistant.

"Do you love it?" She pushed her steepled hands over her lips. "After all the time we've worked so closely with one another, I've gotten to know your dark sense of humor, Sebastian. I knew you would get a chuckle out of it."

I pushed out harsh air through my nostrils. "You give me more credit than I deserve. And it's Mr. Shark, Terryn."

"Of course, of course! Sorry. We should keep up appearances." She gave me a strange little salute, giving me time to turn the object over and over between my fingers. It appeared to be a keychain, but I wasn't sure.

"What is this?" There was a ring with links that were connected to other objects. But beyond that was where my confusion started. "Is this a... tooth of some sort? Maybe an animal's tooth?"

Terryn nodded her head vigorously. Her eyes were so bright, it was like she'd just presented me with the Hope Diamond. "Guess what kind. Guess!"

"I'm not going to guess, Ter—"

"It's a shark's tooth!"

"How original," I muttered before noticing two more charms on the ring. "And what are these other charms?"

While I held them closer for a better view, my assistant's posture stiffened. Her gaze's cartoon-worthy sparkles were a little dimmer. What was this? Nervousness, maybe? Or was that just me?

I scrutinized the little wooden carving, turning it between my thumb and forefinger. Schooling my features was the greatest exercise in restraint I had been challenged with all week. That was saying a lot, considering the week I'd had. Shockingly, my fingers didn't tremble as I examined the intricacies of the miniature work of art.

And that was what it was... really. Somewhere, there was a very talented artist who'd taken a small piece of wood and painstakingly carved it into a very detailed, very accurate, likeness of a piranha. How something like that was even possible was a marvel of its own—but this was not the time to be admiring someone's artistry.

I had bigger fish to fry.

Did I really just go there?

"Terryn?" Her name sprang off my tongue as more of a warning than a question. I wasn't a damn bit sorry.

"Do you love it? Can you believe the detail?" She was almost vibrating with excitement.

Vibrating. Much like my pool water was the night we found Tawny being slaughtered by a school of those little flesh-eating bastards.

Christ.

I shuddered but somehow managed to hide it. For the most part.

"Terryn."

"Wait." Her brows knitted. Her eyes darkened. "What? Are you . . . angry? You don't like it? Why?" She tried to snatch the souvenir from my hand. "Never mind. Just give it back to me. Forget this ever happened. I thought you'd like it. That I could do something nice for you that she couldn't, but I should've known better. Nothing I do is ever good enough for you. For a man like you, from a woman like me."

"Whoooaaa there."

She was coming unglued, and it was a bit frightening. Maybe more than a bit. I could go toe-to-toe with just about anyone, but confronting an insane person when their eyes are glazed over with that *I have nothing to lose* look? No way. Even my drunk father's benders paled in comparison.

But she wasn't getting the trinkets back.

Not when they represented the hugest clue we'd gotten this week.

Once again, Terryn tried to rip the gift from my grasp. Not fast enough. I shoved the keychain into the pocket of my slacks while grabbing her by the wrist with my other hand. But that was the end of my vehemence. I knew the approach I had to take. The woman was like a spooked colt that needed a gentle hand. So that was what I'd give her.

"Terryn," I soothed. "Ssshhh. I just had a few questions. That's all." My stomach turned over at having to be so gentle with this psychopath. "Where did you find such a unique gift? It really suits me. You really do know me well."

Already, I felt her wiry body relax by a few degrees. The woman was starving for attention.

"Someone had it made for me. I mean, so I could give it to you." She turned abruptly and faced me straight on. "It was my idea, though! Giving you this gift, I mean. Okay, not the whole piranha thing." She visibly shuddered. "I mean, let's be honest, just between friends. That stunt was a little over-the-top, don't you think?"

She finished with a laugh, giving me time to mask my shock. Her burst was forced and airy at first but ramped into hysterical cackles before she knocked shoulders with me. I reacted with the same casual camaraderie, but only through supreme force of will.

Holy Christ.

She knew.

Terryn knew what those sick fucks had done to Tawny.

I wanted to vomit but forced back the bile. If I acted like I thought the piranha chow-down was a masterful idea, maybe I'd open her up more. And maybe that little gut spill would include incriminating information about who'd carried the plan out. Maybe even more than that. Now that we were friends and all.

Jesus. This twist could be better than just a clue.

This could be our big break.

"You know, that move was genius, really." I stroked my jaw thoughtfully. "I mean, it took care of that pain-in-the-ass woman and her body in minutes."

"Oh." Terryn blinked. Then again. "You... you really think so?"

"Don't you?" I leaned against the front edge of my desk like I often did when talking to Grant in the morning. Terryn shifted her weight from foot to foot, clearly debating how to react. In some ways, I related. Trying to bait the woman into telling me who was behind all the illegal activities at my home, and even how she was involved, made me feel sleazier than being on the right side of the wrong kind of a business deal.

"I... well..."

"Terryn!" I rose fully to my feet while exclaiming it with mock discovery. "Have you been the mastermind behind all of the things that have been happening? Has it been you this whole time?"

"Pffft. God, no!"

"Why do you say it like that? You're clever, motivated..."

"Sebastian—"

I cut her off with a raised brow. I didn't care if the woman was fucking with my life on a monumental level or not. We were not friends, and I wouldn't willingly allow her to call me by my first name. I had to maintain some sort of control in this ridiculous situation.

"Sorry, sorry." Terryn put her hands up in front of her before correcting herself. "But Mr. Shark... Whoever is harassing you and your girlfriend"—she rolled her eyes while gritting out the designation—"clearly has a lot of money and a lot of connections."

Now we were getting somewhere—though her revelation wasn't exactly a stunner for me. Still, I played her game. "Why do you say that?"

"Well, duh." Terryn could gold medal in eye rolling. "I mean, trucking that many piranhas into your chichi neighborhood? I was horrified and impressed at the same time. Quite the show. I mean, wow."

I took a step closer to her. With a lot of caution. "So you did see everything that night?"

"Hmmm. Mostly." Her tiny shrug prompted me to back away once more. "After I got your email to come to your house that night, I saw everything up to the point your girlfriend fainted, but then I got the heck out of there."

I stopped. Jerked my stare up at her. "Wait. My . . . email?"

"Why, yes. When you asked me to come over to your place for drinks? So we could make a fresh start after the misunderstanding with my cell phone?"

"Terryn." Okay, screw the game. I commemorated the conclusion by raking both hands through my hair in frustrated swipes but stopped when I saw how she eyed my motion with open appreciation. "Does that sound like something I would ever do? An offer I would ever make? Words I'd ever say? And we both know the situation with your phone wasn't a 'misunderstanding.'"

"Umm, well, no." She looked down at the carpet, seemingly fascinated with the toe of her scuffed navy-blue pump. "I . . . I guess it doesn't sound like you at all. Now that you say it like that, with that look on your face . . ."

"And how do you expect me to look, Terryn?"

"I . . . uhhh . . . I don't know, but—"

"How did you really think I was going to accept this little 'gift'?" I was snarling more than speaking now but couldn't stop the tumble of my anger. "Did you think it would be—what? Funny? To give me a gift that reminds me of a night when a woman was literally eaten alive in my backyard swimming pool?"

She jerked her face up, her eyes bright and hurting. "That part wasn't my—"

"My niece swims in that water, for Christ's sake!" I pulled the keychain from my pocket, stared at it, but then jammed it right back in. "You're crazy, woman. Fucking crazy."

"No!" she screeched. "I'm not! Stop saying that. Everyone stop saying that!"

I looked around the room with exaggerated head motions—turning left, then swinging my gaze right. As suspected, it was still just me and the psycho bunny in the ill-fitting suit standing here.

"Like I was saying . . ."

"Let. Me. Finish!"

With ringing ears, I stepped back even farther. And told myself this was one of those "silence is better" situations.

Terryn heaved out a sigh before going on. "I—I wanted the keychain to be a reminder that you're not alone, Seba— Mr. Shark."

She closed the gap I'd just made, and this time I held my ground. She moved in close enough that I could see the pulse in her neck. She was damn agitated. And that was damn alarming.

"I know what you're going through." She gentled her voice and tilted her head. "You may even be scared right now." When she reached for my hand, I recoiled from her palm as if it throbbed with ten amps of electricity. "And that's okay. It would be understandable in this situation."

Alarming was just the start of where this was going now. The nutjob went on like I hadn't just recoiled, making me realize she'd probably played this scene out a hundred times in her crazy-ass mind. She was damned and determined it would go down the way she imagined it. To get what I wanted—needed—out of it too, I had to go there with her. Play the game again, at least outwardly.

"Well, Terryn. I appreciate it. And I do appreciate the gift too. It was . . . thoughtful. But remind me again, because there have just been so many emotions here this afternoon . . ." I sighed dramatically, and she sent back a dreamy smile. "Who did you say gave you this keychain to give to me? The person's name, exactly?"

Her brow knitted. "I didn't get his name. It didn't seem relevant at the time. He had it dropped off here by a courier. It was all very straightforward, really." She retracted her head into her shoulders like a timid turtle. "Although I probably shouldn't tell you all of that, should I?"

"Why?"

"Because it doesn't seem like I put much effort into your gift now."

I couldn't decide if her crestfallen, embarrassed demeanor about having a personal shopper or the fact that the person messing with me was now doing it at my office too, annoyed me more.

Best to just move past it all. Walking toward the heavy door that led back out to the reception area, I said to my assistant by way of dismissal, "Thanks again for the keychain. I'll be working remotely for a few days. You can reach me on my cell phone or via email. I've already handled rearranging my schedule, including the appointment I had with Jacob Cole." I held up my hand in a stop gesture, knowing she would launch into a litany of questions. But she went on with them anyway as she walked toward the door.

"Uhh . . . okay. Are you going on a business trip? Can I help arrange a hotel? A flight? That's what I'm here for, Sebastian. To help you." Terryn trudged through the door, imploring me to allow her to lend assistance.

"For the last time, it's Mr. Shark. If you slip up again, you'll be holding a pink slip by morning. I'm not playing around on this. Now get out of my office so I can finish what I need to and leave for the day." I slammed the door so hard behind her, the framed honors on the adjacent wall rattled in response.

"Siri, call Joel."

"Confirm you'd like to call Joel My Driver."

"Yes."

"Calling Joel My Driver."

The line rang twice before my faithful employee picked up. This man had been with me for a decade, and we had a comfortable rapport. Unlike Terryn, he always knew when to keep it professional, especially in front of other people.

"I'm right outside if you're ready to go home," he said.

"Actually, how do you feel about Twentynine Palms?"

"Personally, or in the way of driving you there?"

"I was thinking about the helicopter, actually. Are you up for it? I know it's already been a full day."

"Yeah, but think about it, an hour and change in the air versus at least three and a half hours and nightmare traffic getting out of the city?"

"Seems like an obvious choice to me too, but I'm not the

one who has to fly or drive. So that's why I'm asking you." And how odd was it that I was giving someone in my employ an option? The Abbigail effect hard at work again.

Damn, I couldn't wait to have her in my arms. Kiss her lips. Smell her skin. Growl dirty promises in her ear. My dick started waking up for the first time in days. I was beginning to wonder what it would take for the thing to feel alive again.

"Mr. Shark? Hello? Shit…lost him," I heard Joel mumble.

"No. No, I'm here. Sorry. I got distracted by an email. We can leave as soon as I come down. I have a bag with me already. We don't have to go out to the house."

"All right, good. I'll call over to the hanger and have the helo prepared. Weather looks good right now. I'll check out my flight app and see what the route looks like. We should be able to stay VFR the whole way, and since we are leaving so early, we'll land before the sun sets."

"Perfect, Joel. I'll be down in five minutes or less." I hung up and shut down my computers. I went through the routine of securing my office for time away—locking my desk and other drawers and file cabinets. I didn't need Terryn in here snooping. I grabbed the duffle I'd brought from home this morning and the smaller bag I'd packed for Abbi. I'd found some things around the house I thought she might appreciate having while she was away, and I'd hidden a few surprises in there for her too.

With a spring in my step, I made the descent to the lobby and out to the front of the building, where I slid into the back seat of the waiting car. Joel whisked us off to LAX and had us airborne with excellent efficiency. The man deserved a bonus for the effort he put into making this journey so seamless, and hopefully, Abbigail would be as happy to see me as I would be to see her.

While we were airborne, I dug through my pocket and pulled out the keychain Terryn had given me. I wanted to look take a closer look at the third charm on the ring. It was a logo or emblem of some sort. I didn't recognize the design at the quick look I'd gotten when I was with my secretary, so I studied it for a few minutes while I had some downtime. I could have Elijah look up the image and see what he could find out when I got to the house in the desert.

We pulled up the long driveway of the safe house a short time later.

Hopefully I'd be able to change Abbigail's attitude and give her a few reasons to smile again.

CHAPTER THREE

ABBIGAIL

The mind has a way of protecting itself in desperate times. Never was that better evidenced than in the dream I was having.

"Finally," my dream-self rasped. "Oh, God, yes! Finally!"

Sebastian was here with me. Here in this house. In my sanctuary.

In my bed.

He moved his skillful lips away from mine. Trailed them tenderly down my neck—at first. But clearly he'd missed me as much as I had him, and his touch got more demanding. He might have missed me even more, if the steely erection stabbing into my belly was any indication. I wasn't sure I'd ever felt him—no, anything—so hard in my life. His incessant rubs were almost painful. His arousal felt more like a fireplace poker than an excited penis.

"Mmmm, yes, baby," I moaned to my dream lover.

"Open your eyes, Abbigail," he crooned. "Let me see you, love."

I writhed against him while squeezing my eyes closed tighter. "No. I don't want to wake up," I mumbled against soft lips. "I hate it here, Sebastian. I don't want you to disappear again."

"Look at me, baby." He brushed a reverent kiss to my forehead. "You're not dreaming." To each eyelid. "I'm here." Then the tip of my nose. "I've come to visit you. I'm here..."

Dream Sebastian covered my mouth with his. Ohhh damn, his kiss was as good as my real man's—especially when he coaxed my lips apart with his own, thrust his tongue inside, and hungrily swallowed my needy cry of passion.

"Don't be cruel," I snarled once he released me. "I can't take it anymore! Not today."

"Little Red," he growled into my ear, just before nibbling the lobe. "Open your beautiful green eyes for me. Silly, silly, girl."

I chanced a peek—but just a quick one. If I were dreaming, I'd be able to sink right back into all the euphoria of him. All the sensual, beautiful glory of him...

Yet there he was. Smiling down on me with the full force of his dazzling grin. Kissing me on one cheek, then up and over my nose to the other. Holy shit. It was really him. He was actually in my room at the safe house—in Godforsaken Twentynine Palms!

He leaned up only far enough to frame my temples with his elegant fingers. He mellowed the grin to a smirk before whispering one word.

"Hi."

One word—that was more than enough for me.

Within seconds, sobs burst from every corner of my body and soul. I wrapped my entire body around him. I held on so tightly, neither one of us could inflate our lungs. The emotional breakdown wasn't just because I missed him, although that was a large part of it. There were so many things represented by each tear from my eyes, each shudder down my body, each desperate inhalation and exhalation.

"Hey. Heeeey. Baby, ssshhh." He hitched up a little higher and looked at me thoroughly. "What's all this?"

I shook my head, hopefully communicating that I needed a second. Maybe more than one. All in all, it took several minutes to expunge all my pent-up emotions, but the purge was past necessary. So much shit had built up inside me over the past week. With Elijah being so terse with me, I couldn't very well open up to him about all the scenarios I'd been creating in my mind. All the feelings that had been eating at my confidence, slowly eroding the foundation Bas and I had worked so hard to build.

Finally, I sniffled—fine, it was more of a deep snot suction—causing Sebastian to let me go and dig into his pocket.

"No," I blurted when he offered me a handkerchief. "I'll ruin it," I croaked pathetically.

"Goddammit. Take it, Abbigail. I want you to ruin it." He thrust the linen square toward me again, inserting a gruff laugh. "I see your stubbornness is still in full force. Elijah wasn't joking."

"Fuck Elijah!" I shouted. And meant it completely.

"Wait. Tell me how you really feel." He chuckled again.

"I'm really beginning to hate him, you know?"

Bas heaved out a sigh. "You don't 'hate' him, baby."

"No; I'm pretty sure I hate him. When he's not treating me like a child, he's barking at me like a prisoner. He goes back and forth between the two, and I abhor them both. I've done nothing to deserve this!"

Seemingly in one movement, he rolled over, pushed his back against the headboard, and pulled me onto his lap. His grinning lips disappeared into the loose hair around my shoulders. "God damn, I've missed the smell of you," Sebastian growled lowly and nuzzled through my tresses to the skin of my neck. "The taste of you..."

As he explored behind my ear with his warm, slick tongue, every corner of my pussy started tremoring... aching.

"Basssss." I tilted my head to give him better access to the length of my neck. This plan was so much better than getting pissed off about Elijah.

"I need to be inside you, Abbigail." In another graceful motion, he moved me from his lap and then stood from the bed. With his dark eyes fixed on me with predatory hunger, he began undressing. His pace was efficient and purposeful but still erotic as hell. Skillful fingers made light work of the buttons of his shirt and tab of his belt. His pants were gone in moments after that. Like always, he was simply taking care of details on his way to me. I never wanted him to change.

"Undress. I need to see your bare cunt. Now. I haven't been able to sleep at night without you by my side." He palmed himself through his boxer briefs. "Without feeling you on my cock before we sleep."

He rubbed himself harder when I knelt up tall and slowly removed my top and bra. His nostrils flared with each breath he inhaled. His voice was a low vibration more than a sound. "I need to taste your pussy on my tongue, my lips," he growled out. "To smell your perfect scent deep in my nose after I've had my face between your legs."

Holy shit, did the man know how to make up for lost time. And I was so damn grateful.

I showed him so by sliding my hands down my torso. Then farther.

His throat rippled. My heartbeat doubled.

In one quick action, he scooped me off the bed and planted me on my feet before him.

"Now you may continue undressing, Red."

After regaining my bearings, I hooked my thumbs into my panties. Began sliding them down, but then I halted. Totally on purpose.

I smiled.

Sebastian didn't.

He shot his black stare to mine. His wordless challenge was like the pull of the moon on my body's helpless waves. I was speechless, completely transfixed with his body's reaction to my playful seduction. The power he'd unknowingly handed me was heady.

"You want me?" I whispered. "You want this?" I slid my palms inward and then dove one hand beneath my underwear's thin waistband. I paused to lift my taunting gaze to his, then slid my middle finger between my folds.

And moaned.

Then again.

"Abbigail." His tone was husky and full of warning, but I was empowered by the lust in his gaze. "Pull your panties down to your thighs and leave them there."

In an effort to push him further, I hesitated to follow his dictate.

"Do it!"

I slid the skimpy fabric halfway down my legs like he ordered and looked at him again through half-lidded eyes.

"Spread your legs as far as your little undies will allow. Yeah, Little Red. Just like that." He continued to fist himself from balls to crown. "Farther, Abbi. Let me see more. Oh, fuck me, you're hot . . . standing there like that."

I swallowed hard. "Hot? That's a bit pot and kettle right now, Mr. Shark."

He jerked up one side of his full mouth, vaguely acknowledging my compliment. The bastard had the most perfect penis in the state and knew it, damn it. With equal insolence, he murmured, "Have you been touching yourself while we've been apart?"

I dropped my gaze. I couldn't look at him after that damn question. Nevertheless, I shook my head. I'd been too sad, too mad, or just not feeling well enough to be aroused. Until now, at least.

Sebastian shifted his stance. He was leaning closer to me but still not close enough to touch. So maddening, yet so mesmerizing. But I was pretty sure he knew that too. The raw edge of his voice said as much.

"In that case, I have a special project in mind for you, girl."

I gulped even harder. Now I really couldn't speak.

"Slide one of your fingers up into your cunt," he issued. "Do it as if it's turned into my cock." As soon as the words were out, he jolted me by thudding down to both knees. As he dropped into the thick pile, he lined up his stare directly with my spread sex. With the hole where I worked my finger inside my trembling body.

Bas reached for the fabric of my panties and yanked them to my knees then, growling with admiration.

"Oh, fuck, yes," he groaned. I was tempted to echo him, but he said then, "Look at you, Abbigail. So juicy and pink and tight. You need to see this too. Do it, baby. Lean forward. Come and look at what you're doing to yourself."

"Oh." I finally got it out while complying with his demand. "Oh . . . God."

"Such a good girl." Bas sat back on his heels. His own self-pleasuring infused the air with erotic slicks that mingled with our heavy breaths. "Such a naughty, sexy girl. Keep finger-fucking yourself. And keep watching. Don't look away. I want you to see every gorgeous thrust."

"Baaassss!" My wetness coated my fingers down my knuckles. For a second, I dared to lift my head and search his face. He was riveted to where my hand was buried inside my pussy. I'd never seen anything more stunning in my entire life.

"Push another finger in," he gritted out.

"A . . . what?"

"You heard me, Abbi. Do it."

"No. I—I don't think I . . ."

"Yes," he demanded. "You can."

"Please, Sebastian. I want you to . . ." I stopped abruptly with his motion toward me. Still on his knees in front of me, he scooted closer until he was inches in front of me.

"Keep your finger inside that tight pussy," Bas demanded while yanking my panties down around my ankles and then tapped the one so I would step out, freeing my leg. "Good girl. Spread wider for me."

From my ankle, my ruthless lover scraped his fingernails up the inside of my leg and left a tingling trail of red scratch marks as he went. When his fist bumped mine, still buried in my wet heat, I made to move out of his way until he barked, "Stay there!"

He ran his index finger through the slickness and brought it to his lips while meeting my fascinated stare. He sucked on his finger, tasting my arousal on his skin. I studied his lush mouth with open envy. Lust and need hit me in fresh waves. I moaned in shameless abandon. Holy shit, I needed some relief. Right freaking now.

I started circling my thumb around my clit. Then even harder. The throbbing bud had become too much to ignore. My desire was too exigent to deny.

"Stop."

"Wh-What?"

"You heard me," he spat. "I said stop."

"B-B-Bas!" I implored. "Come on! I'm desperate here. Please!"

"We'll get there, baby."

Bastard! He actually smirked when saying it. But the look, like everything else about this perfect reunion, was filled with sensual determination.

So was what he did next.

With his dark eyes fixed on my spread pussy, he slid his index finger up inside me. Yes, right alongside mine. Yes, as far as he could.

"Holy shit."

I gasped and writhed. The added fullness was exquisite. And when I bent forward and looked this time, the erotic vision that waited was enough to make my legs weak.

"Oh, my God. Oh, my God, Bas! It's . . . it's . . ."

"What, Abbigail?" His voice was rich yet sharp, an aural version of expensive whiskey. "Tell me, girl."

I rocked my head back, unable to look anymore. I wanted to focus on the cataclysm of sensations taking over my sex. "Feels . . . so good . . ."

"You're so warm inside here. So tight and wet. Fuck, baby. My dick is so hard for you right now."

A spasm took over my whole body. "Ooohhhh," I moaned.

"Help me, baby," Bas encouraged. "Help me finger-fuck

you into the best orgasm you've ever had. Let's make you come apart, Abbigail. Then I'm going to stuff you so full of my cock, you won't be able to see straight."

"Sebastian! Stop! It's happening so fast. I'm . . . I'm going to come!"

"Yeah, you are, Red. All over our hands. Then you can taste yourself on my fingers."

He rammed his hand in harder, pushing mine along with his. Fuck! It felt so good. I'd never be able to masturbate on my own after this experience. The orgasm was building in my belly, a tidal wave of erotic ecstasy. My pores were flooded with heat. My mind was drowning in delirium.

"I'm going to come. Bas, I'm going . . . I'm . . . I can't . . . it's too much . . . shit . . . Bas!" At my warning, he leaned in and sucked my clit between his lips, flicking his wicked tongue over the hard button. A beautiful black curtain descended over my senses. I stuttered for air as wave after wave of electrifying pulses surged through my limbs and across my chest. I swore I even felt my eyelashes tingle! My knees buckled, and I crumbled into Sebastian's arms.

He whisked me off my feet in an effortless move and onto the opulent bed where I'd cried myself to sleep night after night since I'd gotten here. When I finally opened my eyes, he was positioned between my legs and supporting himself on his forearms on either side of my head.

"Hello, gorgeous." He smiled, satisfied with a job well done.

"My God. That was amazing." My eyes grew heavy with contentment. My body was limp and lax, now relieved of all its pent-up tension from my lonely, restless nights.

"I'm going to fuck you now, Abbigail."

"Hmmm. Please do, Mr. Shark." I quickly added, before he had the chance to make the claim, "I know, I know; you're not asking. Neither am I."

He dipped in, lingering his lips atop mine in a tender but torrid kiss. "Demanding red devil."

"But the one who's all yours." I grinned as I finished, just before tilting my hips to just the right angle. Sebastian groaned low while sliding deep into me, not having to use a hand to guide his shaft inside or wait for me to adjust. Our bodies simply knew one another's that well and accommodated for what they wanted. What they needed.

No. More than just our bodies.

Our spirits. Our instincts. Our hearts. We were each other's home. Each other's safety. We fit together as though we were meant to be one. Because we were.

"My God, woman. I could die here and be a happy man. You. Are. My. Salvation." Each word was punctuated with a thrust of his pelvis. "I'm going to come inside you now, Abbigail."

"Bas…"

"What?"

His rejoinder was a croak of need, so clearly betraying how hard he was holding back, that I bit back my protest. Still, the smarter part of me knew I should stop him. But the wiser woman in me already staged a return argument. Every time he'd done this recently, we'd been rolling the dice. Even though I was taking my birth control pills religiously, they weren't foolproof.

But the foolish, fantastical girl in me held on to another idea. The sweet dream of carrying his child. I would love to grow and nurture a life that we'd created together. To build a family with this amazing man. A little boy with his dangerous features . . . or a little girl with my crazy red strands . . .

But I didn't tell him any of that. Instead, I showed him. I wrapped my legs tightly around his hips and held him close to me while he depleted himself deep within my channel. Sebastian buried his face in the crook of my neck and chanted my name over and over as he finished. It sounded like he was praying. I wanted him to be. I knew I truly was.

Finally, he rolled to the side and then tucked me against him. Our breathing slowed in tandem. For the first time since I'd arrived, a real sense of calm settled into my heart. A real peace blanketed my soul. Both had been missing without this man nearby.

Maybe that should've frightened me. I tried examining the sensations and seeing them as huge warning flares. I'd gotten way too close to him. Had let myself depend on him too much, too quickly. But the heart wanted what the heart wanted.

And apparently mine wanted Sebastian Shark.

And apparently I was done fighting that fact.

★ ★ ★

The next morning, I awoke to an empty bed.

The realization wasn't reassuring. Not in the damn least.

I'd slept in much later than usual, my exhaustion finally catching up with me. But my body ached in all the best ways, and my cheeks ached from my wide, ridiculous smiles.

So all the physical evidence was here. Sebastian had been here with me. But for how long? And what if he had left already this morning?

At once, I cast out the concept. He wouldn't do that. The

man was a bastard, but not a heartless one. Well, not most of the time.

Quickly, I kicked off the sheets and surged to my feet. I was officially on a Shark hunt.

I found the en suite bathroom empty, but the shower was freshly used. The air still carried his distinct bergamot scent. He was definitely up and about the day already, though I sensed he was still somewhere near.

I breathed out with relief—but my new inhalation also brought my stomach's normal morning pitch and roll. I gripped the counter's edge, thinking I had some sort of Pavlovian reaction to this bathroom. Every time I went near the toilet, I seemed to have to drop down in front of it and empty my stomach—even when there was nothing in it to empty. Sometimes a splash of cool water from the sink helped. Not this morning. Swiftly, I made a new contribution into the toilet bowl.

I sat on the floor for a few minutes before I chanced standing to brush my teeth and hair. I wasn't in the mood to answer a list of questions from Bas or Elijah about not feeling well again, so I made sure the color returned to my face before I went out into the hall.

At once, I heard voices in the kitchen. Elijah and—thank God—Sebastian. Their baritones were modulated a bit, giving away their animated discussion. A smile breached my lips as I followed the volume, though I attempted to tread lightly in hopes of catching part of their conversation.

Of course, they noticed me and fell silent.

"Good morning," they said in unison.

"And good morning to you too." I chuckled while darting my gaze between them. "As you were, gentlemen. You don't have to stop talking just because I walked into the room."

They stared as if I'd ordered them to go sit on a pair of cacti outside. But only for a second. "Would you like some coffee?" Elijah asked, as if my comment had never existed.

"And you don't have to be nice to me all of a sudden because Sebastian's here."

Well, that got the man to react. "That's not really fair, is it?" he stated evenly. "I've been nothing but kind to you since we've arrived."

I pushed past him to get a mug from the cupboard and then helped myself to a cup of tea instead. I wasn't about to get into another argument with the man, especially after the fabulous mood I'd woken up in. But I couldn't even enjoy that for two seconds, because I'd now reminded myself about being concerned about Bas's schedule.

"Hey," I murmured, turning toward him. "How long are you staying? Do you have to go back this morning already?"

I already dreaded the answer. At once, he seemed to sense that. He always did. The man could read me like his own illuminated manuscript. It was why I didn't hesitate as soon as he held his arms open for me to come to him. I snuggled into his chest and just enjoyed the feeling of his embrace. I hated how much I didn't want to be sequestered in this house with his best friend. How much I hated not being invited to pack my things and leave with him. Whenever that might be.

When would that be?

"So I trust you slept well?" He smirked down at me, heating up the crackle of energy between us. The mutual understanding about exactly how good my sleep really was.

"I did." I grinned too. "How about you? What time did you get up?" I leaned in, flattening a hand to his chest. The move was blatantly needy, but I didn't care. "I didn't even hear your shower. I would've been happy to join you." Yeah. Needy. Still didn't care.

"Hmm, I like that idea. Maybe tomorrow morning?"

He studied my features closely while we spoke. Shit, maybe the color hadn't returned as well as I thought. But I liked the intense focus of his attention. A lot. "You're staying?" I blurted. The happiness in my voice couldn't be missed.

"For a few days, if that's okay with you?" The mischief in his couldn't be missed either.

"Well, you better clear it with that one." I motioned to his buddy with a tilt of my head. "He's the heavy around here."

"That's not the story I'm hearing."

Bas was still teasing, but I wasn't amused. Not in the least. I jerked out of his arms, planting my hands on my hips. "Oh, really? And what have you heard? Exactly?"

I started a new ping-pong match of my accusing glare, back and forth between the formidable men in front of me. But not for very long. Elijah's groan swiftly broke the moment.

"Oh, dude," he groused. "Why did you say that? I'm the one who's stuck here with her."

"And it's such a hardship," I countered. "I mean, right? I've told you before, Mr. Banks"—I all but spat his name—"I'd gladly like to declare your post done. I didn't ask for this bullshit. You recall that little fact too, yes?"

Elijah didn't answer me. Well, not in words. He said enough by raising a brow at Sebastian.

And that was more than enough of that. "What?" I seethed.

Sebastian let out a long breath. "Baby," he finally murmured and held out his hand. "Come here."

He turned his hand over and hitched his outstretched fingers. I didn't move. I just stared at his offering. His damn bidding.

Until he raised an expectant brow of his own.

I probably looked like an obedient little dog coming to heel. But the second Sebastian folded me back into his embrace, my spine relaxed. My breathing evened. My ire leaked out through my toes and fingertips. In Sebastian's arms, I barely had a care in the world. He was the Abbigail Whisperer.

My boyfriend kissed the top of my head and gently stroked my hair. That didn't stop my awareness of Elijah's new assessment. The man's hazel eyes were practically boring holes into my back. Before long, I was visibly squirming against the confines of Bas's hold.

"Hey. What is it, Little Red?"

I twisted my lips before whispering, "Tell him to stop staring at us."

"Huh?" His voice was hushed, as well. "Why does that bother you? He's interested in the way we interact. He's never seen me in love with a woman before. He and I have known each other for a long time. Elijah cares about me."

"Yes, but he doesn't care about me. Not in the slightest. Quite the opposite, I'm afraid."

"Is that what's bothering you?" His breath was warm atop of my head. There was a distinct smile in his tone. "You two are like oil and water, aren't you?"

"It would seem that way."

"And that irks you. Or . . . confuses you?"

"Both." I smushed my nose to his sternum. "I'm not used to not getting along with people."

"I know, baby." But after his tender rebuttal, Bas pulled a

one-eighty on me and changed the subject completely. "How about we go for a walk. Would you like that? You and me? Around the property?"

"That would be nice. I haven't really been outside all that much," I said.

"That's true," Elijah said, injecting himself into our conversation again. Sebastian and I both turned to look at him. "You haven't done anything but hide out in your room."

Glaring at the man, I said, "You know I haven't been feeling well. I've told you twenty times. And why are you still standing here? Don't you have something better to do?"

"Actually, I do. But because you're being so sweet around Sebastian, I'm enjoying your company this morning. In fact"—his eyes glittered with mischief—"maybe I'll go along with the two of you."

"No." Sebastian and I fired it in unison.

Just as quickly, he added, "Go get dressed, baby, while I finish my conversation with Elijah. I'll meet you out by the pool."

After he kissed me again, I set off to dress for our walk. I considered lingering in the hallway to eavesdrop on their talk but inwardly talked myself out of it. Spying wasn't cool. Besides, I trusted Sebastian. Just because I couldn't say the same thing about Elijah Banks . . .

Beside the point. At least right now.

And my ace in the hole? I'd just ask Bas about their talk while we took our stroll. The sooner I was dressed, the sooner I'd have my answers. But more importantly, I'd have more alone time with the man I adored.

And maybe, just maybe if I was extra charming, I could convince Sebastian to take me back to Los Angeles with him.

And if pigs had wings, they would fly.

CHAPTER FOUR

SEBASTIAN

This walk had been a good call.

I could tell Abbigail needed some more one-on-one time. While last night had been the hello-again-is-it-me-you're-looking-for I'd been dreaming of for a week, she and I hardly had time to reconnect anything other than our bodies. From the second she stepped into the kitchen this morning, I could tell she needed some physical distance from Elijah, as well as a chance to unload her version of what had been happening out here.

And boy, did she ever.

She talked almost nonstop while we walked, and I let her. It was good to see the color finally returning to her cheeks. Whether her new glow was from the fresh air, the sunshine, or just the joy of getting to vent her frustrations, I didn't really care. I was just glad to see her looking lively—and even a little saucy. I'd take it all, considering how deeply she'd scared me when I first saw her last night.

Her discernible pallor substantiated all the claims Elijah had made to me. She'd been irritable and moody, spending most of her time cooped up in the master suite of the house. She hadn't been eating much. Banks also told me he'd heard her crying. A lot. Though I ensured him that she released her anger and frustrations through tears, he'd been concerned. It was more than what should be expected.

I hadn't fully believed him but gave him the green light to turn up the heat about her at least emerging to eat. My decree had been effective in that regard but unfortunately had torpedoed any hopes of the two of them forging a friendship.

But I needed to try to smooth things over between them. They were two of the most important people in my life, and now they were constantly at each other's throats. Unacceptable.

"Bas?"

Her prod came with a slight squeeze of my hand, nudging me back to the moment. "Hmmm?"

"I was asking if you've managed to find out anything. I mean, anything? At all? About who may be doing all of this." She clarified the point as we sat down on a wrought-iron bench in the shade of a Palo Verde tree. "I don't see how anyone, or even a whole group, disguises all their tracks after pulling stunts like these. It's not like dead sharks can be picked up on Rodeo Drive. Or a few hundred live piranhas . . ."

"You're right, of course," I said. "But . . ."

"But what?"

I looked up and gazed across the villa's extensive grounds. The landscaping on the property was a mix of naturally occurring desert trees, bushes, and cacti. There were so many varieties we didn't usually see near the Pacific in Los Angeles. The Palo Verde over our heads was an old, sturdy tree. It stood close to eighteen feet tall, its sprawling branches providing perfect shadows against the day's mounting heat.

I pulled in a long breath while I twined my fingers with Abbi's slender ones. Damn it. How much should I tell her at this point? Definitely not everything. If half of what Elijah was telling me was true, she was too fragile for a complete confession.

"It seems like the deeper we dig, we just come up with more questions instead of answers," I finally confessed. "It's very frustrating."

"And who are 'we'?" she pressed. "You and Elijah?"

"Yes. And his team."

"His . . . team?"

I couldn't decipher her reaction as incredulous or impressed, so I just went on. "He has a small but trusted corps that he works closely with in LA." I phrased everything carefully. "But there's something that's happened . . . beyond what they've dug up."

Abbi swiveled to face me more fully. Her reaction was surprising. I expected a jolt forward followed by a demand for every last detail. Instead, she watched me closely while waiting patiently.

At last she asked, "Something . . . how?"

"Baby? Do you want to go back inside? Are you feeling okay?"

"Yes, I'm fine. I'm just tired. Please . . . just tell me what happened."

Mentally, I vowed to call a doctor once we got back inside. My sister, at the very least. Something was definitely wrong with my woman, aside from typical stress about a situation like this. But she wasn't being honest with me—and likely herself—about it.

So maybe piling more weirdness on her wasn't the best call at the moment.

I was on the brink of vocalizing exactly that, when Abbigail compressed her lips and stated, "Damn it, Bas. Just tell me. Don't treat me like a fragile child. Please!"

With a heavy sigh, I gave in. I figured I always would with this woman. "Terryn's . . . been acting very strange."

A dozen tense lines of her face evaporated. She chuckled with gusto. "Sebastian, that's not breaking news."

"Normally I'd agree with you."

"But?" she filled in the word that my tone implied.

"Yesterday morning, she came into my office acting squirrelier than normal. To be honest, I was actually uncomfortable about it."

Abbi narrowed her gaze. "Why?"

"Well, she had a *gift* for me." As soon as I put air quotes around the word gift, she straightened.

"A gift?" she charged. "Okay, what was it?"

"A keychain."

She knitted her brows. "Like . . . a souvenir or something? Did she go on vacation? Or make it in some kind of arts and crafts—" She interrupted herself at the start of my "get real here" look.

"It had some charms dangling from it," I explained. "Seems harmless enough, right?"

"That depends," she said slowly. "What were the trinkets, exactly?"

"One was a shark's tooth." I rolled my eyes. "Really original, right?"

Abbi barely cracked a smile. She was really invested here, despite my attempt at dry wit. "And what were the others?"

"The second one . . . is a carved piranha."

"A . . . what?" Abbi bugged out her gaze. I would've been surprised if she hadn't—but her uptick of distress had me scrambling to play down the disturbing implication of my revelation.

"If it weren't so creepy, it'd be awesome. I'm serious."

She eyed me like I'd just confessed to liking anchovies straight out of the can. "Oh, I can see that."

"The artistry of the thing is amazing." I held my fingers up to estimate how small the charm was. "Anyhow, Elijah is researching the last charm now."

"Which was what?" she prompted.

"A flatter disk that displayed some sort of insignia… maybe even a corporate logo or a family crest. Neither one of us was familiar with it."

"But you think it might mean something? And if so, then what?"

I squared my shoulders. "The simplest explanation is often the truth, so we're going for that first. Clearly it's meant to be some sort of message to me."

Abbi screwed her face into a confused frown. "But how would Terryn, of all people, have known about the piranhas? We were the only ones in the backyard that night." Her throat visibly constricted. There was a new flare of her gaze. "Holy shit, Bas. Did she have something to do with all of this?"

I maintained calm across my own mien. Fortunately, I'd had over twenty-four hours to sit with this knowledge. "We don't know," I told her. "At least not yet. I mean, this is definitely where the woman's shit gets really suspicious."

"And it wasn't before?" Abbi injected.

I took half a moment to again steel myself. "She said… she was in the backyard that night," I explained. "Terryn said she stuck around long enough to watch you pass out. That was when she left."

"Long enough?" Abbi spewed. "Because she wasn't inspired sufficiently to take off before then?" As her voice pitched higher, she went on. "You've got to be kidding! Honest to hell! What was she doing there?"

Once more, I struggled to crank down my blatant surprise. This was the most animated I'd seen my Little Red all morning. I hated that it had taken raw anger to accomplish that.

"She said she got an email from me asking her to come over."

A new flurry of her open agitation. "And now this is getting weird. No, scratch that. It's getting outright messy."

"I know." I worked on modulating my composure now, since there was nobody else around to help modulate Abbi. There was animated, and then there was outright spun up. "I know, baby, and Elijah's working on—"

"So you've said," she snipped, looking ready to break free and pace any second. But she didn't. Instead, she challenged, "Aren't you worried about Pia and Vela now? Didn't you say you were going to bring them here, too? For their safety? Where are they, Sebastian? Are they being secured?"

Since I sensed she had more questions left, I said nothing. But I sure as hell listened. Her pitch was still escalating, but if I wasn't mistaken, her angle now seemed... hopeful. Was this the key to the ongoing health problems Elijah kept telling me she was having? Was my sweet, outgoing Abbigail suffering from loneliness? Feeling isolated?

"Elijah has a detail keeping watch over them, but so far, there hasn't been a reason to be concerned about them," I said. "I've been trying to have minimal contact with my sister to keep her off their radar."

Abbi dipped a terse nod. "Okay. I guess that makes sense. But what's the plan now? I mean, what's the new direction, given this development with Terryn? Clearly, she's involved somehow . . . in all of this."

I emulated her nod but replied, "Yes and no."

"What do you mean?" she demanded.

"Terryn told me that she'd corresponded remotely with the keychain's supplier. When it was ready to give to me, they had it couriered to her at the office."

"Is that how she's explaining the freaky email too?" Abbi charged. "That all of that was done . . . remotely?"

"Of course not." At once, I hated myself for barking it. My sourness was entirely due to what I had to tell her next. "Apparently, somewhere along the line, my email account was . . . hacked. Those bastards used the originating address to set up the message to Terryn. The email only looked like it came from me."

Abbi absorbed that information with terse lips and a probing gaze. "So what does that mean?"

"That it seems Terryn is just being used as a pawn. The woman hasn't exactly been secretive about her . . . crush on me." I dragged a hand through my hair. "Or whatever the fuck it is."

"Crush?" Abbi pushed out a bitter laugh. "Ohhh, Bas. That woman is more than just crushing."

"Like I said," I bit back, "whatever the fuck it is . . . the bastards took advantage of it to get directly to me. They leveraged her."

"Yes, but she let them." They were the words, laced with bitterness, that spurred her to pace away. When she turned back to face me, her arms were folded and her shoulders were stiff. "Maybe you should let her go, Bas. Once and for all. They can't use her to get to you if she's no longer near you."

"Well, I'm waiting to see what Elijah comes up with

regarding that third charm, and then I'll go from there. As much as that woman is a creepy psychopath, I think whoever used her once may use her again. Now that we know that it's happened, we can watch her closer, too. That was definitely our mistake to not take her seriously."

"At what point are you going to get law enforcement involved in this?" The pale shade had returned to her cheeks.

"I don't know that yet either."

Her scowl warned me of an incoming argument. At the very least, a spirited protest. But by this point, I was looking forward to it. The fire in her fight usually led to one in my loins. But more than that, I needed to know her flames still existed. That my fierce, determined girl was still in there somewhere.

The conflagration never came. Instead, Abbi simply snuggled back into my side. "Hmmm," she murmured while resting her head on my shoulder. "Okay, then."

What the hell?

As the thought hit full force, I pulled back. Probed my stare down at her. In return, all I received was the vast emptiness of her huge emerald eyes.

"What?" she asked. "What's wrong?"

"Who are you, and what did you do with my Little Red?" I tried—and failed—to make it a joke.

"What do you mean?"

"I was expecting a full PowerPoint about why we should have the Feds involved in this." I couldn't help but frown.

"I trust you, Bas. I'm sure you know what's best." She snuggled back into my side, but I pulled away again.

"What?" she asked again, this time getting a little snippier. But barely.

"Seriously, Abs. What's going on?" I pressed, more stern

about it. She was really worrying me.

"Seriously." She mocked my concerned tone. "Nothing."

I squinted my eyes at her, not buying her bullshit for a second.

"Don't look at me like that," she retorted. "I'm not working an angle here. It's simply called acquiescence, Sebastian. Resignation, if you'd rather."

I rocked back. To be honest, I was stunned her two-by-four of an admission hadn't knocked me completely to my ass. How was the word *resignation* even in the woman's vocabulary? "Explain."

She sighed. "Bas—"

"Explain." I gritted it this time, though she barely seemed to care. A listless shrug preceded her listless plop back to the bench.

"I don't know." She waved a hand around with aimless uncertainty. "I guess . . . this. The whole situation." She sat up straighter as I lowered back next to her. "Look," she said, turning so we directly faced each other again, "I'm not trying to be evasive. Right now, I'm simply trying to be coherent. I've just spent an entire week locked away in my room, crying my eyes out until I was sick to my stomach every goddamn day. It's not a good feeling, Sebastian."

"I know." No way could I pull the heartless bastard card right now. Part of me prayed that was still even possible, but it wasn't. My twisting gut confirmed the inevitable truth. Abbigail Gibson held the damn thing in the palm of her hand, now and forever. "And, baby, I'm so sorry." I took her hands and reverently kissed each one. "I'm just trying to keep you safe here."

"I understand that. And I also understand that no matter

how much I cry and kick and yell, you are going to leave me here again. You're going back to your life in Los Angeles, and—"

"My life?" I deliberately punched out the second word. Barely resisted adding an acrid laugh—because right now, that term was truly a joke to me. "What makes you think I have any kind of a life without you?"

Abbigail didn't say a thing. She just stared, still eerily calm. Scarily resigned. "But you're still going back without me. And we still won't even talk on the phone for days on end."

"Damn it." I shoved back up to my feet. Grabbed the back of my neck. "I'm doing my best here, Abbigail." But at once, even I realized how ridiculous that sounded. "I . . . I thought I was doing the right thing by keeping my distance."

And now, beyond ridiculous.

Further proof? Abbi's continued stillness. And palpable, discernible tension.

She threw me one shred of mercy by speaking again.

"Wow."

Okay, only one word. But I could work with that. "What?" I softly demanded.

"You weren't joking." She shook her head, exposing the wet tracks across her cheeks even as she wiped with visible frustration. "You really don't know how to be a boyfriend, do you?"

"No." I grimaced. "I guess I don't." As I dropped my hand, it felt like a goddamned anchor of grief. "I'm so sorry I made all this harder for you. I thought that if we talked a lot, it would just make us miss each other more."

She dropped her hands too. Gripped them to the edge of the bench. "So you thought not talking at all was the answer?" She searched my face as disbelief washed over all her features.

"Uhh . . . yes?"

"Jesus Christ, Sebastian Shark." A laugh spilled from her. She rocked her head back. "You're a fucking idiot. Do you know that?"

"Well, I do now." I emulated her grin. "Come on." I stepped over and pulled her to her feet. "I have the very sudden urge to fuck you senseless."

"Is that so?" She went for coy with the smile now.

"Oh, it definitely is."

"Hmmm." She averted her sparkling gaze from my hooded one. "I don't know."

"What do you mean, you don't know?" I started tugging her along the path back to the house. When we got there, her giggles filled the terra cotta courtyard—and I rejoiced in the magical sound. A lost treasure unearthed.

"Well, you screwed up the easy part of boyfriending pretty monumentally," she continued explaining. "Who's to say you even know what you're doing in the bedroom?"

I halted, making her do the same, while growling out, "Watch yourself, young lady."

She only laughed harder. "Hey, I'm serious! Talking on the phone is Boyfriend 101!"

I hauled her back to me so swiftly, she thudded into my chest. I dipped her back and kissed the exposed valley between her breasts. She moaned out my name as I continued suckling up her neck—at least until I got to her lips. Those succulent pillows were shiny and ready, all but begging for the plunge of my tongue. Her eyes were glassy and mischievous, surely matching my own.

The recognition brought a brand-new grin to my own mouth.

She was back.

At least for now.

And to see this new life breathed back into her, to know I'd brought it, made my heart ache—and my soul agonize.

Please. Please whoever the fuck is listening to my hopeless soul... don't let me destroy this perfect creature. I'm begging you, don't let me ruin her.

"So at what grade level does the student get to learn about the fucking stuff?" I asked, grateful for the humor—and the lust beneath. Both were damn good smokescreens for the deeper emotions that vied for pole position on my tongue.

"Oh, that's the senior thesis project, I'm afraid," she answered, obviously trying to stifle her impending laughter. "You may have a lot of research to do before you're ready for your final dissertation."

"And that's an interesting analogy, Ms. Gibson."

"And why's that, Mr. Shark?"

"I got straight As in every class I ever took, you know." I set her down but didn't let her get far. With my hands lowering around her ass, I ground my growing shaft against her warm, welcoming cleft. "I make an excellent teacher's pet."

"Well, then." She traced a fingertip across my bottom lip. "We'd better hurry inside then, before the bell rings. You don't want detention on your first day, do you?"

With that, she took off running. She squealed with laughter as I playfully growled, chasing hot on her heels. We ran through the house to her room, where I tackled her onto the bed. She was facedown, and I was instantly turned on. I pinned her there by sitting on top of her, holding her arms above her head. Her chest pumped heavily from the exertion of bolting away from me.

"I love you, Abbigail." I rasped it into her ear before dipping down to drag her pants over her hips. Despite my tender declaration, I was feeling anything but soft and sensual. I needed her—in every way—and right now.

"I love you too," she moaned, and the sound gained a notch of volume as I pulled her clothes all the way off. On my way back up, I caressed her round, luscious ass. As I swatted it, she giggled.

"I'm so glad you're here," she said, turning her face to the side. "Just in case I haven't told you in the past hour." She bit her lip seductively. "It just feels so good . . . to laugh."

Except that now, she wasn't doing that. Just like that, her eyes brimmed with tears again. Not only one or two. The angst came in a full torrent, the huge drops coursing down her flushed cheeks.

"Fuck! Not again!" She buried her face in the blankets. Her whole body shook from the deluge. I moved with my sole instinctual reaction, immediately gathering her into my arms and holding her against my chest. My erection deflated with each sob that racked her alarmingly thin body. I could feel the sharp outline of her shoulder blades as she reached up and clung to me—resulting in me backtracking over the calendar, reminding myself it really had been only a week since I sent her here.

No. I had to be wrong. This had to be wrong. And if it wasn't . . .

How was it physically possible?

How could she have lost so much weight in such a short amount of time? Had she gotten this sick, this fast? Was something going on before she'd left? Something I hadn't noticed? Or was all of this more than simple stress?

My God.

What if she was dying? What if she had some sort of terminal disease and hadn't told me? What if she knew that I was falling in love with her and that I'd be left to grieve for a life that could've been?

Christ. And I always thought she was the one who got spun too far up?

There had to be another explanation. A logical one. But when I tried to tilt back and better assess her, Abbi refused to let go. She clung to me even tighter.

"Baby?" I prodded. No answer. "Abs?" Still nothing but shuddering sniffles. "Abbigail Eileen." Okay, that got a moment of stillness, at least—to which I took full advantage. "Okay, you're scaring the living shit out of me. What is going on? And don't you dare fucking say 'nothing.' So help me, I will spank you on top of everything else right now."

She jolted her face up. "I'm—well, I'm just stressed out. This is a lot to deal with. You get that, right?"

I cupped her cheek. "Yeah. I already told you—"

"What you thought I wanted to hear." Though she remained where she was, her voice went cold. Her gaze was dull and hard as jade. "But do you really understand this, Bas? Until you got here last night, I've had no one to talk to. No one! He— Elij— That man won't even let me use the phone! So do you really know how the hell I feel?"

I slid my touch down. The ball of her shoulder felt like a sparsely padded coat hanger. "I know that I want to, okay?"

"Then start believing me." In an angry lunge, she was off the bed and back on her feet. "You need to know about all of this, damn it. Do you know he did something to my cell phone so it won't work in this house? Do you know that, Mr. Shark?"

She stabbed her feet back into her pants. Once they were on, she stomped around the room. "He plays Mr. Innocent when I ask him about it, but he's a liar about it all—and not a very good one! He doesn't even try to be convincing!"

By now, her chest was heaving with fury—proving that fate really had it in for me now. Every new breath thrusted her nipples harder against her T-shirt. It was pure torture, and I was only human. The human who was hopelessly, helplessly smitten with every inch of her . . .

"Oh, dear God. Are you even listening to me? Or are you staring at my tits?"

"Red. Baby. I'm sorry. But you seriously can't blame me. You're magnificent . . ."

"Oh, for fuck's sake." She stomped over to the door and whooshed it open. As I glanced over, checking to make sure she hadn't torn it off the hinges, she hollered, "You know what? Get out!"

I nailed my stare back on her. "Excuse the hell out of me?"

"You heard me," Abbi snapped. "Just go hang out with the asshole. He's your goddamn friend!"

I maintained my position on the bed but gaped at her like she was possessed. "I'm only going to warn you one time, lady. Check yourself. And the attitude."

"Fuck you." Abbi hiked up her chin. "And your warning! And your buddy! And his attitude! How does all of that sound?"

Finally, I stood from the bed—though I never unpinned my stare from hers. Invisible electricity zapped between us, intensifying as I approached her. One calm step. Another and then another and then another, until I had her backed up against the wall adjacent to the open doorway she'd so adamantly insisted I use. The terminology was my version of benevolence, though likely for my sanity more than hers. If I thought of her tactics as a pure order, she'd be getting different treatment than this already.

But I was feeling benevolent.

I continued reminding myself of that while pressing the entire plane of my body against hers. I moved in as though I were going to kiss her but continued past her mouth to growl into her ear, "I understand you're not feeling well, and I also understand you're under a lot of stress, but this behavior is uncalled for. I'll be in the office when you're ready to apologize."

With a measured step backward, I held her stare, then turned and left the room. I didn't bother closing the door, figuring she'd slam the thing behind me in her fury. Surprisingly, after getting about fifteen feet down the corridor, I heard it close softly. Instantly, she engaged the lock, as well.

★ ★ ★

In the office of the Twentynine Palms estate, I sank into an overstuffed leather chair with a tall vodka tonic. Not my usual drink of choice, but nothing about today had been usual.

I watched three lizards battle for the prime sunning spot on a flat rock in the late-afternoon sun. They took turns with their dominant displays of what looked like push-ups, until one daunted the other two into backing off. He lifted his head, seeming to crow while spreading out unchallenged.

Not much different than humans.

The conclusion made my lips quirk. Not a lot. Just enough to acknowledge the stupid truth here. Living creatures were all pretty much the same. The strongest survived. The beast who could intimidate all the others into tucking tail and running was left with the best sunning spot in the end. The old phrase from the eighteen hundreds, "To the victor belong the spoils," came to mind.

Victor.

No. Viktor.

My smile faded.

Viktor Blake.

My pulse thundered.

"Jesus fucked a lizard," I muttered—as a new fact of life smacked me in the face like a wet towel.

The charm. On the key ring. It was associated with that bastard. The hairs on the back of my neck, all sporting instinctual erections, confirmed it. The recesses of my brain just couldn't put the exact details together. Not yet.

Not that I was about to waste time waiting on my goddamned gray matter.

I dug into my pocket, eager to grab my phone and get a text off to Elijah. He and Joel had gone out to town—if that was what it could be called—for restocks on groceries and other supplies.

When my fingers met nothing but pocket lint, I swore beneath my breath. I must have left the device in Abbi's room—but I'd be damned if I was going back into that hornet's nest anytime soon.

So, I enjoyed my drink and looked out at the property. For all of the five minutes I could stand it. Okay, so not much happened around here. As in, not at all. I could appreciate why the boredom might drive someone a bit to their limits. At the same time, being forced to unwind for a few days carried some of its own merit too. Abbi was going to have to find something to do with her time here. I really thought the gourmet kitchen would give her pleasure. If she wanted ingredients for culinary adventures, experimenting with new recipes, or just to cook for enjoyment, all she had to do was ask Elijah to get them. I'd given him, and the rest of the staff, carte blanche on what they had to spend. I'd ransom one of my own kidneys just to make the woman happy.

But she wasn't.

At all.

And Elijah had helped make her that way.

I leaned my head back and let out a heavy sigh. Where had I gone wrong with those two? They were at each other's throats with a stunning level of intensity. They either really hated each other that much, or—

I swore again and ordered the thought to fuck off. Too late. The nagging voice persisted, wondering if something was actually going on between them. As insane as the idea seemed, I couldn't bury my head in the sand. Elijah was one of my best friends. And Abbigail was—

Well, Elijah knew what she was to me.

And while the man was sarcastic, arrogant, and annoyingly bold, he was also loyal, smart, and valued his testicles.

Which was why I could officially quash that stupid misgiving.

"Christ," I muttered, slugging back more alcohol. I'd just used misgiving in a complete sentence. About myself.

I drained the last of my drink, rose, and then headed to the kitchen. I could no longer ignore the aromas emanating from there, filling the entire house with savory spices. My stomach growled loudly enough to echo back from the tile floor.

I nearly dropped my tumbler upon finding Abbigail

cooking side by side with one of the estate's staff members. I wasn't sure if I should quietly turn in the other direction and just leave her to it or engage her in conversation. The decision was taken from me when she abruptly lifted her gaze, as if sensing my presence.

"Something smells fantastic," I said with a natural smile, hoping to test the waters between us. "I came to investigate."

Abbi copied my look, though it was an automatic expression. She could just as easily have been smiling at a stranger on an elevator or waving at the nosey neighbor from her Torrance condo days. "Martha was making mole sauce and asked if I wanted to help. I told her the other day that I'd never made it before, so she's teaching me."

"Well, don't let me interrupt. I left my phone in the bedroom, and I just had an idea about that third charm."

"Of course you did." Her reply matched the neutral nothingness of her smile, but I stowed my irritation. Right now, I had to focus on deciphering that symbol. The sooner we found these mysterious bastards, the sooner I could give Abbigail what she wanted. What I wanted more than anything too. Her, back with me every day and night.

"Well, I'm going to call Elijah. We're going to move on this shit as fast as possible."

Abbigail simply nodded, not breaking the pace of her stirring. While tamping deeper aggravation, I headed down the hall.

I found my phone on the bed and saw I'd missed a call from Elijah. I hit redial without listening to the voicemail. He picked up after the first ring.

"Hey, man. We're almost back to the house. Hope I didn't interrupt anything."

"Unless you're talking about an epic argument or the tirade that got me banished from the bedroom? Nope, not a thing."

"Damn." His tone was sincere. "Sorry, my friend. What's gotten into her now, you think? Maybe she's OTR?"

"Don't be so crass," I spat. "And it's definitely not that. I have firsthand knowledge. She keeps saying it's stress. I'd suggest her sister-in-law coming out for a few days, but the woman is a powder keg."

"Yeah, but also the powder keg who's holding Abstract Catering together."

I grimaced. Scrubbed a hand up my jaw. "I fucking hate this," I muttered. "I'm the reason that's even having to happen. The cause of Abbigail being away from her business."

The company that was her own version of Shark Enterprises. That she'd built with her bare hands and raw passion.

"Well, the sooner we can get her out of Twentynine Palms detention duty, the better."

I almost questioned if the guy was referring to himself as much as Abbigail but decided I probably wouldn't like the answer. Instead, I said, "I've had a brainstorm about the keyring. Maybe it can help."

"Outstanding," Elijah stated. "Because I've got something too, but it's definitely only half the puzzle."

"Let's meet in the office when you're back."

"We're pulling into the garage right now."

A few minutes later, he and I sat at the desk in the study, looking at the computer monitor to which he'd connected his laptop. The gift from Terryn lay on the hardwood desk between us, and an image of the charm was on the display, blown up so the detail could be seen.

The symbols matched.

But right now, that was all we knew.

"So, talk to me, Banks. How did you find this online?" I asked.

"Easy." Elijah shrugged. This was his wheelhouse, so he spoke like the discovery process was simple and reasonable and anyone could do it.

Except it wasn't simple and easy. I paid him a ridiculous amount of money to do his job because he was at the top of heap at what he did.

"I scanned the charm, then searched for the image and found a handful that matched. Certain things about the image stand out, you see? Like the colors, the points here and here." He motioned to the screen while he explained. "So, all of the supposed matches had those things in common. From there, it was a matter of weeding through the images and looking at the finer details and picking out the actual match. The words around the outside of the triangle were the key."

Victori Sunt Spolia

Each word spanned the outside edges of a triangle, which served as the framework for a twine of laurel leaves.

"So were you able to locate this company? This is a logo for a company, right?" I leaned in closer to the monitor to read the small lettering around the logo.

"Unbelievable." I shook my head as the growl emanated from the pit of my throat. I peered closer, just to make sure I was really right about this.

"What?" Elijah leaned in too. "What is it, man? Have you

seen this symbol before?"

"I think so." I steepled my hands. "But I don't think it's a symbol."

"What is it, then?" He fidgeted with tension, struggling to be polite about it. "Because I'm still coming up empty on anything beyond the match. I've had a few hits, but every thread I follow comes up as a dead end. Big fucking wastes of time. It seems like they're intentionally misleading."

"I'm not surprised."

"So you want to share with a brother?" Elijah rubbed the back of his neck, more open about his frustration. I understood his agony. We'd been friends for a long damn time, and like me, he was a take-charge fixer. He was as pissed as me that we hadn't won this game yet.

But I sensed he'd be more enraged by what I had to share next.

"That's not a symbol," I asserted. "I think it's a logo."

Elijah narrowed his gaze at me. Swung it back to the monitor. "A . . . huh?"

"That phrase is in Latin." I pointed at the screen. "It basically means, 'to the victor goes the spoils.' In the eighteen hundreds, it was more famous as 'to the victor belong the spoils.' Basically, the strongest person wins and takes all the treasure, right?"

I waited for Elijah's nod. He didn't take long for the acknowledgment.

"Earlier, I was sitting over by that window—"

"With ice on your singed pubes?" Elijah smirked.

"Something along those lines," I went on without giving him more kerosene for that fire. "And along came these three lizards, onto the same rock. As I watched them fight for the alpha sunning spot, I had that same thought. How the biggest asshole reptile won the right to sun himself."

Elijah chuffed before affirming, "To the victor go the spoils—and the sun."

I rocked back in my chair. "Well, guess who I thought of right after that?"

"Well, shit." Elijah settled back against his own seatback. "Viktor Blake?"

I pointed at him. "Ding, ding, ding. Stuffed shark for the winner."

He rested his head against his upturned fist. "Man, your mind is a complicated and crazy place."

"I love you too, honey."

He pinned his stare back on the monitor. "So you think that son of a bitch is behind this?"

"I'd bet you a few lizards on it."

"Well, you can keep those—but just this morsel may help a lot in my search. If I cross-reference his name and known aliases with the logo, it might pull up something interesting."

"Good."

I meant it. Goddammit, at last we might be getting somewhere with this crap. *Thank you, Terryn Ramsey*. But the celebratory grin I expected from Elijah was a no-show. The guy still seemed stuck on a pause button as he sat back, thinking, before rising and then turning to face me.

"Bas. Let me ask you something."

I gave a single nod and then waited for him to continue. I had no clue what to expect next. The look on his face shifted like storm clouds rolling across a prairie sky.

"What happens if you confirm Blake and the logo are connected? What are you going to do?"

I remained still. That was a good question. My immediate instinct led at once to an outrageous plan, but I didn't have to state that out loud. Elijah already knew it too. But killing the bastard wouldn't get us anywhere. I'd be every authority's first suspect if Blake turned up dead.

"I think we need to figure out his motivation," I said at last. "Is this all still the bullshit from the old neighborhood? If so, it's gone way too far at this point. People are dead now."

"Agreed," my friend declared. "Which means we've got to follow the dots to something else." The storm on his features turned darker. "In this case, probably some*one* else."

My instincts flared again. This time, in the most tormenting ways. "What the hell are you getting at?"

"I think you know, man." He waited as I plunged my head into my hands. "I know you don't want to, but you do." Then as I heaved in a lungful of air. "It's Abbigail. At some point, we have to acknowledge that."

I still didn't say anything. I barely moved—until my violent flinch when Elijah lowered a brotherly clasp to my shoulder.

"Bas?"

He gave me a gentle nudge. I jerked up my head, leveling my gaze to his.

"What do you want from me, Elijah?" I asked plaintively.

"I want you to face the reality of the situation."

"And you think I'm not, damn it?"

"Blake has an unhealthy fixation with her. I watched him at that groundbreaking, and it was disturbing." Elijah's voice was quiet and eerie, and chills ran up my spine. At the same time, rage kept boiling my blood and balling my fists.

"I know that, you fucker," I seethed. "I was there too!"

"But you haven't processed anything past that, aside from

going off on Blake like a caveman."

I swallowed hard. Didn't do a damn thing for the sting behind my eyes and the lump of lead in my throat. "Processed it?" I flung. "In case you can't tell, I've been busy processing a few other matters at the moment, Banks."

"And I'm not debating that." He was still speaking like the goddamned reincarnation of Mr. Miyagi, trying to quietly coax me into walking across his ridiculous rice paper. "But maybe, while you've got the chance, you need to step back and evaluate where you're going with all this. Where you're actually going with Abbigail too."

I stomped my way back over to the window from this morning. More than anything, I wished there was another vodka and tonic waiting for me there. "What about Abbigail?"

"You tell me, man. You never really talk about it. About her."

"What the hell are you– I talk about her all the damn time!"

"About how to protect her. About how to get her to behave the way you want her to. But what about how you actually feel about her, dude? About how much she means to you? About your plans for a future with her?"

I turned my back on him. Slammed my hands to my hips in lieu of smashing one through the plate glass window. "I'm not a touchy-feely asshole like you and Twombley, okay? Just because the two of you sit around braiding each other's hair and shit doesn't mean I do. I'm not wired that way."

"And look where it's gotten you."

"What's that supposed to mean?" If he didn't tread carefully, the next place I put a fist would be in his mouth.

"Well, while you've been busy with your world domination

plans and studiously ignoring your feelings, your arch nemesis is trying to take your most prized possession," he rebutted. "And said possession has now gotten incredibly ill, yet you still don't seem to think any of it's important enough to pay attention to."

I spun back around. Elijah had folded his arms across his chest. Mr. Miyagi, in all his self-satisfied pride, was still in the house.

"Important enough?" I gritted out. "What the fuck more do you want me to do, Banks? Open a goddamned vein? Because I will. Because the woman in that bedroom is that important!"

As he rolled his eyes, I longed to knock him so hard that his pupils flew to China. "And of course yelling at me will fix everything. That's the answer, huh?"

As soon as the patronizing words were out, I fought the craving to deck him again. To smack his head into the desktop until he started really hearing me. But that would help nothing.

Fucker probably knew that too.

Not that he'd get the satisfaction of my admission.

I stumbled back to my chair. Fell back into the thing as I let fly with a long, conflicted groan.

"Shit. I brought her here to keep her safe. I had no idea she was this sick."

Elijah grunted. "Well, she's this sick."

"It's been tearing me up to see her like this. I planned on calling a doctor this afternoon to come out here and look at her, but then I found her in the kitchen, content and cooking, and she looked completely fine. I'm so damn confused!"

"No." He shook his head. "You're a fucking idiot."

I glared harder at him. "What the living fuck are you talking about?"

"Are you really that blind, man? Or that stupid?" When I just continued staring, he facepalmed himself. Hard. "Okay, yeah. I guess you really are."

I slammed my hands to the tops of my thighs. The wrath in my move catapulted up my body, landing solidly at the center of my chest. "You going to spit it out sometime this century, Banks?"

He lowered his hand. Glared like we were in third grade all over again and he was having to explain new math to me. "Just…call the doctor anyway, okay? And stop evading the important stuff with Abbigail. Something tells me you two will need to be solid on that shit, sooner rather than later."

He wasn't going to divulge more than that. Which definitely left me stranded in the dark about the new math.

Which meant I still felt like decking him.

As soon as I remembered how to add two and two.

CHAPTER FIVE

ABBIGAIL

Parting is such sweet sorrow.

Romeo and Juliet could both suck a bag of dicks as far as I was concerned. Sweet sorrow? More like absolute hell. Full-on gut-wrenching misery was even more accurate.

Bas and I finally had sucked up our egos and made up for our terrible fight. I apologized for my "impertinence"—his label—and he did the same about his "breast-obsessed distractibility"—my label—which led to some of the best sex of my existence in the giant master suite bed. Afterward, there was a different energy about him, as if the last of his rage had spilled out along with his orgasm. In its place was a quiet watchfulness that I couldn't figure out but wasn't sure if I wanted to. I kind of liked it.

We spent the rest of the afternoon lazing in each other's arms, trading off between an oversize float in the pool, a large lounge chair on the deck—and just about every other surface in the master bedroom. We made love on every surface that was available and even some we improvised.

Memories I battled to keep close in my heart, instead of the crushing ache threatening it as soon as Joel started up the town car that night. A pain that swelled and grew as I watched the vehicle—and in it, the man I was hopelessly in love with—

disappear down the driveway. I didn't stop watching until the red taillights were nothing but tear-blurred stars in the far, far distance.

Thirty minutes later, it was still a toss-up which ached more: my head from crying so much, my stomach from dry heaving over the toilet bowl, or my heart from shattering yet again. Every shard felt irreparable this time—and I honestly didn't know how much more abuse the organ could sustain before refusing to beat any more.

Curling into a smaller ball didn't help. I tried my left side and then the right, tossing from one end of the bed to the other. I couldn't get comfortable. All I smelled was Sebastian's scent. It wasn't just his cologne wafting up from the sheets. It was all of him. The smell of the heady perspiration that slicked his skin while he fucked me. The expensive hair products he artfully fingered through his dark waves to demand their submission.

"Damn it." I drew out the last vowel, making it a groan into the pillow. As I closed my eyes, I swore I could even smell his smile, his laughter, his passion. It sounded insane, but I could so easily picture him. Could so easily be engulfed by all the memories of him. The mischief in his eyes as he loomed over me. The devious slant of his lips as cunning thoughts pursued his mind. And oh yes, all the beautiful ways he made those fantasies come true, arousing and tempting me with his lips, fingers and tongue... until I begged. Begged for all of it. Every wicked, depraved way he could drive my need so high and hot and urgent...

But I couldn't beg him anymore. Because he wasn't here anymore. My whispered pleas met nothing but heavy, empty air. It was all so unfair.

So. Freaking. Unfair.

I'd entreated him to stay. Pleaded for just one more night. Asked in my sweetest, most desperate voice for him to stay with me for one more night and have Joel drive him back early in the morning—but nothing worked. The man had a resolve stronger than the hull of a modern-day battleship, and now he actually had a direction in which to steer that big barge. I knew that even before I tried changing his mind, but I also knew I had to try. I had to do everything I could to keep him with me instead of lying here lonely and afraid and unsure.

Exactly like I was feeling now.

A laugh burst from me as I considered that. *Afraid.* Afraid of what, exactly? I didn't fear for my own safety. Elijah had me locked away in this fortress as though I were a damn prisoner. No, my fear was for Bas himself.

At least I thought that was what it was. The guys kept me so carefully closed off and in the dark, believing I was too fragile to handle any information they had uncovered on the case, I had to fill in the blanks on my own from the tidbits I overheard or that were accidentally shared in front of me.

I only knew all this "investigating" had gone on for months now, and the most viable culprit they had right now was Viktor Blake. The concept still seemed like grasping at straws to me, but I had resigned myself to leaving the investigation to Bas, Elijah, and their team. Those men knew way more than me about what made Viktor tick. I simply had to trust Bas. And surprisingly, that was something that came very easily.

Oh, yes. *Surprisingly.* Since my mom's death, trust was something I had a hard time dispensing—until that morning I stood in the Inglewood kitchen with Rio, watching the morning news about a suicide jumper in Long Beach. Soon after, Sebastian Shark strode into my world and changed everything.

The man made trusting him as natural as breathing—almost from the first moment we met and absolutely from the first moment we touched. He had a way about him that just said, *I've got you.*

But this whole situation felt like he was asking for more than trust. Something even beyond blind faith. And I was tired, deep into my bones, of trying to generate it all the time. It was easier to just be resigned to the circumstances. To give up the fight. If I couldn't even keep my eyes open, what was the point in caring about anything beyond this compound? Hell, I barely even cared about combing my hair anymore. At least once a day, Elijah found me in my window seat, softly snoring with a book on my chest. Bas had brought me most of the paperback TBR stack that normally sat on my home nightstand when he visited.

God, how I missed that nightstand. And the luxurious bed it was next to. And the house in Calabasas. Our house. My normal life.

But would anything be normal again?

The men still refused to restore my cell phone's calling capabilities, insisting someone could easily trace my incoming calls. But Sebastian had told me if I wanted to make a phone call, Elijah would allow me to do so without a hassle.

First thing the next morning, I decided it was time to put that acquiescence to the test.

I set off to find my warden in the grand expanse of the estate. Elijah was usually in the office, by the pool, or fussing around the kitchen. The kitchen staff was patient with his relentless meddling and persistent "helping," but to me, he just seemed underfoot.

But just the walk to the kitchen took its toll on my system.

By the time I came into the wide-open space, my eyes danced with bright white spots and my mouth watered with the telltale burn of nausea.

"Abbi—"

I stopped Elijah, and his concerned rush, with an upturned hand. I couldn't deal with his third degree and the queasiness at the same time. A panicked wave of heat flashed over my skin, knowing I wouldn't make the distance from the kitchen to the nearest bathroom.

"Ohhh shit," I moaned. "Shit . . ." I covered my mouth and looked frantically from side to side for something to vomit into. In the nick of time, one of the staff women was there with a trash bin.

A few minutes later, the episode was done. A short one this time—thank God—since I had an audience witnessing it all, though Elijah left the room about halfway through. Thank God for small favors, I guessed. The man and his watchful eyes unnerved me more than anything else, especially because he reported everything directly back to Sebastian. My man had more things to worry about than my ongoing sour stomach. I had to learn how to handle this stress better.

Goals for another day.

Right now, it just felt nice to accept a damp dish towel from the woman who'd helped me through the episode. After smiling in gratitude, I blotted my parched lips and flushed cheeks before pressing the cloth to my forehead.

"Thank you," I murmured.

"Of course," she gently returned.

"You've been so kind. I'll take care of the trash. Where do you keep the larger can outside?"

"Don't be silly, Miss Gibson. It's already been taken care

of. Why don't you rest?" The woman nudged me toward the great room and the inviting sectional sofa.

"Mmmm, that sounds like a good idea." From firsthand experience, I knew that like every other piece in the home, the couch was magnificently comfortable. "Maybe for a few minutes, at least."

I slipped my shoes off before putting my legs up and stretching out across the cushions—but before I could close my eyes, Elijah emerged from the office.

"Feeling any better?" he asked quietly. It struck me that this might be the kindest I'd ever heard his tone.

"Yes, thank you." I gave back as good as he'd offered, even managing a small smile. "Hey... uhhh... do you know that woman's name?" I asked then. "The one who just helped me?"

Elijah chuckled while walking over and then hitching a thigh up on the arm of an oversize chair. "Well, you've come to the wrong guy. I'm terrible with names, to be honest." With a self-deprecating smile, he admitted, "I've tried every trick in the book to be better at retaining names when I meet people, but none seem to work for me."

"Same here." I phased my smile into a soft wince. "And I always feel bad. I think it makes me seem self-centered."

"Abbigail Gibson, you are the furthest thing from self-centered."

I batted a hand to the bottom of my neck as a gasp of mock surprise burst from it. "Elijah Banks, did you just compliment me?"

He started to scowl but stopped himself. With slick ease, he slid all the way into the chair. "You know I genuinely care about you, Abbi." He securely held my gaze with his steady hazel one. "Right?"

"Right." I pulled the quilt up to my chin, using the blanket to physically gird my emotional vulnerability. "Of course I do."

Only then did I notice the brown shopping bag he'd brought in and discreetly stashed at his feet.

"So, hey. What's in the bag? Is it yours?" I was more than ready for a subject change.

"Yes, well . . . it's for you, actually."

I gave in to a double-take. "Huh?"

"I set it down earlier when you came out from your room looking as green as the Grinch," he explained.

I sat up taller and eyed the discreet package with new interest. "Really? It's for me? You got me a gift?" I deliberately stressed the pronouns, wondering if I should even be circling the day on my calendar in red. God only knew when this would ever happen again.

"Mmmm . . ." Elijah tilted his head, succumbing to a weird version of a wince. "I . . . wouldn't call it a gift, per se."

I scowled. Not necessarily in anger. More like puzzlement. And a little irritation. Maybe more than a little. I should've known the guy had stipulations. Even for something so minor it could be contained in a small, innocuous brown bag. I drummed the fingers of one hand against the back of the other, waiting for him to either explain or just hand over the parcel.

"First, I want to tell you a story."

"That so?" But I regretted my snip as soon as I took in the glance he gave me—from beneath worried brows.

Wait a second. Well, holy shit. Is Jailer Man Banks . . . uncertain about something?

"Let me amend that, actually. First, I want you to eat something. Oatmeal? Yogurt? Please, Abbigail."

My good mood quickly soured to match my stomach.

"Not this again."

"Abbig—"

"Damn it, Elijah. I have a stomach bug, okay? Don't be so dramatic. I'm drinking fluids and resting more than any person should need to. This thing's just taking a while to run its course because I'm under a lot of stress." I shrugged for good measure. "It's really not a big deal."

Silence settled between us for several minutes until his phone signaled an incoming message. He tapped out a reply and stuffed it back in his pocket without comment to me. I fought the urge—with every cell of my body—to ask if it was Sebastian.

Instead, I prompted, "So . . . the bag? Or, should I say, my gift? Come on, give it over, Banks."

"Not until you eat something."

I flopped back against the overstuffed couch pillows. "Oh, my God. Seriously?"

"Yeah, seriously. Just a few bites."

"No."

"Do you normally take vitamins?"

"No!" I spat it this time. "I don't usually take vitamins. They bother my stomach." I chuckled at the comment—and meant it. I couldn't imagine what a multivitamin would do to my stomach in its current condition. "I normally eat a very balanced diet. I'm a chef, remember? I cook exceptional healthy food, and I always ensure the meals I prepare are nutritionally balanced."

We were quiet again for a few minutes before a woman from the kitchen entered the room. She was younger than the saint who'd just helped me get rid of everything but my stomach lining but her face possessed the same open warmth, her smile the same friendly dimples. She carried a tray with a steaming bowl in the center of it.

"Martha prepared this for you, Ms. Gibson," she said while lowering the tray to the coffee table. "She said it might help to settle your stomach."

"Thank you." I nodded and smiled in return. "And please, just call me Abbi."

"All right." She had a charming blush. "Abbi."

"Would you mind telling me your name?"

"I'm Dori. It's short for Dorinda. But that's a silly family name that's awful!" She laughed, and I found myself joining in with a weak giggle. "There is vegetable broth and toast. I put the butter on the side in case your stomach isn't ready for that. There's some mild cheese there too. Maybe some calcium would be good for you right now?"

I looked up to catch the happy twinkle in her gaze. Her kindness and generosity, with the food as well as her spirit, made tears threaten the backs of my eyes.

"Thank you, Dori. This is very thoughtful."

"Well, we've all been worried about you, Ms. Gib– Abbi. Please, try to eat a little bit before you rest. I'll take the tray when you're done, okay?"

"Okay."

Elijah and I watched her disappear back into the kitchen before he turned back to me. "Sit up a bit," he directed. "I'll hand you the bowl."

"Actually, the toast sounds better at the moment."

"All right. Do you want butter on it?"

"No. I better just stick to plain for now. I'm not sure the fat is a good idea."

"Agreed. Here you go." He handed me the small plate

with the four triangles of toasted wheat. Never had two measly pieces of bread looked so daunting. "Just do what you can," he urged. "I'd rather see you keep down one-half than return all four."

My keeper sat back in his cushy chair after getting me situated. I glared at him and huffed. "Sheez, Elijah. You don't have to sit and stare at me to make sure I eat. I'm not playing some game here."

"I know that," he countered. "But I also told you that I wanted to talk before giving you this." He nudged the elephant in the room, masquerading as that damn brown bag, with his toe.

"Does this story have something to do with the... interesting... shift in your mood here?" I asked it carefully, lest my spotlight on the difference make him change his mind about giving it to me.

"Maybe." He sighed and pushed his hands through his sandy brown hair. "Okay, yes. Probably."

"Which means what?"

Elijah leaned forward. Did that digging-through-his-hair thing again. Shoved back. Leaned forward. I almost said something about his fidgeting endangering my tentative sense of balance, but he finally settled for bracing his elbows on his knees—just before asking, "Has Sebastian... ever mentioned a woman named Hensley to you?"

So much for my restored equilibrium.

My stomach lurched. Holy shit. There was a woman in Bas's life I didn't know about? One Elijah was so concerned about, he had to sit down and tell me a story with her as the main character? And then offer up a consolation gift afterward?

"No." I dropped the toast onto the plate and shoved the dish away.

"Stop," he ordered, using that same take-no-prisoners tone Bas used with me.

I flared my nostrils. "Don't you dare tell me to—"

"Don't get all worked up! She wasn't his woman." He held my gaze for a few beats before declaring, "She was mine."

I exhaled audibly. As much as I didn't want to be so petty, his confession flooded me with gratitude. On top of everything else, my heart couldn't handle yet another tale about one of Sebastian's past conquests.

"You loved her," I said knowingly. The pained look on Elijah's face already spoke a thousand words of its own.

"I did. More than I knew I was capable of," he agreed quietly.

"What happened?"

He shrugged. "Things . . . didn't work out."

I narrowed my eyes. Tilted my head a little. Waited.

Elijah was the one to sigh then, scrubbing his hand down his face. He looked like he was reconsidering his insistence on this story hour after all.

At last, he went on. "You and Bas . . . remind me a lot of us. Hensley and me," he clarified. "Sometimes . . . it's hard to watch the two of you. Brings up a lot of shit I didn't realize I had buried. I'm sorry; I'm just trying to be honest . . ."

"It's okay." I was so sincere about it, my voice shook. "Really."

He rubbed subconsciously at a phantom pain in the center of his chest. "Hensley was . . . beautiful. And sexy. And smart as hell. Fuck, probably smarter than me."

"Imagine that," I deadpanned with a smirk.

"She was everything I could've ever wanted in a woman. Every damn thing. I wanted to give her the world, you know?

And I tried to. She had a restless spirit, though. I always felt like I just wasn't enough. Like maybe one day it would all fizzle out for her. She always said I was crazy, that I was acting so insecure..."

"Now there's something I really can't picture."

He grinned slyly, but I saw a new hollowness to the guy's once-cocky swagger.

"Well, as luck would have it—or so I thought—she got pregnant."

I grabbed a smaller pillow and clutched it close—to hide the tension that broadsided me. "Oh." It was all I could eke out, past my suddenly deafening heartbeat.

"It just...happened," he continued. "I mean, we were careful. Seriously careful. She always got some shot or something... at her doctor's office. I never went with her when she got it, but she always assured me everything was fine."

I tilted my head. "Nothing's a hundred percent effective."

"No shit." He grunted out a laugh. "Regardless, I was fucking over the moon about it. I've always wanted a family. With the shitty childhood I had, I wanted to give a kid the life I never knew. Hensley recognized that too. We used to talk about it."

I softened my grip on the pillow, realizing I was mesmerized by his anecdote now. The rapt emotion on his face had become a glow down his entire body. "So, what happened?" I asked gently. "She didn't want the baby?"

"No, she did," he insisted. "But she was so sick in the beginning. Throwing up all the time..." He shot me a pointed stare. "Of course, that's not abnormal, and the doctors assured us things would mellow out. We went to all the appointments and did all the right things. I even proposed. I mean, sure, it accelerated all our plans, but it wasn't like I didn't plan to already. And shit, a baby! Right? It was time to get serious. Lock it down, and all that." He waved his hand through the air, encompassing all the usual rituals for a couple when a baby is on the way.

"So, what happened?" I prodded again.

His glow dimmed. "Hensley was about five months along, maybe six... starting to really show... so she could no longer hide it from her friends and family. She'd been putting off telling people, no matter how many times I asked. She kept saying she 'didn't want to jinx it.'" He twisted his lips. "Bullshit like that."

Oh, yeah. His light was officially out now. It even fled his face as he sat deeper into the chair and dropped his head back onto the cushion. Finally, when he spoke again, he didn't even meet my eyes. He just kept staring up at the ceiling fan, whirling obliviously above us.

Then he dropped the bomb I could never have planned for.

"She told me the baby wasn't mine." His voice cracked on the last word. "And then she left."

Silence. Deafening silence. I wished I could give him more, but I couldn't. Sheer shock had taken over my thoughts... my heart. There was no sound in the air beyond the fan's persistent *wwhhaa wwhhaa wwhhaa*. The blades sliced, heartless as daggers, through the pea-soup-thick air hanging between us. Emotions so asphyxiating, neither one of us was capable of inhaling or exhaling for a few long beats.

My human instinct told me to go to him. Hug him. Comfort him. But the relationship we shared wasn't like that. I was paralyzed with indecision.

"Elijah." I sat up and scooted to the end of the sofa, nearest to where he was still so eerily frozen. "I— I can't imagine… I have no words—"

He cut me off when he raised his head. I lurched back, unable to hide my astonishment. The agony and bitterness of a hundred broken hearts were etched on his handsome face. I'd never seen him like this before. I wanted to tell him I was sorry, but suddenly that seemed wildly inappropriate.

"Don't," he nearly barked before a grimace contorted his features. "Just don't," he said in a softer tone. "Sorry. Honestly. It's raw. It's been three fucking years, and it's still so raw. I keep thinking it will get easier, and it doesn't. But that's not your fault. So I apologize." He took an intentionally long breath. Then again. He closed his eyes, clearly working to calm himself. I watched him, frozen in my spot on the sofa.

"Thank you for sharing a part of your past with me," I finally said. "I can only imagine how difficult that was."

He gave me a forced half-smile. "Well, there is a reason for doing so, Abbigail. And it wasn't just to exorcise my demons or forge some bond between us or whatever."

"Gee, thanks for clearing that up," I muttered tersely. That at least had him shifting back into his usual asshole demeanor, navigating us into familiar waters. Floating on those currents was my abject curiosity. "Why flay yourself open like that, then? What's this all about? If you're going to go right back to this?" I waved my hand up and down his seated frame.

Elijah let half a beat go by before reaching down and finally grabbing the small shopping bag at his feet. He extended it my way. "I picked this up for you the other day when Joel and I were running errands. You and Sebastian seem to be the only two people on the planet who haven't figured it out yet." He shook his head and nudged the bag toward me again.

"Figured out wha—"

My vocal cords surrendered to a choke as I opened the bag and pulled out the box inside. The words *pregnancy test* all but throbbed in purple lettering on the long container in my trembling grip. I stared at them. Hard. Then looked at him. Back again to the box. One more time at the determined man in the chair—this time not disguising my disbelief.

"You and I both know how that's going to turn out." Elijah nodded at the box. "Don't we?"

I opened my mouth. Shut it. Shoved the box back into his cute little brown bag. "You think this is clever, Mr. Banks?"

He arched his brows. "I think this is smart, Ms. Gibson. The faster we find out, the quicker we can get you some proper care—"

"I have a stomach bug, damn it! I'm not even late. Not that it's your business." I hurled the pillow across the room. "Any of it!"

He shot to his feet. Threw his hands in the air while bumping his voice up to match my shout. "For Christ's sake, woman. Be serious right now. I mean, I get the whole virgin thing and all—but shit!"

I surged up to mirror his stance. "You know what? Fuck you. I know you have some shit you haven't dealt with from your past. And honestly, you may want to talk to a professional about all that, as long as we're being assholes to each other. But don't put your shit on Sebastian and me. We have more than our share of drama at the moment, in case you haven't noticed."

He narrowed his glare. "Of course, I've fucking noticed. That being said, do you really think I did this just to be 'cute'?"

I shoved out air through my nostrils and stomped across the room.

The bastard did the same, stomping the opposite direction.

"Abbig—"

"No," I spat. "Just. Don't." Neither of my snarls helped to dissipate my outrage. I was just more pissed off now—enough to fire at him, "Next time you want to get me a gift, buddy? A candle or some fucking flowers will suffice!"

Only then did I realize that I still clutched the brown bag, the offensive purple box sticking out the top like a wino's stash. I whipped it away like it had turned into a snake—right at the asshole across the room. The top of the box hit Elijah's head so hard, it bounced off his hard skull and smacked into the large window beside him. It *shooshed* down the glass and thumped to the floor. The box fell free from the bag, its brilliant violet letters landing face-up. Taunting me.

And now driving me into a full fight-or-flight.

I stormed down the hall to my room and slammed the door. The entire wall shook, and I watched the hanging artwork tremor with a vaguely satisfied smirk. Which, of course, quickly dissolved into rolling, raging tears.

How dare that bastard stick his nose into our personal life? How dare he insinuate I was so naïve, I wouldn't know if my own damn body was with child or not? And how dare he possibly be right?

And in that case . . . how dare I?

I couldn't even comprehend it. How dare I? How could I? How could I bring a child into this dangerous situation? Into this world where I couldn't even be with its father right now? In which we wouldn't be able to share any of the happy, exciting... terrifying times with him or my family or friends?

I angrily wiped my face. Desperately pushed the horrible thoughts away.

Elijah was wrong. He had to be.

Nevertheless, I pulled up the calendar on my cell phone. Swiftly, I searched for the last time I'd had my period. I usually kept careful track, even in the days before Sebastian, so I'd know to be "prepared" on the Abstract delivery runs. But time had gotten warped since I'd been at this house. Everything was out of sorts. I barely knew what time of day it was anymore, let alone how it related to the passing days and weeks. My period had been the last thing on my mind.

Three weeks.

Four.

Five.

"Oh, God," I blurted. No. Nooo! How could this be happening? How could it really be close to six weeks since I had my period last? How had I not have noticed I was late?

That answer came with agonizing speed. I had been so wrapped up in everything else, I hadn't been paying attention. But how could I possibly care for a child if I couldn't even count fucking days on a calendar?

And now that the possibility was horrifically real, I didn't even have the test to take for clarification. It was back on the floor, next to where I'd thrown it at Elijah like a child confronted with the truth about Santa Claus. I'd have to wait a bit and sneak back out to the great room and see if he left it sitting out somewhere. Or maybe I could ask Dori to bring me a test next time she went into town. Oh, yes! Much better idea.

I cracked my door open to go find her. I paused, like a naughty kid listening for—why not—Santa Claus on Christmas

Eve. If I heard Elijah moving around anywhere, I'd just tuck back to my room.

I didn't hear a thing.

Except the crunch that resulted when my toe hit the damn shopping bag—which had been placed just outside like a sentry guard.

I was really starting to hate him.

But I swallowed my pride and snatched up the little package. After locking my door, I hauled the offensive box all the way out. There was only one way to restore my peace of mind—whatever that was anymore—and to prove him wrong, as well. That happened right now.

I went into my bathroom and peed on the damn stick.

Five minutes later, and two solid—and I mean very solid—blue lines later, the truth was confirmed.

I definitely did not have a stomach bug.

CHAPTER SIX

SEBASTIAN

"You scored how many goals? Are you sure it was that many?" I laughed as Vela's version of a girl growl stretched across the miles between us and tugged at every string of my heart. Good-naturedly teasing her, even over the phone, was one of my favorite pastimes. By contrast, there were still too many damn papers on my desk left to sign.

"I am! It was! Ask Mom!" Vela insisted. My answering smile was a welcome stranger to my face, making me not want to end the call.

"Actually, little star, is your mom there? I need to talk to her before I go into a meeting."

"You work too much, Uncle Bas. We haven't seen you in soooo long. And when is Miss Gibson coming back from her trip? I miss her too."

"You and me both, baby," I muttered.

"Okay, here's Mom. Love you."

"I love you more. Study hard."

"Of course! I'm a Shark!"

I was still chuckling when my sister came on the line.

"You bring out the fire in that girl's soul, Sebastian." Pia laughed softly. "I don't know what it is, but I swear she stands an inch taller after she talks to you."

"I will always be here for her. You know that." I vowed it to my sister with an ache in my chest that always swelled for these two ladies.

"I do. What's going on? How have you been? How's Abbi?" she asked tenderly.

"I think we've been better. The separation has been difficult for both of us."

"I can only imagine." But her tone told me something different than the pledge. That she didn't have to imagine. That she understood the solitude of my spirit all too well. Not that she was about to dwell in that emotional space. "Well, I'm continuing to stay extra vigilant and watchful, though there's nothing new to report from this side of town. I do appreciate Elijah dispatching an extra man to assist during Vela's games. The parks are a little tougher for me to watch over than simple school pickups and playdates."

"Of course," I said. "Say the word, and I'll have him give you an extra guy for those too."

"No." Her voice was adamant. "You know where I stand on all this."

"Oh, I definitely do." I didn't hide my exasperated sigh. "But you're not going to be giving Vela any sense of normalcy if you or she are taken by these bastards—or worse."

A beat of heavy silence from her end. Another. "So… exactly how did you say Abbi was doing again?"

I spared her from the sigh this time. Wouldn't have done me any good. When Cassiopeia Shark was determined to change a subject, the ruling was law.

"She's okay," I finally said. "I mean, as good as can be expected, given this clusterfuck of circumstances…"

"Annnd?"

"And what?"

"What are you not telling me?"

I whooshed out a long—but resigned—breath. "The desert isn't exactly . . . agreeing with her," I muttered.

"In what way?" Pia pressed.

"She picked up some sort of . . . virus . . . or something. A stomach bug, I think. Still, she's thinner. And paler. I'm worried, Dub."

"Sounds like you should be," Pia returned. "It sounds like you're both under a lot of stress—and it's not doing you any good."

"Her more than me." I rubbed my forehead, which was already throbbing at ten o'clock in the morning. "Elijah isn't exactly the nurturing type, so I'm very thankful the staff at the safe house is mostly women. They've been mothering her like crazy."

"Yeah, that is good," Pia concurred. "Something's definitely going around. That's why Vela is home today. I mean, she seems fine right now, but the midnight blow-and-go session wasn't so pleasant."

"Thanks for sharing," I deadpanned.

"Just keeping it real, Your Majesty," she teased back.

"Ugh. The poor kiddo," I lamented. "I'll have some of those flower fairy books delivered to her. I think she was telling me that a new set came out this week."

Pia sent back a grateful sigh. "Best. Uncle. Ever. Thanks, Bas. That really will make her day."

"Done," I said. "But listen, I need to hang up right now. Grant will be here in five minutes."

"And that means we have to hang up?" she jibed.

I grunted. "He and I have some scheming to do. We've got

serious problems brewing in the Malaysia corridor again."

"Oh, no! Now what?" There was genuine curiosity in Pia's tone. "I thought you just finished working that deal out."

"This is different than what I was there working on. There are maritime pirate stories in the mainstream news this morning. Never a good sign when the big cable channels catch wind of stories with buzz words like 'pirates' in them. I mean, everyone in the business knows that shit is going on every single day, but the rest of the population does not. Once it leaks through to the folks sitting around the dinner table watching the nightly news, the criminals start attracting too much attention for their screwed-up causes. Just encourages more of the bad behavior."

"Ugh." She huffed. "No kidding. Well, let me know if I can help. Tell Abbigail we were asking about her, okay?"

"I will, Dub. That will make her happy to hear. Hopefully I can bring her home soon." I hoped she could hear the smile in my voice.

"Talk to you soon. Love you, Bas."

"Love you too, Pia."

After we hung up, I quickly reread Grant's earlier email. I'd given it a harder perusal on my first pass, making sure I separated the actual facts of the situation verses the media uproar about what was happening in the world's southern hemisphere. But I wasn't sure that feat was completely possible, given all the information being skewed in every outlet's story. I needed to contact my sources on the ground in that region and get the data from the horse's mouth, so to speak.

My COO's unique knock—two quick raps, one short pause, two more quick raps—sounded on my office door. We'd used the bootleg Morse Code signal since we were kids, showing up at each other's houses at all hours of the day and night. Whether we were in trouble, in need, or just plain lonely, Grant and I always had each other's backs. We were into our second decade as brother-close best friends, and I couldn't imagine my life without the man in it.

"Enter," I called out.

"Hey." Grant issued his usual response while efficiently shutting the door behind him.

"Hey, man. How you doing?" I didn't look up, instead focusing on finishing a final email before I could give him my full attention.

"Not too bad."

"But?" I spoke it because his tone already implied it.

"But just once, I'd love to walk in that door and have you look at me. Like it mattered that I just came in the damn room."

Immediately, I dropped my face into my palms. "Excuse me?"

"I just don't get why you're so rude all the time."

"Are you serious?" But when I looked up, the truth was there across his face. "Holy shit. You're serious."

He shook his head, giving in to more of his apparent hurt. "Forget it."

But that was the thing. Now I couldn't.

Was all of this actually happening?

"It's called familiarity, Grant," I finally stated. "I've known you longer than anyone else in my life. Other than Pia, obviously." I rubbed my temples and decided to get some ibuprofen from my bathroom while I defended myself. "I just assume there is a level of comfort between us that I can't have around others. Is that wrong now? Do you want me to treat you with the formality of a stranger?" I emerged from the bathroom with my arms spread. "Fuck, man, give me some slack. You act like a woman on her period sometimes."

Grant was already stretched out in his usual spot on my black leather sofa. Thankfully, he didn't have his feet up on the coffee table, so we could avoid beating that dead horse this morning.

"Damn," he muttered while I lowered into the chair facing him. "You're right, man. I'm sorry for jumping your shit the minute I walked in."

"It's fine," I grumbled. "We're all tense, for obvious reasons. And you've had one of the shittier shifts too."

"Hmmm. Might have to agree with you there." Despite his sardonic words, the guy laughed out the delivery. "Seriously, I think I've been spending too much time around Rio Gibson. That woman . . . is a demon."

I narrowed my gaze. "But you're laughing about that too."

"I . . . I am?" Grant stood. Sat. Stood again, Okay, the guy was always restless, but this was an even bigger dose of his nervous energy than usual. It continued as he beelined to the kitchenette to fetch a bottle of water. As he turned and tossed one to me, I took a chance to eye him with curiosity. "Probably overcaffeinated," he explained. "I've been up since four a.m. at the kitchen. Those women work their asses off, man." He took a big gulp from his bottle. "It's shocking how much effort goes into the lunch run alone—all for demanding bastards like us, who don't want to be bothered with getting their own damn lunch."

"Well, I can have Elijah put one of the other guys in the kitchen," I offered. "If the schedule, or Rio's attitude, are becoming too much to deal with . . ."

"I can handle her, damn it." Grant's protest had me

double-taking again. I couldn't figure out if his vehemence was defensive or offensive, and that alone was strange. Twombley was usually one of the straight shooters in my life.

But what about my life had been usual lately?

But now wasn't the time for cosmic questions. I cut to the core of the matter at hand here. "To be really honest, man, I'm not even certain the tight surveillance on her is necessary anymore. It doesn't seem like anyone has been sniffing around since we moved Abbi out to the desert. Whoever took those pictures of her seems to know she's not in LA anymore." I thought quietly for a second, attempting to be more relieved than troubled about that, before adding, "I mean, nothing new has been sent to me. And there have been no more wildlife visits in my backyard either. That's a good sign, right?"

Grant didn't respond right away. He took a full beat to compress his lips and flare his nostrils. "I'd rather stay near Rio, if it's all the same."

"Of course." I kept my response neutral.

He relaxed his stance. "Thanks. I think it's for the best. Even though she won't admit it, she's spooked. And, believe it or not, she's finally starting to trust me." He inserted a new chuckle, seemingly as an afterthought. He was doing a lot of that in this conversation, I'd noticed. "Besides, I don't think there's any way we can really guarantee whoever is behind this—"

I cut him off with a hard huff. "It's Viktor. Damn it, why are we all still dancing around the problem like we don't know who's causing it?"

"Fine, fine." He flung up his hands, palms out. "But if that's the case, I'm still not convinced he wouldn't do something to Abbi's family—Rio, Sean, or even any of her brothers back east—to flush Abbigail out of hiding."

He finished the last of his water and tossed the empty bottle in the recycle bin beside the trash can. As he finished, my best friend lifted his stare back to me. We held the mutual regard for a couple of moments.

"What?" Grant prompted at last. "What is it?"

"I just don't get it, man," I confessed with a grimace. "I mean, the dude can have any trim he wants in the state. Probably anywhere. Why is he playing with me like this?"

"You're right. It doesn't make a lot of sense, does it?" He parked a hip on the corner of my desk and folded his arms. "Don't get me wrong; your woman is beautiful, and I know there's a lot about her that you love. But to go this far out of his way for someone else's girl?" He studied the skyline with a slow shake of his head. "Moreover, Abbigail's made it very clear she's not interested in him."

"Exactly. None of it is adding up, by even a fraction," I said. "The efforts he's already gone through... they're over-the-top, even for him. And why? Just to taunt me? Or scare her?" I recognized how crazy the words sounded, even as they tumbled out of me, but I was still trying to make all the puzzle pieces fit together here. My instinct was still casting a mold my logic couldn't fill.

Grant pushed back to his feet. He walked all the way back over before pausing again, his stance braced with somber stiffness. "Bas? Has he contacted you in any way you haven't told us about?"

"No!" I spat. "Of course not!"

"Don't get snippy. You've had a crappy few weeks, which means you could've overlooked something. Just a stupid detail somewhere."

"You seriously don't think I'd remember something like that?"

"Just turning over every stone, man. Nowhere has there been any phone message or skipped email? Anything that could be the terms of a deal? No actual threat, no quid pro quo type of bargain?"

I motioned him back toward the sofa. "Nothing," I retorted. "And yeah, I know it's odd. So unlike Blake. You and I have been dealing with that bastard nearly as long as we've known each other. We've negotiated with him enough times by now to know how he operates."

Grant stretched his long legs out in front of him. "And this definitely isn't it, my friend."

I gripped the chair arms until my knuckles went white. "The bastard I know would've come out of the gate flaunting his goddamned terms. Typically, he lays down his hand as soon as all the cards are dealt. He's a straight shooter when he wants something."

Grant folded his arms again. Knocked his head back and stared at the ceiling. "All right, so what if…"

"What if what?"

A new exhale from him. "What if we're following the wrong trail altogether?"

"Explain."

"Nothing to explain, really. You know I might be right, though… right?"

I dropped my hands atop my thighs. They didn't fare much better than the armrests. "Okay, let's set all this on the back burner to simmer for now. We still have to deal with the pirate situation."

"Yeah. Fucking bastards." Twombley gave it enough growl

for both of us, allowing me to be the all-business guy in this part of the exchange.

"How bad is it?" I demanded. "I got a few hits online, but they were buried around the fourth or fifth result. I'm in the damn dark here."

The guy sat up straight again. "Our brokers seem to think the problem is significant."

I clenched my jaw. "How so?"

"A freighter was boarded overnight. Six crew members were taken hostage. I spoke to the freight company's PR rep right before I came in here, and she said communications with the ship have been cut completely."

"Well, at the risk of sounding mercenary, do we have cargo on that ship?" I asked.

Grant pulled in another sizable breath. His face was set in stern lines. "Unfortunately, we do. But you know as well as I do that this is the MO for these bastards. They hold the freight and crew as collateral until their demands are met."

"Christ," I bit out. "Has anyone cross-referenced the cargo manifest? Looked to see who else's shipments are being delayed—and how we might be able to coordinate recovery with them?"

"The route was scheduled from Kendari to Port Klang, with at least one stop in Palembang."

"And?" I prompted.

"And that's all I can remember, man. Sorry." My friend dug his forefinger and thumb into his eye sockets, seeming to be fighting the same impending migraine as me. "I know they unloaded some containers in Palembang, but that's it. The dispatchers are trying to figure what was still onboard. Additionally, if other freight was taken on in Sumatra and so on... Well, we're still trying to untangle a big fucking mess."

Well, that sealed the deal. By now my head was pounding. I leaned back in the chair and ground my fingers into my temples. Of all the times for this kind of shit to be happening. When it rained, it poured—only this was all a damn hurricane.

And with her usual awful timing, the next band of the storm knocked on my office door.

Grant joined me in gritting out our favorite F-word. Even the sound of Terryn's timid knock annoyed me, but I didn't dare permit her full access to the room. I gave up my comfortable position and strode to the door. My freak show of an assistant visibly startled when I *whooshed* the panel open.

"What is it?" I asked through clenched teeth.

"Oh. Umm." She fluttered a hand to her necklace, her usual nervous reaction. "Ex...cuse me...for interrupting, Mr. Shark..."

"What. Is. It?"

Terryn forced an awkward smile. "Mrs. Gibson is here with your lunch."

A quick look at my watch showed more than an hour had passed since Grant had come in. "Christ, this day is slipping away." I looked over to my COO. "Are you having lunch in the office today?" While he scrolled through his phone, presumably to check his schedule, I told Terryn, "Show her in."

While I gave Rio a decent smile as she pushed the Abstract Catering cart in, it was rough not to add a visible eye tick, as well. I craved the sight of my woman's smile behind that conveyance instead. I ached with a thousand kinds of remorse, knowing she hated being away from her business.

"The usual spot there?" Rio motioned toward the seating area but pulled up short when she saw Grant sitting there. I looked on, instantly riveted, as the two of them locked gazes for a second. A long damn second. A second in which a wave of discernible electricity charged the air between them.

As they both recovered, hurriedly returning to their tasks, I raised a finger. Lowered it. What the hell was I going to say about that crazy bullshit? If I hadn't just witnessed it—felt it—for myself, I wouldn't have believed what just happened.

Interesting. Very interesting. And as replacement for focusing on a migraine, it didn't suck one bit.

"Mr. Twombley."

"Ms. Gibson."

"It's Mrs. Gibson, remember?" Rio stabbed her left hand into the narrow space between their forms.

"Blink and you'd miss it," he said with a roguish wink, causing the woman to answer with a huge eye roll. "If that's the sort of thing that matters, I guess."

"It matters." She visibly seethed.

Grant only widened his grin.

Mother. Fucker.

"If you have mine there, I'll just eat here with Mr. Shark, please."

"Whatever Your Highness desires."

She performed a dramatic curtsy, much like a prima ballerina during a grand curtain call, but the overture just seemed to spur Grant on. Again, if I wasn't watching it, I'd never believe it—but my best friend was already in motion, sliding in to loom his six-foot-six frame over her feisty little one.

Then he leaned in even closer. Ducked his head and uttered, in an intense but quiet timbre, "Submissive looks damn good on you, Blaze."

Rio sputtered and choked like she'd gulped water wrong. "You are so barking up the wrong tree, dog." She stared up at him, openly defiant. Her eyes were huge and round—and as undeniably dark as espresso beans. "In fact, you're in the wrong forest altogether."

Once more, Grant's grin was nothing but broad playfulness. "I'm not so sure." He looked her over slowly, from the top of her pixie haircut down to her Dr. Martens-clad feet. "But keep telling yourself that."

As the woman dropped his tray of food on the table beside mine, I raised my finger again.

As a bunch of his pasta salad spilled out onto the table, I decided to lower it again. Slowly.

Rio, after all, was taking full charge of all the brash behavior in the room. "Oops," she spat past a saccharine smirk before spinning on her heel and ramming the cart back out of my office. She didn't bother reclosing the door, an opportunity that had Terryn all but salivating in let-me-save-the-day glee.

"Oh, my God," she huffed. "How dare she? That woman is so rude! Do you need help with anything, Mr. Shark? Anything at all?"

Before I could bark out something in return, Grant cut in. "We're fine, Terryn," he said while smoothly shoveling his food back onto the service tray. "Would you mind just closing the door when you go out, though? Thank you."

We ate in silence for several minutes.

Long. Damn. Minutes.

That I should've let lie.

I mean . . . hell. The man was my best friend—but Christ, Rio was, in all likelihood, my future sister-in-law. If he wanted to tell me what I'd just witnessed, then—

No. Screw it. There was no fucking way I couldn't say something. Anything.

"Dude."

"Cool your jets, big guy," he said around a mouthful of food. "I was just messing with her."

"Bullshit."

"She's married. You know I don't play that way. Even I have standards."

I tilted my head a bit. Then a little more. Calling his bluff without words.

"Christ," he growled. "Ease up. She's like catnip. I can't help myself. All that spunk and fire and . . . well, yeah."

My buddy shifted in his chair, and I recognized the move. Things were likely getting uncomfortable in his slacks, but I'd show him some mercy and not point it out. Or maybe I would . . .

The fucker was saved by my phone's distinct chirp. It was a text from Banks.

Call me re: Abbigail

My stomach surged into my chest. At once, it shoved my heart into my throat. "Crap," I spat beneath my breath before activating my office's computerized assistant. "Siri, call Elijah."

While the line was connected and then ringing, Grant abandoned his cavalier bit to quickly ask, "What's going on? Everything okay?"

"We're about to find out. He just said to call him regarding Abbi."

Elijah picked up just after the second ring. "Hey, man. Thanks for calling so quickly."

"No problem. Grant's here too. We were just inhaling lunch."

"Hey, Twombley."

"Hey, man," Grant returned between gulps of the bottled iced tea Rio had left intact.

"You ever actually work these days?"

"You ever try getting up at four to make a few hundred artisan grilled cheese melts?"

"What's going on, Elijah?" I charged. "Is she okay?"

There was a weighted pause from the other side of the line. At last Elijah revealed, "In all seriousness, Bas? I think you should get your ass back out here as soon as you can."

I leaped to my feet. Stayed braced there, hands on hips, as if threatening to lose my shit at any second. "What the hell is going on? Tell me right now!"

"Yeah, yeah . . . okay." He punctuated with a strangled sound. "I really think she needs medical attention, man. I mean, I've pushed to take her to the hospital, but she's refusing—yet she won't let me call a doctor to come to the house. That is one stubborn woman you've got on your hands."

I felt like tearing out my own hair. Instead, I barked, "Let me speak to her."

"She's sleeping. She won't get out of bed nor will she speak directly to me." The concern in my friend's voice was palpable. It was likely what saved most of my hair follicles. "She'll only allow the women in and out of the room. But Dori told me she looks worse every time she goes in there."

"Wait. What do you mean she's not speaking to you? What the fuck, Banks?" I scrubbed my hand down my face. "You said you'd ease up on her."

"And I swear, I have. We had a long talk yesterday, and

everything was fine. I even told her about Hensley."

"What? Why? Why the hell would you do that?" My head throbbed again, five times worse than before. I could barely wrap my mind around actionable thought, let alone a rough comprehension of why Banks had all but sliced his soul back open and let it bleed all over my fragile, beautiful woman. "Never mind," I snarled. "It doesn't matter. I'll have Joel bring me in the helicopter again. I'll text you the details, but don't share them with Abbigail."

A deep grunt from the overhead office speakers. "Remember that part where she refuses to see or speak to me?"

I simply nodded. I didn't care that he couldn't see me. Right now, I didn't know whether to be moved he'd gone out on such a limb and shared his secrets with Abbi or to tell him to keep walking until he fell out of the tree. "I'll be there as fast as I can."

"Sounds like a plan. See you soon."

We hung up, and I swung my stare up at Grant. "Feel like making a trip to beautiful Twentynine Palms?" I couldn't believe I laughed while asking it, but suddenly, the company sounded terrific. And this pirate dilemma wasn't going away anytime soon.

"Sure. I probably have an overnight bag in my office."

"Imagine that," I quipped.

"Let me go see what I have. By the time you scramble Joel, I'll be ready too."

He was already halfway out the door, but I was thankful for his decisive move. I needed the galvanizing force right now—despite what he said as a follow-up.

"On the way there, you can tell me what the hell is really going on. Because I can only think of one reason why he'd tell

Abbi about Hensley. And then the fact that she is throwing up that much . . ."

I whipped up a hand, stopping him there. Like me, he was already putting the pieces together. And honestly, I just wanted to get to her, get a doctor to come to see her, and find out what we were really dealing with.

★ ★ ★

We were winding up the long driveway of the desert estate by dinnertime. When we got inside, I headed straight for the master bedroom. I didn't bother knocking on the door, just pushed through the entrance to find the big bed rumpled and empty.

"What the—" I choked into silence, my heart again lodging in my throat, until I breathed long enough to hear the ricochets of the running shower against the master bathroom's sprawling tiles.

A setup like this didn't get more perfect.

"Nowhere to hide now, Little Red."

As I murmured it, I shed my clothes. And then entered the steamy room.

Abbi was standing under the spray, head tilted back, rinsing soap out of her thick, fire-red tresses. The suds flowed over her full, lush breasts and down over her sleek, wet thighs. They swirled around her feet, with their toes painted a color to match her hair.

I was smitten by her all over again. And proved it with a low, savoring growl.

Her eyes popped wide—but, thank God, she stifled her alarmed screech.

"Oh, my God!"

Okay, most of her screech.

"Sebastian! Wh-What are you doing here?"

I answered by opening the shower door and stepping inside the stall to join her. Though she fish-gaped her mouth, no words emerged up her throat. I was just fine with that. "Happy to see me?" I murmured while wrapping my arms tight around her wet, gorgeous body. And then slicking my fingers into her warm, secret crevices . . .

"Hmmm. Yes. God . . . yesss." Within seconds, she returned the heat of my eager embrace—many minutes passed before we were done just enjoying the feel of one another.

Finally, she pulled back a bit to look up at me. "Wow. I'm so surprised to see you."

I regarded her past a hooded gaze. "Good surprised?"

"What do you think?" She batted my chest, spattering my face with the splashing result. "I just had no idea you were coming. Did Elijah know? Oh, my God. He's such a—"

I cut her off with a firm but lingering kiss. "How are you feeling, baby?" I murmured when I was done.

"I'm okay," she said at once—though never met my gaze while doing so. I decided not to push her on it, though.

Not yet.

"Are you finished in here? Or . . . can I help you?" I decided it was a rhetorical question. Washing her sexy body was one of my favorite things to do, and damn it, I deserved a little reward after my dusty flight. Even if she was already squeaky clean, I wanted my hands on her. She'd have to endure another round.

As she watched, I squeezed body wash into my palm and then made a lather between my hands. I started with my flat palms against her shoulders and upper arms, stroking her skin with sudsy fingers.

"Mmmm," she moaned. "That feels so good."

She tilted her head back under the spray again. I took a moment to simply gaze at her, captivated by her gleaming and brilliant glory. My hands were guided by the force of my need for her, washing across her chest and collarbones and then carefully down over her breasts. Her nipples stood at attention through the bubbles when I skated my fingers across them. She winced when I grazed the tight buds, and I studied her features as I did it again.

"What's wrong, Abbi? Sore?"

"Uhhh…yes. I guess you were a little rougher than I realized, Mr. Shark."

As she blatantly referenced our marathon lovemaking from a few days ago, I merged my mischievous smile with hers. But not for long. I was too distracted. "I do love these tits, baby. So damn pretty."

I touched her nipples again, wanting to thumb the stiff peaks, but she startled backward and covered them. "No. Too much. I'm…sorry. I'm just hurting everywhere. I'm really sorry."

She frantically dropped her gaze. I didn't miss a second of it.

Hmmm. The floor was mighty interesting to her tonight. She couldn't seem to keep her eyes off it.

I washed the rest of her body with even more care. Knowing we weren't in the shower as a precursor to a lovemaking session, the movements were purely me caring for her. I didn't want to put her on edge.

I pushed her back a step so she could rinse off, making sure she was free of all the soap suds, and then shut off the water. Two towels were hanging over the door, so I pulled one down and wrapped her hair up in her cute turban style. We both grinned when the wrap was in place, enjoying a quiet remembrance of the first time I'd done that for her. Our love story—and yes, that was what it was—had moved at five times the speed of most, but in so many ways, I felt like I'd known this extraordinary human for a lifetime. The thought of her not being in my world was completely unacceptable.

The resolve was a welcome helper as I patted Abbi dry, making sure every drop was wicked from her sensitive skin, and then grabbed a towel off the rack and secured it around my waist. I wasted no time in guiding her back into the bedroom.

"Do you have some pajamas you want to put on?" I asked her along the way, deliberately ignoring the slight shrug she gave as response. "Perhaps a T-shirt and some leggings?" I pressed and started opening the drawers of the dresser, one after the other, until my increasingly frantic search finally led to stuff that resembled pajamas. I grabbed the most conservative pair in the stash and walked back over to the bed.

"How about these?" I offered the light-blue cotton sleep set to her.

"Thank you."

I let her quietly dress before I spoke again. I feared the next bit of news would send her over the edge, but my decision was irrefutable whether she liked it or not.

"Abbigail."

"Hmmm?"

"It's time, baby."

She sighed while letting her hair tumble free from the towel. "For what?"

"I told Elijah to make a call. There's a doctor on the way

to examine you."

She shot her eyes up to mine. Took in a huge, meaningful inhalation. My gut wrenched when she probed my features with her stare. "Sebastian . . ."

"We have to figure this out, okay? You're not well. If anything awful happened to you . . ."

My world would end.

I would end.

She waited for a moment to say anything more, seeming to think better of it. She dropped her head again. "Oh, Sebastian."

"Baby." I plunged to my knees at the side of the bed and pushed my way between her knees. "Talk to me, Abbigail. What is it?"

She dipped her shoulders but managed to raise her head—at least high enough that I could see the tears brimming in her eyes. Every one of her tears was a new sting in my heart, even as they collected on her lashes then spilled over onto her cheeks. As they plopped, over and over, onto the cotton fabric lapel of her pajama top, she started to speak again. Stopped. Started. Then again.

I circled my arms around her waist. Flattened my face along her belly. Barely managed to hold in my own bewildered sob.

Holy. God.

Our child was inside her body. Right now. The thought was so fucking amazing and terrifying at the same time. When she threaded her fingers through my hair and held my head tighter against her, the moment froze in time. I didn't deny its importance. The crest upon which we stood. Maybe what I'd been working and waiting for my whole life. The edge I'd really been looking for.

A new beginning. A chance to start life over again.

"Sebastian," she whispered at last. "I'm pregnant."

"Abbigail." I turned my head, lifted her shirt an inch, and kissed her soft skin. "I know."

"You... what?" she croaked.

"Well, I had an idea."

She started breathing faster. I lifted my head to look at her. Her beautiful eyes were still filled with tears, but now they were luminous with fear.

"Hey. Abbi—"

"I swear I didn't do it on purpose."

I crunched my brows. Gripped one of her hands. "Why would you say that? Or feel you needed to? Of course, you didn't get pregnant on purpose."

She pulled her hand free and joined it with the other, cradling the sides of my face. "I... I was so afraid," she confessed. "So terrified you'd think I was trying to..."

"To what?"

"To trap you."

"Trap me?" I showed her every shred of my bewilderment.

"Bas," she chided. "You didn't even want a girlfriend, for God's sake. And now you're going to have a child."

"We." I covered her hands with my own while stressing the word. "*We*, Abbigail. *We* are going to have a child." I actually chuckled by then. "And God help us all, there's a part of me that wants to be a father. That wants to raise a family."

Abbi flared her gaze. "There is?"

"Yes. But I would never have given that wild idea a second thought with any other woman besides you."

Her bottom lip wobbled. "I'm... I'm so scared." She

stopped the trembling by biting hard into her full flesh. "The timing of all of this . . ."

"I know, I know." I rose to sit beside her on the bed. "And I don't have a poetic sentiment to cover that one up. The timing is completely shitty. But baby, life is like that sometimes."

"I guess you're right."

For the first time since I sent her to stay at this house in the desert, she gave me a genuine smile. As I cherished the swell of warmth in my chest from it, she abruptly stood. When she marched to the bathroom with such purpose, my mushy feelings fled. I was afraid she was about to be sick again. Instead, she returned with a small brown shopping bag in her hand. She returned to her spot next to me and pulled out the pregnancy test and handed me the white stick.

"Well, would you look at that." I couldn't help the grin that spread across my face. "You passed this thing with flying colors, baby."

"I did, didn't I?" She laughed. "God . . ." She rubbed her stomach. "I just wish I felt better. This little person has your temperament already, I can tell you that much."

"Or possibly yours?" I gave her a disapproving scowl. "I hear you've been quite the fierce housemate still."

"Elijah Banks is not exactly Mary Poppins," she said with bite.

I burst out in a full laugh. "Oh, I know. Trust me, I know."

★ ★ ★

The doctor arrived a little early, and Abbigail asked to be left alone with the female obstetrician so she could be examined without me hovering. They both promised to give me a full report as soon as they were through.

When I went out into the great room, I found Elijah and Grant sitting on the sofa, sipping glasses of whiskey.

"How is she?" Grant asked.

"She's okay. She's with the doctor now. Guess we'll have a definitive answer soon enough."

"Dude." Elijah tilted his head, adding a bemused smirk. "This is—"

I held up my hand, already stopping the lecture. "Save it, man. I don't need it right now. I could use a glass of that, though." I pointed to the drink as he lifted the tumbler to his lips. "And I will warn you fuckers now," I added, becoming lethally serious. "The first one to make a *Daddy Shark* comment or sing that damn song will get cut in his sleep."

I fell into the armchair across from my two friends, and the three of us burst out laughing.

CHAPTER SEVEN

ABBIGAIL

"Since your period was due two weeks ago, you likely conceived about two weeks before that."

As Dr. Landon explained all the details, Sebastian and I listened carefully. I looked up at my man's intense profile, already able to read his mind. He was trying to remember where we were precisely at that time, wanting to commit every single moment of our child's history to memory. He was combing through the same details I'd already reviewed—in painstaking detail. Since I had nothing but time on my hands these days, I'd been able to devote a good chunk of brain space to the process. Thanks to my uncooperative stomach, no way had I been able to use my downtime for perfecting recipes or working on the restaurant's business plan.

The expression on the doctor's face said that special free time still wasn't about to happen. "For now, we need to start some IV fluids, Abbigail. Just from testing your urine, I can see you're definitely dehydrated. That's not good for you or the baby. I know you're having trouble keeping things down"—she patted my hand with compassionate care—"so we can do things this way for now. After twenty-four to forty-eight hours, you should feel remarkably better. Maybe then you can start back on eating bland foods."

“Can we hear the baby’s heartbeat?”

Sebastian’s question surprised me but in a good way. His excitement, already so palpable, touched a deep place in my heart—and then even deeper than that. I had to close my eyes to will away the emotion—but even with my eyes shut, I discerned the smile in Dr. Landon’s answer.

“It’s still a little too early, but that doesn’t mean there’s anything wrong.”

I gave in to my own soft smile. Boy, did this woman have my man’s number already. That definitely would’ve been the next question from his mouth.

“At around eight weeks, we will be able to hear the heartbeat. If Abbigail has the conception date correct, she’s only around six now. We should be able to hear your child in two more weeks.”

“I can’t wait.” He leaned over and squeezed my hand. “You doing okay, baby? Warm enough?”

“Yeah, I’m fine. Just tired. But what else is new?” I laughed a little, but the burst was forced. Dr. Landon was competent; I already knew that much. But I still wasn’t looking forward to having an IV in my arm. I sucked down a long breath, struggling to stay calm about this whole thing.

“I’m going out to my car to get the necessary supplies to start your IV,” she said. “And then you can rest. If you want to take a quick shower or do anything that would be easier while you aren’t tethered to a pole, I suggest you do it now.”

“I’ll have one of the staff show you out to your car.” Bas walked out the door with the doctor.

Slowly, I got up from the bed, holding on to furniture as I went, and moved into the bathroom. Bas came in with a panicked look, having worked himself up between seeing the empty bed and finding me in the bathroom. I put my flat palm on his chest and said, "You have to calm down. It's going to be the longest nine months on the planet if you keep acting this way."

"Sorry. Christ, I'm sorry." As he dragged a hand through his thick waves, worry twisted his handsome features. "I thought you were throwing up again."

"No." I stroked his arm, glad for the chance to focus away from my condition and onto his comfort instead. "I thought I'd take her advice and shower, even though I just had one. The hot water feels so good on my overly sensitive skin."

"Need some help?"

"No. You're sweet, Bas, but I can manage—and I may need you more in a bit, when I'm not able to move around so easily."

"Fair enough." He conceded much easier than I expected, though there was already fresh purpose in his eyes. "I'll go find Dori to change your linens, then. Elijah said you and her seem to be getting along really well? And you've mentioned she makes your bed just the way you like it."

I answered him with an indulgent smile. The man was seriously like a German Shepherd sometimes. At his best when he had a clear purpose.

As soon as he was gone, I closed the bathroom door and flipped the lock, ensuring some privacy when he came back. With my back against the door, I closed my eyes.

And finally, for the very first time, let all the information sink in.

Deeply.

We were really going to have a baby.

Actual human life was growing inside my own.

If there was any time to be justified in throwing up my

guts, this was it. But I wasn't nauseated. Not even a faint wisp of the stuff.

That glaring clarity had ushered in a bigger revelation. A purpose that split open my senses like a giant diamond had been lobbed into my chest, scattering a thousand prisms of decision through my being.

I couldn't stay here any longer. Not in this desert. Not in this house. Not this far from my baby's beautiful, beguiling father.

But weirdly, I knew that my pregnancy wasn't the only pivotal factor here. As well as he wore impending fatherhood, that wasn't the sole turning point for my determination.

I needed to be with him. Period. In my heart, in my soul, with all of my body and mind. And I refused to accept his mandates about the matter anymore. When he went back to Los Angeles, whether it was tonight, or tomorrow, or in a week, I was going with him. I wouldn't take no for an answer. If he was still convinced I was in danger, he could surround me with five ex-football players if he pleased. But my sanity—and now the wellness of our unborn child—would no longer pay the price for his paranoia.

I needed to go home.

The resolve brought me a new surge of energy. I took a shower and even did the extra things I'd been ignoring lately. I shaved my legs, used the sugar scrub on my dry skin, and also went so far as the second lather of shampoo before conditioning.

I'd lost track of the fact that Dr. Landon was waiting to start the IV until I stepped back into the bedroom and five pairs of expectant eyes were waiting for my reentry.

"Whoa, shit," I muttered, glancing around the crowded

room. "Well, the gang's all here."

Not an understatement. They really were. Sebastian, Elijah, Grant, Dori, and Dr. Landon were all present. Perhaps blushing and shifting more uncomfortably than me—which was kind of funny, since they weren't the ones wrapped only in a towel.

"Wh-What's going on?" I blurted. "Why is everyone—"

"Nothing's wrong, Red." Bas rushed forward with such fervency, I got panicky all over again. "Baby," he soothed. "Honestly; everything's fine. The guys just wanted to give their official congratulations to us."

"And I just finished changing out the bed, Miss Gibson," Dori offered.

"And Dr. Landon's ready to start the IV," Bas finished. "So nothing's wrong at all."

I still side-eyed him. "All right…"

"Do you want pajamas?"

I watched, stunned, as he pawed through my nightwear drawer for the second time this evening, and came up with a set decorated in cartoon cooking utensils this time.

Once dressed, Dr. Landon instructed me to sit on the bed and get comfortable while she checked my arm for a good place to stick the needle. I wasn't a fan of the process but knew it needed to be done for the sake of the precious bean inside my belly. The men were talking among themselves in the corner, not paying attention to my distress, so that helped as well. I hated being the center of attention when I was showing weakness. Who didn't, really? No one liked all eyes on them when they weren't at their best.

In a few minutes, I was all set up and lying back against a stack of pillows. Sebastian had broken away from his friends and was back to fussing over me.

"Why don't you try to get some sleep, baby?" He bent down until we were at eye level, piercing me with his intense blue stare. "Can I do anything to help you get more comfortable?"

I reached up and flattened a palm to his strong, stubbled jaw. Holy God. The man was normally beyond beautiful, but in this moment of our connection, he'd never taken my breath away more. "Can you . . . will you . . . lie down with me for a while?" I whispered.

"Of course," he husked. "But I want you to try to sleep."

"I don't think that's going to be a problem." I forced a smile, and that was enough to have Bas turning toward the small crowd in the room. Our guest count had grown by a few, as the other staff members came in to start up their own conversation with Dori.

"All right." His voice was back to its commanding boardroom best. "Everybody out."

He herded our company into the hall. That included the kind doctor. He followed Dr. Landon out and paused to speak with her for a few minutes. They'd cut their tones to considerate murmurs, so I was unable to hear their exchange.

When Bas came back into the room, he removed his shoes and shirt and then stretched out beside me. Taking care not to strain my IV line, I snuggled against him. His broad pecs rose and fell beneath my cheek. I focused on pulling in a matching breath, gratefully filling my senses with his familiar scent. As the crisp blend of cedar and my man calmed my nerves, I murmured into his skin, "Congratulations, Papa."

He lifted a hand to my hair and started stroking his fingers through it. "I love you, Mama."

I hummed in bliss. I think. His rhythmic motion, along

with his strong and warm proximity, was lulling me to the land of the sleep comas. "I . . . love you . . . too . . ."

When I opened my eyes again, the room was dark. And quiet. And empty.

I told myself not to panic. He wouldn't have left without saying goodbye. Not this time.

After hauling the IV stand across the room and using the restroom, I found my phone on the nightstand. Less than a minute after I texted him, Sebastian bounded back into the master suite and hauled me into his arms.

"My Little Red." After kissing my forehead, he pulled back a little to dazzle me with his full smile. "How was your nap? How are you feeling?"

"It was good. I'm fine. I don't even remember falling asleep. Were you working?"

"Yes. There's always something." He smiled halfheartedly. "And I was also on the line with Pia, giving her an update."

"Oh." I felt my own lips curving upward. "I miss her. How is she?"

"Asking about you," he supplied. "Both she and Vela wanted me to forward their love."

His smile widened—as it always did when he spoke of his sister and niece. For several seconds, I sat and simply absorbed its stunning magic, from the sexy gleam of his perfect teeth to the pure happiness in his dark-cobalt gaze—and I recognized the blessing with which I'd been bestowed. When most of the world talked about the power of Sebastian Shark, they referred to his corporate drive and his commanding swagger. For the rest of time, I'd think of him exactly like this. Radiating the love in his heart. Exposing the huge capacity of his soul.

Which was why I already dreaded having to crack him

open in both places.

"How . . . how sweet of them," I stammered before hoisting on my proverbial big-girl panties and spurting in one long rush, "Sebastian, I want you to take me home."

His grin faded. His face tightened. "Baby—"

"I'm serious."

He glowered. "So am I."

"I understand that." I straightened my spine against the pillows. Jerked my chin higher. Most importantly, I met his gaze without a blink. "But it's time for you to understand my perspective too. We belong together, especially now. But even if that wasn't the case, we'd be having this exact conversation. I refuse to stay here by myself while you go—"

"You're not by yourself," he spat.

"With all due respect, Mr. Shark, that's bullshit."

"Christ, Abbigail." He paced a contorted figure-eight across the floor. "Please don't argue with me!"

"No." I raised my volume but—miraculously—kept my tone level. "This time, you don't argue with me!"

He stopped and rushed out a weighted sigh. "I still have no idea if it's safe. And now, other problems have come up that will require my time. It's really not—"

"Then call in a battalion of security if you have to. I'm going with you, Bas, whether it's on that helicopter or on my own two feet."

He spun around. His chest was pumping. The only other time I'd seen him breathe so hard was during his wildest orgasms—an image I really didn't need right now, with my system flushed in fresh sleep, half a bag of IV hydration, and a bunch of pregnancy hormones.

"I need to start care with my own doctor, Sebastian—the

one who will be following me through the whole pregnancy, especially if the nausea is going to continue." I capped that point by holding up the arm that housed the IV.

He didn't let up with the hard breathing. Or the tormented look that now went with it. "Abbi, please," he gritted. "I'm not trying—"

"I know you're not, baby. But I've been more than patient with all of this." I waved my untethered hand around, letting it symbolize my frustration with every part of the sequestration. "But my feelings don't matter anymore. This child is the most important detail in the picture now."

"And you don't think I get that?"

"Do you?" I rebutted. "I mean, I can't help but feel like this has been easy for you in some ways. That you've kept me conveniently hidden away out here, and now? Well . . ." I swallowed so hard, it felt like there were golf balls lodged in my throat. "Yeah, well . . . now this."

I drifted off, barely saying the last words loud enough to be heard. If I had to raise this baby on my own, I would. And could. If I had to. But this child would never believe he—or she—was a mistake. Ever.

"Woman." Bas and his growl punctured back into my consciousness. "What on fucking earth are you talking about? 'Hiding you away'?"

He stared like I'd just sprouted a second head—until clearly, the full brunt of his anger set in. "Tell me one goddamn time I have ever treated you like my *hidden secret*. One. Damn. Time."

I gulped again.

He glowered harder.

Right before folding his powerful arms across his chest,

which showcased the rippling definition of his muscular pecs and biceps. Down lower, his thighs were flexed and his stance was braced wide.

No more gulping now.

My mouth was too dry.

His body, so taut and coiled and furious, was officially doing some crazy things to my bloodstream. And my nervous system. And my hormonal, confused libido.

Sexual, primal things.

At once, I knew that Sebastian had seen the shift in my gaze, a direct result of my heated thought process. I watched it in the blaze through his eyes. The way he suddenly flared his nostrils. The decision with which he took a slow, menacing step toward me. Then another. I held my ground, defiance stiffening my spine while lust spiked hotter through my blood—and zapped straight to my pussy.

As the arousal struck, wetness rushed between my legs in a startling tingle, and my lips fell open. I wasn't sure if I was shocked or unnerved; maybe both—but it didn't matter when my man covered them with his possessive, open kiss. It was wicked and sinful. Vehement and perfect all at the same time.

I told him so by answering his erotic growl with my entreating sigh. Bas gave me what I wanted at once, gripping my hair in his dominant fist before cranking my head back for his complete plundering. The moan that crawled up my throat was needy and loud, and I wasn't ashamed. I was desperately aroused and entirely consumed by the swell of natural chemicals in my system.

And confused. Oh, yeah. Definitely that.

I was so. Damn. Confused.

"Turn around. Stand beside the bed. Hands on the

mattress," he growled after nipping down the front of my throat.

"Whaaa? What?"

"Do it, now, Little Red."

"But . . . but the ba . . . ba . . ." I tried to form a coherent thought. And it just wasn't happening. I was so aroused, I could only think of his dick and my pussy and how they needed to come together in the most instinctual way.

"Oh. Don't you worry, Little Red. We can still fuck. I already cleared it with the doctor." His voice was so low, it vibrated across my whole ribcage. "Now do what you're told."

He seized my hips and spun me toward the bed, adding a gentle push for emphasis. I had to bend at the waist a bit to place my hands on the mattress, but the maddening, mesmerizing man had probably anticipated that.

Ohhh, how he had.

I heard the familiar sound of his belt *whooshing* through the loops of his slacks, and my pussy registered the noise as a promise of impending pleasure. Next came the *thunk* of the buckle as it hit the thickly padded area rug beside the bed. But the best sound of all was his sensual moan, scraping the air like a hummingbird's wings but impacting my skin like a condor's talon.

"You ready?" he prompted.

"Oh." I frantically nodded. "Ohhh, yes."

"You sure?" he warned. "This is going to be fast and rough, Red." In one forceful move, he grabbed my pajama bottoms and then yanked them to the floor. "Out." The one-word command was accompanied by a tap to my lower leg.

My folds gushed while I stepped out of the pants. My senses swam—this time, in all the right ways—as I watched

Sebastian toss them to the side. When he stayed in a kneel, my nerve endings sparked like stars. Holy shit, I hoped that meant—

"Oh, God!"

I whimpered it as he shoved his face into the gap between my thighs. Then louder as he darted his tongue deep into the crack, bestowing a languorous sweep from my pussy to my tailbone.

"Fuck, Bas!" My God, he wasn't kidding about the fast and hard. He'd given no warning of his intentions; he was simply diving in and going for it! His finger prodded at my entrance, pushing up into me before he commanded, "Spread wider for me. Let me in this cunt."

And I did. Quickly too. But not quietly. I cried out even louder when he joined a second finger to the first. "Yeesss!" I writhed and bucked as he thrust both demanding digits into my clenching, wet opening.

"Mmmm, that's right, baby," he murmured into the sensitive place at the base of my spine. "You like it that way, don't you? When I just take what I want?"

I hung my head between my outstretched arms, not bothering to answer. His question was rhetorical anyway. And my pussy felt too damn good. And my muscles quivered too damn hard. And my head spun with too much pleasure. So . . . much . . . pleassss . . .

Until sharp teeth sank into my ass cheek.

"Answer me, Red," he snapped.

"Y-Y-Yes," I managed in a rasp. "I . . . I like it."

He fingered me harder. Faster. "No! Say it all. Tell me what I want to hear from your pretty mouth, or I'll shove my cock into it so you can't." Faster. Harder. Fluid dripped down the inside of my thigh because I was so turned on. "Look at this pussy. Abbigail, your body's crying to be fucked by me."

Abruptly, he stood behind me, going completely still and silent. He pulled my head up by a handful of my hair, causing my back to arch and my ass to thrust up. Angling my sex for his pleasure now . . .

He dipped his lips against my ear. And then challenged in a lethal whisper, "I'm waiting."

"I— I . . . can't think. I don't remember what you said now." Just as I finished my plea, he shoved his cock into me in one ruthless motion.

"I said you like when I just take what I want from you," he panted.

"Yes. God, yes, that's it. Just take what you want from me, Sebastian. Please . . ." While I all but sobbed it out, I reached between my legs. With jerking circles, I started pleasuring myself.

"I take what I want, Abbigail." Bas circled his hips and then shuttled his length deeper inside me. "Like this?"

"Yes . . . just like that."

"And what are you going to do while I'm at it?" His voice held sensual challenge. I was already hypnotized by his dark baritone grate. "That's right love, touch yourself."

"Mmmm. Hmmm."

"Keep going, my good little girl. Rub yourself hard while I ride you harder."

"Yes," I groaned. "Ohhh yes."

"Put this knee up on the mattress." He tapped my right thigh to indicate what he wanted. I obliged at once and wanted to cry in gratitude to him. Changing position, even subtly, opened my channel for a new angle of his long, throbbing length. His next stroke penetrated so deep, stars danced before my eyes.

"Holy shit. Oh, Bas. God. My God . . . so good. Feels so good."

"I'm so deep in you, Abbigail. Can you feel that? I want to crawl inside you. Be as deep as I can get. Fuck. Yes!"

What this man and his filthy mouth and carnal imagery did to my libido. I was moments away from climaxing. Now milliseconds.

But before I could say anything about it, Sebastian stopped moving altogether. His dick was buried so far into my pussy, I was certain his cock pressed against my bladder.

"I love you, Abbigail. I love you so completely."

"I love you too."

"Don't ever forget it," he gritted into my hair.

"But Bas?"

"Yeah?"

"I . . . I need to come so badly . . ."

His low chuckle had me twisting raging handfuls of the comforter. "I know, baby."

"Th-Then why did you stop?"

"Because I want to come together. And I want us to do it like this. Without moving."

"Without . . . but how . . ."

"Squeeze my cock with your pussy. Let me feel your walls convulse around me. I just want to be still when I shoot off deep inside you."

"I still don't get . . ."

Oh, but then I did.

From the moment he leaned forward and licked my neck, just under my ear. It was the perfect place; the one spot that aroused me more than any other spot on my body. Sebastian knew that, too.

When he added some fast but sharp bites to the effort, I was gone.

At once, every inch of my sex squeezed around his shaft. Then harder. Harder still.

Sebastian groaned low in his throat. "Yesss, baby, that's it. Feels so . . . fucking . . . good."

"Oh, God." I kneaded the comforter like bread dough, focusing on the motion so I didn't start bucking against him. "Oh . . . I'm going to . . ."

"Yeah, you are. Come on my cock, Abbigail. Fuck me, baby. Yes! Goddammit, just like that!" His stiffness jerked inside me. When he moaned again, he dug his fingers into my hips with bruise-inducing intensity. I didn't care. All of them would be so damn worth it. So damn worth it. "Can you feel me, baby?" he husked in a voice spun of lusty shadows and dark desires. "Do you feel me coming so deep inside you?"

"I do, Bas," I said with wonder. "I do. That's amazing. I've never felt anything like it before."

He backed out and thrust back in only an inch or two, milking the last bit of his climax. When he'd pulled out altogether, he tumbled onto the bed with an incredulous laugh. At once, he pulled me down beside him. We were a sweaty, sated bundle of limp limbs and colliding heartbeats, coming down from someplace higher than the summit of Everest. Kind of an odd metaphor, considering we were in the middle of the California Desert—and that I was barely capable of remembering my own name at the moment.

"That was . . . that was . . ."

"Hmmm. Yesss?" Bas teased. "Go ahead. I'm listening."

I stroked up and down the arm that was wrapped protectively around my middle. "Let's just say that you never cease to amaze me."

He laughed into the base of my neck, but not for long. "Are you okay?" he asked, his voice full of gentle concern. "That wasn't too much? Or too rough?" Since he was lying behind me, I couldn't see his expression, but I could picture it clearly in my mind. All the troubled frown lines . . .

"Bas, I'm pregnant, not injured," I insisted. "I will let you know if something hurts or is uncomfortable, I promise."

"I know you mean that. Thank you."

I didn't bother with returning the protocol. There were important things to discuss right now—first and foremost, securing his agreement about my return to LA. That was going to best be done face-to-face, so I turned over—but damn it, the IV tubing got tangled around something on the bed frame and yanked my arm back.

"Ugghh!" I groaned.

"Just hold on a sec," Sebastian ordered. "Before you pull this out."

His distraction with the tubing was my sickroom version of a golden egg. As he worked the line free, I went ahead and stated, "When these twenty-four hours are done, I'm going home with you."

"So you've said." Since he was leaning over me, it was easy to see the little pinches at the corners of his mouth.

"Good," I said, lifting just high enough to kiss both of them. "It's settled, then."

The pinches snaked inward, and he compressed his lips tightly. "Do we have to start this again? So soon? I mean, I'd be happy to fuck the sass out of you again if you push me."

"Oh." I giggled. "Is that what that was?"

"Mmmm. Maybe? But in all seriousness, I've got a meeting downtown about some changes to the Edge's parking garage layout. I have to go back tonight. And you, have to stay on that"—he motioned to the IV—"and also see Dr. Landon tomorrow afternoon. So you need to hold tight here for a few more days at least, baby."

I flattened my own lips but waited for him to settle back against the pillow before I seethed with words again. "You remember that scenario about me hiking across Joshua Tree?"

He huffed. "Abbigail—"

"Once Dr. Landon takes this thing out of my arm, I'm leaving, Bas. Period."

"All right, all right. Let's not be ridiculous."

I jumped my brows at him. "Because it wasn't ridiculous to make me come out here in the first place?"

"A decision made in love, damn it—before fate even gave us this treasure." He flattened his hand across my belly and pressed in until our faces were an inch apart. "Are you listening to what I'm saying to you, Abbigail? Because I'm listening to you. And I do understand all your reasons for wanting to go back to Los Angeles. I wish you'd look at things from my side, though. And I don't think you're even trying."

I yanked away and sat up. "Are you joking?" I retorted. "You really have to be joking, right? Because you really have no idea what you're talking about."

"Please don't get all worked up ag—"

"You haven't been here, Sebastian. You have no concept of what this has been like for me. My business isn't here. My family isn't here. Despite that, I've tried it your way—but now this bullshit has run its course. I can't use your reasons any longer. Do you see that?"

"Give me a few days. Can we just agree on that? A few days to get security around the house in place. I would feel so much better."

"Three days," I agreed but then added, "At the most."

"You drive a hard bargain, Miss Gibson." He kissed the end of my nose. "How do you feel? Do you think you could eat something? Broth? A smoothie?"

I thought about it for a moment while I snuggled back into the pillows. All of our . . . activities . . . were quickly catching up with me. "Maybe some toast?" But when he started to get up, I hung on for dear life. "You don't have to get it. Dori gave me her cell number. I can just text her, and she will bring it." I held up my phone to show him we didn't have to leave the bed. "Please stay with me. Just a little bit longer."

But the infernal man swung his legs over the edge to pull on his boxers and pants. "I'll be back soon," he promised. "I need to go talk to Elijah about the new plan. He's got to make arrangements if we're all going home."

"All right. For that, I can excuse you." I grinned, knowing I sounded like a full-blown queen, issuing orders to her loyal subjects.

"Well, thank you kindly, my lady." He leaned over and kissed the top of my head. "I'll send Dori in with your toast."

He buttoned up his shirt and ran his fingers through his hair. The man was so damn gorgeous. It was still hard to believe he was mine. And now we were going to have a little boy running around with his good looks and charm. And between the two of us, one hell of a defiant attitude. I don't know why I had such a strong premonition that it was a boy growing in my belly, but for some reason, I was almost positive it was.

"I hope our little boy has your dark hair, and not this . . ." I flipped the ends of my unruly mane up with a scowl.

"Little boy, huh? Are you sure about that? I think it may be a girl. And she'd be beautiful with that flaming red hair, just like you."

"Well, we have a while to wait, so we can come up with a good wager to see who's right." I grinned, just thinking about all the exciting things that were in store. It wasn't all going to be feeling like crap and worried about keeping food and water down.

"Hey, what would you think about bringing Dori back to LA with us? You seem to get along with her really well. You haven't really bonded with any of the current staff at the Calabasas house the same way you seem to have with her."

I thought about it but then frowned. "We can't just ask her to uproot her life, Sebastian."

"Well, it couldn't hurt to ask. You never know. I mean really, Red, think about it. What does a place like this have to offer a young woman? She could live in the pool house if she doesn't want to stay in the staff wing. Or until she can afford something of her own."

I thought about how nice it had been to have Dori around. Her easygoing nature was so much more relaxed than the stuffy, formal staff Bas had around his house now. Other than Craig, I always felt like I was just "visiting" in their eyes. I probably served as their current wager topic. *Everyone place your bets; how long until Mr. Shark tires of this one?*

"I'll ask her, and I'll send her in with some toast. You rest. You gave me a workout."

I smiled and watched him leave the room, feeling a glimmer of actual contentment for the first time in months.

CHAPTER EIGHT

SEBASTIAN

Three days.

Seventy-two hours.

Forty-three percent of a week.

That was all I was given to get enough security into place for my comfort level with Abbigail's homecoming.

Which, of course, wasn't enough time—so saying I felt uneasy about the situation, even while guiding her out of the villa hand-in-hand with me, was the understatement of the century.

In the long run, there were a few factors that did help. Elijah had sweet-talked the whole security team from the Twentynine Palms property to transfer with us, so Abbi was reasonably at ease with them. A bonus: many of them already hailed from LA and knew the city well. On that end, details were transitioning as smoothly as could be expected.

Bonus number two: Dori agreed to come along too, as I suspected once I quoted the monetary incentive involved. Additionally, she had no family or other outlying commitments to keep her in the desert. The cheerful girl seemed excited about a change of lifestyle. She was happy to help Abbi pack everything up, and they were both ready to go when Joel pulled up with the car.

Dr. Landon gave the travel approval, saying the two days' worth of IV fluids had been the perfect boost for Abbi's hydration and energy levels. She asked Abbi to ensure her chosen provider contact her office for her clinical notes, and I watched Dori tap out a note on her own smart pad. When I pulled the young woman off to the side later to ask her what she was keeping on the pad, she told me she was just making a list of things that needed to be handled when we got to LA.

"You know, just to make sure she doesn't forget anything. I think she's more tired than she's letting on, and a lot of information is being passed back and forth right now." She bit her lip then, sneaking a furtive glance up at me. "I'm... umm... not overstepping, am I? I was just trying to help, Mr. Shark. Honest."

I wrapped a reassuring hand around one of her shoulders. "I know, Dori. And I'm not upset."

Beneath my hand, her tension finally released. "Are you sure?"

"Quite the opposite," I assured her. "Actually, I'm impressed with your initiative." And then, I even smiled—and meant it. "I think you're going to be a great assistant for Ms. Gibson."

"Good. Thank you so much, Mr. Shark." Her reply was taking a bath in pure relief. With the same happy gusto, she stowed her smart pad in her backpack.

"Let's hit the road." The exhortation belonged to Abbi this time. She tugged me eagerly toward the car—after hugging Joel like he was a beloved cousin she hadn't seen for ten years. "It was nice knowing you, Twentynine Palms, but I'll be happy if I never see you again." She swung up a hand, already playing the diplomatic disclaimer. "No offense to the fine folks who call this place home. It's just not mine."

But her sardonicism disappeared as soon as the villa staff gathered to see us off. Abbigail joined Elijah in issuing personal farewells to each and every one of them on the front drive. My tenderhearted woman was tear-streaked and exhausted by the time I got her settled in the back of the car.

Abbi slept in my arms for the majority of the ride home. Traffic was light until we got back into our own city. By the time we wound up the hill into our neighborhood, we had been in the car over four hours, making only one stop for gas and snacks.

"Home sweet home," I whispered to my sleeping beauty, and her emerald eyes popped open immediately.

"Hmmm? We're here already?" she asked sleepily.

I chuckled into her hair, and then kissed the top of her head. I was certain everyone else in the car commiserated with my impression: that we'd been counting the minutes to get out of the damn vehicle for good.

But as soon as we got out, Dori froze in place again. "This is your house?" She openly gasped. "It's . . . so beautiful!" She gawked while absorbing the sight of my home, from its wide sienna clay tile roofline to the dramatic, arched front portico.

"Well, the place in the desert wasn't too shabby either," Abbigail returned while linking arms with the girl. "Come on. I'll show you around inside." At once, she'd shifted into her happy zone of welcoming hostess. "After that, maybe we'll rustle up a snack for everyone in the kitchen, and then we can get you settled in the pool house out back."

"Abbigail . . ." I focused on making it more a friendly nudge than an ominous order. She literally hadn't even stepped inside yet.

"Hmmm?" She smiled at me over her shoulder. "Did I forget something in the car?"

"No. But Dr. Landon specifically said you have to rest. And it's been a long drive—"

"That I slept through?" she rebutted.

"Doesn't matter." I moved in, wrapped my hand around hers, and tugged her close. So it was more like jerking her back and forcing her to slow down, but civility be damned. I'd given in big-time about this; it was time for reciprocation. "Why don't you go to lie down, and I'll have Craig show Dori where she'll be staying?"

She clenched her jaw. "Oh, for Christ's sake, Bas."

"He's not here." I flashed an I'm-not-kidding smile. "There's only me to please right now, and I'd rather you rest."

"But I just slept for"—she looked at her watch—"four damn hours. I won't overdo it, I promise." She held up her fingers in a Scout's oath. "It will feel good to stretch my legs and get some sun on my face without the scorching heat. Plus, I've missed this place so much."

I grunted hard. She batted those big greens harder. And I was gone.

"All right, Dori; you're in charge." I sighed in concession. "First sign of dizziness or nausea, and she's back in the house. Understood?"

"Of course, Mr. Shark."

Elijah and I headed straight to my office, where we were going to address the security team. As we walked, I mumbled, "Why do I already get the sense this was a bad idea?"

"Because you're paranoid." My friend shoulder-bumped me. "It's going to be fine. *She's* going to be fine." When I didn't ease up, Banks reached over and gave me a full-on reassuring clamp. People rarely touched me, but Elijah and Grant had freedoms others didn't.

"How can you be so confident?" I growled.

He shrugged. I wanted to both deck him and hug him for it. "I don't know. Call it intuition, man."

One by one, Elijah's men filled my study. Their oversize bodies quickly made the room seem small. Fifteen men would patrol the house and grounds around the clock, seven days a week. The other ten, comprised mostly of men from my existing LA security detail, would patrol the neighborhood and help relieve the house team when necessary. The neighborhood's security force agreed to allow me to add an extra guard of my own at the entrance gate of the community itself, as well as an extra man at the lesser-used back gate. The association board had been understanding of the request upon my explanation for the heightened security, a necessity considering recent publicity surrounding the Edge and publicized deaths of women I was associated with. Of course, my sizable donation to the neighborhood's private park initiative went a long way toward opening their minds—and cooperation levels.

"Thank you all for taking this matter seriously," I said to wrap up the security briefing. "Now if you'll excuse me, I need to catch up on some things I missed while we drove home. Elijah, can you email me the team's schedule each week? That way if someone doesn't show up for a shift, I'll know who to fire." I made sure every man in the room heard what I said to my friend.

"Uh, yeah," Elijah assured me at once. "Of course, Bas. But these men were hand-selected for this assignment. No one in this room will let you down."

"I'm counting on that."

The men filed out, some shaking my hand and thanking me for the opportunity, while others just pushed past and set off toward their duty stations.

Back in front of my computer, I pulled up my email and scrolled through the incoming messages I hadn't yet caught via my phone. I needed an update on the commandeered freight vessel and had been trying to avoid mainstream news channels for that information.

Only a handful of new emails had come in during the security meeting, and I got busy scrolling to those but was interrupted by an incoming text.

At once, I smiled and murmured, "Well, that didn't take long." It could be no one else but Abbi, ensuring me she'd already settled Dori in and wouldn't require me hog-tying her down for a nap.

Within the next second, my disposition became a storm cloud.

Not Abbigail.

The message was from Terryn.

Terryn, who'd been instructed to contact me today only if the damn office was burning down.

Terryn, who preceded her little missive with a red car, a jumping shark, and a smiley face wearing sunglasses.

Going to the Edge building site to take some pics for social media. Want any shots in particular?

I answered with furious speed.

PR firm is handling that. Stay at office.

Do your own work. Job site is dangerous.

Don't be silly! But I'm touched you care, Sebastian.

What did I tell you about calling me that? Don't go to the job site.

Don't be such a nervous Nelly, boss.

She concluded with another string of emojis, but I didn't give them a glance. I didn't have the time or the energy to care about this infuriating person—not when the woman I did care about was likely in need of some avid oversight. Abbigail had assured me she wouldn't overdo it, but I wasn't sure she knew the definition of personal pacing. On most days, her drive was what I loved and identified with the most. On days like this, the concept alone gave me an ulcer.

Before I got too frustrated with Terryn, I deleted every one of her text messages from my phone screen. After that annoying box was checked, I stood, tucked the device into my pocket, and left my office in search of Abbi.

The first place I looked—and should've found her—was our bed. It was empty. There were no signs she'd even sat on it yet either. She also wasn't in the bathroom taking a shower, nor down in the kitchen fixing the snack that she'd mentioned.

I rounded the counter into the breakfast nook, already jamming my hands to my hips. As the sun dipped over the nature reserve beyond the backyard, my agitation climbed. No way could she still be out back, giving Dori the grand tour of the pool house. The place was all of eight hundred square feet.

Nevertheless, I stomped out the sliding glass door, across

the patio, and down the pool deck before coming to a halt at the entrance of the little casita. After giving the door three harsh raps, I heard quiet shuffling on the other side.

Dori appeared in the portal, at once lifting a helpful smile my way. "Mr. Shark. Hello."

"Hi." I wanted to feel crappy for the terse snap but didn't. "Listen, is Abbi still here with you? She was supposed to be lying down by now."

"She is right here, and she is fine." The interjection came from the mother of my baby, who now stepped in to stand beside the other woman. "Look. See? I'm fine. You need to calm down, Mr. Shark."

She patted the center of my chest with her delicate hand. I scooped it up in mine and kissed her fingers. "Come on," I said. "It's time to go."

Just as swiftly, she wrenched off from my grasp. "Sebastian, stop. You don't have to tow me around like a child."

She ended it with a scowl. I refrained from doing the same, though hated how I likely looked more like her reprimanding father than her concerned boyfriend. But my patience was wearing thin. I didn't like treating her like a child but didn't want to feel like I had to. She'd heard the doctor's instructions as clearly as I had.

"Why are you being so defiant?" I muttered, impaling her gaze with mine. "Dr. Landon gave you specific, essential instructions for taking care of yourself today, yet you're parading around like everything is normal."

She exposed her locked teeth. "I. Feel. Fine."

"But you aren't! Do you want to end up in the hospital? Jesus, Abbi. You haven't eaten a thing all day."

"That's not true," she argued. "I had..." But then she

trailed off, not able to name a single thing that had entered her mouth today. Because nothing had.

"Bed. Now." I ordered it with a full glower. "Then some food. No options, no detours."

She abandoned her feral fury for a bottom-lipped pout, tempting me to bite her, spank her, and kiss her at once. I didn't give myself a chance to succumb, pulling her back through the dining room and den, toward the front staircase.

"Oh, God, it's so good to be home," she said as we walked.

I squeezed her hand. "And it feels good to have you home, baby."

She wrapped an arm around my waist. "Thank you for this," she murmured. "For bringing me back where I belong. It feels so right to be here. To really call this place home."

"Oh, don't try to butter me up now, young lady." Though my tone was teasing, the statement was more truth than I let on. My body, heart, and soul were wrapped around this woman like rubber bands on a glue stick. Not that I needed to tell her that. Not right now, when I was maintaining the upper hand by mere fingernails.

It was seriously time to change the subject. Or maybe just segue it.

"Does that mean you want to raise our family here?" I asked as we headed up the stairs. "Or would you prefer finding a new place together?"

"I love this house. I can't see a point to moving. And there's certainly enough space here. We could have ten children and still have room," she said while we reached the top of the stairs, giving her a perfect chance to spin in a giddy circle—which resulted in her dizzy little stumble and my not-so-little panic attack.

"Fuck!" I seized her waist and pulled her against my body. At once I had a hand braced to the side of her head, compelling her stare right up into mine. "All right, into bed with you. Before you bring my early death."

I took no pains to turn that one into a joke, but Abbi snickered anyway. "Maybe I can talk you into joining me?" She waggled her eyebrows while grabbing her bottom lip under her teeth. Christ. The little minx really was going to put me six feet under before our kid saw the light of day.

"Convincing will not be necessary," I husked back. "I can definitely assure you."

She let out another laugh. Her eyes twinkled like lusty fireflies. "Ohhh, really?"

"But later," I emphasized.

"You're no fun."

"Because that's not resting."

She tried a new pout, but I gamely ignored it while getting her settled into a nest of pillows. During her ordeal with the IV treatment in the desert, I'd fast learned how she liked the security of the extra cushions. I'd seen a full-body pillow in one of those airline catalogs always filled with extravagant products for silly people, but I fully admitted I was now one of those dorks. I needed to learn where to get a few of those things. Sounded like a good job for my sister. Pia always knew about this sort of thing.

By the time I closed the shutters and then turned back to the bed, Abbigail was asleep. "Somebody's 'just fine,' hmmm?" I whispered before kissing her temple and then pulling the quilt up and over her.

After leaving the bedroom, I jogged downstairs again. On the way back to my office, my cell phone rang in my hand. It was a local Los Angeles number but one I didn't recognize.

"Hello? Sebastian Shark?"

"Speaking," I stated. "Who is this?"

"Name's Bob McKenzie. I'm—"

"Right. I know who you are, Mr. McKenzie. We met briefly at the groundbreaking for the Edge."

"For all of ten seconds. Damn, you have a good memory."

"Essential for my business, Mr. McKenzie. You're one of the shift foremen, correct?"

"That's right," McKenzie confirmed. "I'm the primary night foreman at the site."

I filled a brief pause with my respectful hum. The man deserved it. What McKenzie did for a living was just as intricate a job as mine, with different moving parts. "What can I do for you this evening, Mr. McKenzie?"

"Yeah, umm, look... I just came on shift here, and the security guys were up in my trailer right away, freaking out..." He cleared his throat.

"Why were they freaking out?"

"Well..." Another gruff grunt from the man on the other end. "They told me they found a body."

I lowered my ass to the surface of my desk. Shook my head, hoping to clear it of the word I thought he'd just uttered. "A what?"

"Down in the pit," he continued. "Where—uh—down where they're prepping to pour the foundation."

"I'm sorry, Mr. McKenzie. Maybe we have a bad connection." But we didn't. The line was crystal clear. "I thought you just said a body." I forced out a laugh—while painfully pinching the bridge of my nose. Jesus fuck. Had he really just said—

"You heard me right. Mr. Shark. A body. It looks like a young woman. Either she fell, or slipped—or shit, I don't know—guess she could've been pushed or jumped—"

"Pushed?" My incredulity finally surfaced as ire as I lurched back to my feet.

"Sorry I can't be more specific." McKenzie's sincerity was discernible. "But we don't have cameras up in that area yet. Not much going on over there but a big hole in the ground and some forming. Well, they started the rebar and tying at the beginning of the week. We're right on schedule for you, Mr. Shark."

"Yeah, okay. That's great, Bob." I pushed my hand up, spreading my fingers to massage my whole forehead. "Can we get back to the body?"

And would the universe ever cut me a fucking break? Ever?

"Well, we haven't touched a thing," the guy informed me. "I just thought I should call you first, you know—before we notify LAPD. I mean, we have to notify them; there's no way around that."

"And I wouldn't want you to do it any other way," I ensured him.

"But they'll be swarming in here right away, and I know the press will be right behind them. We have your personal number here in the trailer in case of emergencies, and I'm sorry if I'm interrupting your personal time, but—"

"Nah, man. It's fine." Now that we were bonding, I felt okay about the casual turn. "You definitely did the right thing."

"Appreciate that, buddy," he said warmly. "But yeah, well, I just thought maybe you'd want to handle this . . . initially? Or have your people handle it. Or whatever?"

"Thanks, Bob." While stating that, I moved around to face my laptop. I opened the messaging app to Elijah's name and tapped out three exclamation points, our way of stating the obvious. That he needed to drop everything and get his ass in here. "Can you do me a favor and keep the rest of the crew away from the... incident site... until I get there? Or until a man named Elijah Banks gets there? Do not let anyone else near the area beside the two of us." I mean, now that we were buddies and all.

"Sure, Mr. Shark. Anything you say. I mean, you're the boss man here."

I ground my molars together at that fucking nickname but held my shit together. I needed to talk to Elijah. About five minutes ago.

"Well, Bob, I appreciate the call, and I will see you as soon as I can get across town."

As soon as I disconnected the call, Banks strode back in. Thank fuck.

"What's going on?" he queried with a smirk. "Miss me already?"

"You're not going to believe this," I huffed.

"Uh-oh." He dropped into a leather chair, changing out the smile for a hard stare. "I don't like the sound of this already."

"And rightly so," I asserted.

"What the hell's up now?"

"I just took a call from the site foreman at the Edge."

"McKenzie?" And of course he had committed the man's name to memory, as well. I hired the best. I made friends with the best of the best. "Why is he calling you at home?"

"Apparently there is a body that needs to be dealt with at the site. In the pit where they're prepping to pour the foundation."

"Wait. What?" Within seconds, the man was back on his feet. "Hold up. Did you just say body? As in a dead human? Nooo. You did not just say—"

"I did."

His shoulder sagged. He pushed out an exhausted grunt. "Did he say whether it was—"

"It's a female. On the younger side."

Banks dropped his head between his shoulders. "Of course it is."

★ ★ ★

When we got to the job site, I was surprised to see how much activity was still going on at that hour. Workers milled around, all making a big show of looking even busier when they saw me approaching. Despite all that, Banks had ensured security was tight on the property since day one. Whomever was lying lifeless in the pit had to have checked in at the trailer before going on to meet her maker.

My friend greeted the guard on duty with an enthusiastic handshake and back smack. The officer called Bob McKenzie over a two-way radio.

"How do you know this guy?" I mumbled to Elijah while the walkie-talkie conversation took place.

"You think I let just anyone on this job site?" he replied at once. "The building's too big and too important. I sat in on every interview myself. Every single one of these workers has been interviewed, screened, and then thoroughly investigated before being offered their jobs. If someone wasn't qualified, seemed shifty, out of place, or just felt off in general, we passed them over."

As he spoke, my gape of disbelief kept widening. "Don't we have human resource people for things like that?"

He looked at me like I'd asked how gravity worked. "We had more applicants than we knew what to do with," he explained. "The process was interminable, but it was one way to make sure we had the best crew here at all times, sharing a singular goal." My buddy grew more passionate as he spoke. "Making this project the best it could be."

If I were a more effusive, emotional man, I would have embraced him then. Instead, I put my hand on his shoulder and squeezed. "Thanks, man," I uttered. "I mean it. And I probably don't say it enough."

I was saved from having to wax on with any more mush than that, as a thick-mustached man lumbered forward. I recognized him at once. It was tough to forget Bob McKenzie's distinct style.

"Mr. Shark! Mr. Banks! So good to see you again." Bob grinned. He was clearly the kind of guy who did that a lot. He looked like a good family man, the kind of guy who spoiled his grandkids and took his wife to Hawaii every other year.

"I'll need you to put on these hard hats to go down to the site. OSHA and all. We don't need them sniffing around the job. Once you get one of those inspectors interested in your project, you can't shake them for the duration." He made a face like he'd just smelled something foul.

"Better get some vests then too," the security guard chimed in. "I think I have a few floating around here somewhere." The guard shuffled through a cabinet and produced two caution orange safety vests and handed them to us.

Once we were appropriately outfitted, we headed out with Bob leading the way.

He pointed to a piece of paper jutting out of his shirt pocket. "The woman had this in her hand. It was crumbled so tight in her fist, she didn't drop it when she fell. Still, that's pretty incredible. Considering what it says, it might be a clue about who she is or why she was here. I didn't want it blowing away or anything, so I grabbed it. I had my work gloves on, so there shouldn't be any fingerprints."

"That was smart thinking, Bob." Elijah grinned at the guy.

"Hey, the Mrs. makes me watch *CSI* every damn night. It finally paid off!"

I pulled the handkerchief from my slacks and wrapped it around my fingers and then reached into Bob's personal space and plucked the note from his pocket. We all stopped walking while I carefully unfolded the letter and read it. Elijah stretched his tall frame to read along with me.

This is all your fault. I hope you're satisfied now.

After staring long and hard at the paper, Banks and I traded confused expressions. Bob finished speaking into his radio, informing the crew he was bringing us over to the pit, and then re-clipped it to his belt.

"The pit's just up ahead. It's . . . uhh, the b— Well, it's over here."

He motioned to the wide-open area in front of us. Bright spotlights lit up the area like a UFO was about to land in the deep crevice.

"She's there off to the side, closest to the equipment," Bob said. "So really, if she was a jumper, that's all she could've jumped from. But I would think one of the guys would've seen her climbing up there. And given what she's wearing? I mean, wouldn't it be hard to climb an eighteen-ton Caterpillar in heels and a business suit?"

Another trade-off of puzzlement with Elijah, and then we were skidding down the bank of the pit, toward the intricate crisscross of two-by-fours that were helping to shape my building's foundation. I was so close to chuckling at my friend, who openly cringed as the mud and dirt trashed his fancy loafers.

"Be careful here," Bob cautioned from right behind us. "This rebar is sharp and rusty. If you get stuck with that and haven't had a tetanus shot lately, you'll be sitting in the ER all night waiting for one. And let me tell you, those sons of bitches hurt! Right in the ass!"

He rubbed his backside as if remembering the last time he had to get his booster, but I was happy to have the mental image. It was a momentary relief from what we were about to look at. A sight that already seemed unbelievable. Christ. I'd seen more dead bodies in the last six months than a man should have to view in an entire lifetime.

"Her head is on that end." Bob pointed, saving us the trouble of having to uncover the whole body. Elijah was closest, so he dipped in and pulled back the scratchy burlap material.

We both sucked in a breath.

My crazy assistant, Terryn Ramsey, was the lifeless woman in the dirt. Her lips were blue and her skin was gray, but it was definitely her. That gaze, normally brilliant with her borderline insanity, was now a dull blank study of the city's uncaring skyline.

Elijah respectfully recovered her face with the dull brown sheet.

As Elijah stood back up fully, Bob asked, "You know her?"

"Yeah," I answered.

We crawled back out of the trench.

And then tried to come up with a plan.

"Thanks for everything here, Bob. Do you mind if we have a few minutes?" I said to the foreman.

"Oh, yeah, sure. I'll see you up at the trailer. I'm going to take a lap around the site, though. Just to check on the guys. You know, make sure everyone is doing what they're supposed to be doing." He laughed good-naturedly and headed off toward some men who appeared to be welding.

I looked at Elijah and then scrubbed my hands down my face. "Seriously, bro, what the hell? This bitch has always been crazy. This can't be pinned on me. Everyone knew she was off her rocker."

"The media is going to have a field day with this. No matter what. And the fact that the body is here..." He held his hands up like the Messiah and turned in a semicircle. "So fucking bad."

"We have to involve the cops, though. I'm not burying this and looking more guilty later if it comes out. No way in hell."

"Agree one hundred percent. I'm just saying it's going to be a shitstorm. I wish I were still in Twentynine Palms."

That sentence made me burst out a sardonic laugh. "I never thought I'd hear those words come out of your mouth."

"Right?"

"Okay. I need to call Abbi and let her know it's going to be a late night. Once we call the police, we're going to be here for the rest of the night."

Now my friend was the one rubbing his hands across his face. "No wonder I have zero social life."

★ ★ ★

"Well, Mr. Shark, you just can't seem to stay out of trouble, can you?" said the detective to whom LAPD dispatch connected me. Surprise, surprise; he was a member of the same task force that had been out to the house investigating Tawny's murder. The City of Angels must have been severely understaffed for wiseass murder investigators these days.

"More like trouble can't seem to stop finding me, Detective." I kept my reply even. "I had nothing to do with this. At all."

"Didn't you say this woman is, or was, your administrative assistant?"

"Well, yes."

He snorted softly. "And her body just happens to show up at the site of the building you are very publicly erecting in our fine city?"

"That doesn't make me guilty of murder, Detective. It would probably do you well to remember that."

"Are you threatening me, Mr. Shark?"

"No more than you're unfairly accusing me, Detective."

The line went quiet for a few beats while Elijah shot death rays at me with his glare from across the room.

What? I mouthed and flipped the phone my middle finger.

"I'll gather a forensics team and be over as soon as I can. You know the drill at this point. Don't touch anything. Don't move anything. This is an official police investigation at this point," the man droned on.

"Right. We'll be in the security trailer when you arrive." I disconnected the call and flopped down in the nearest chair. What I wouldn't give to be at home, in bed, with the warm, willing woman who was carrying my child.

The woman I should've never brought back to this fucked-up mess of my daily life. But it was too late now for that clarity, wasn't it?

CHAPTER NINE

ABBIGAIL

Uggghhh.

After being used to sleeping in and doing nothing all day, I'd forgotten how painful four thirty a.m. really was.

It was called an ungodly hour for a reason, I guessed—and now I knew why. There was nothing holy about my phone's vibration buzzing incessantly in my ear. But I had only myself to blame. I'd purposely put my phone's alarm to the setting, already knowing what kind of a skirmish I'd get from Sebastian if he knew I was getting up and going into the kitchen today. Fortunately, fate had intervened with some kind of an emergency he had to deal with at the Edge's construction site, so he'd crawled in beside me only an hour and a half before. Now, a freight train could've barreled through our bedroom and he wouldn't have moved a muscle.

Or so I thought.

For good measure, I'd put my work clothes in one of the guest rooms. I also planned on showering and getting ready for work in there. If Bas even sniffed what I was up to, there'd be hell to pay—but I had no intention of sitting in the house all day, every day, like I had in Twentynine Palms.

Besides, this wasn't complete freedom. Bas and Elijah had set up a security network that could likely be seen from space.

It covered the property, the neighborhood, and likely every pore of my body. No matter where I went, I would be safe. I'd have to be okay with that. But so would he. It was that simple.

Or so I thought.

This was Sebastian Albert Shark I was considering, after all.

I set aside that thought while climbing into the guest room's shower. It wasn't so easy to ignore how I felt physically when finishing up the task. As I got out of the stall, I was already a little nauseated and lightheaded—a troubling recognition, considering my minor amount of activity, but I was determined to push through and actually accomplish something in my day for once. I'd delivered lunches while battling allergies, fevers, and once, even a sprained ankle. A tiny upset stomach wasn't going to hold me down, damn it.

I used my silent pep talk for strength to start fluffing through my hair, getting rid of the excess water in my unruly curls.

Until I ran directly into the brick wall of a man standing just outside the shower door.

I was pretty sure the whole neighborhood heard my startled yelp.

"Jesus Christ, Bas," I blurted. "You scared the crap out of me!" When he replied with nothing but a sleep-deprived glower, I went on with my nervous stammering. "Wh-What are you doing up? You just came home a little while ago. You should be in bed, babe."

That still didn't earn me any spoken reaction, though he ticked up one eyebrow and crossed his arms in a foreboding pose across his bare chest.

Clearly my only option was to ignore his sexy-as-hell brood.

I continued with my after-shower routine, though I had to step around him several times to look into the mirror. He followed every move I made with his stony, unyielding expression. He didn't falter the look by an inch, and I could tell he was gearing up to dole out a lecture, and I could also sense it was one I didn't want to hear.

"Go back to bed, Bas. You don't need to hover here while I get ready."

"And what exactly do you think you're getting ready for?"

That made it official. I was unnerved. His calm tone was eerier than a poltergeist's howl. By now, I wished he'd just yell it out and be done with it.

"I'm going to work." I held back the "duh," but barely. "I have a business to run, remember? And I've taken more than my share of time off. I've been leaning on Rio way too much since the Edge's groundbreaking. It's time to get back to it."

"It's time to—" He saved me from having to stomp on his snarl by interrupting himself. "You can't be serious."

"Of course I'm serious." I smoothed more concealer in under my eyes. Then a little bit more. Then just huffed, giving up. Clearly, I wasn't going to be fresh and dewy and bright-eyed today. "Things have been so chaotic lately, and it's been so unfair to her—"

"Fuck fair." He loomed in until he was angled between the mirror and me, forcing me to confront the dual laser beams of his glare. "Abbi… goddammit. This is your health we're talking about—and now the baby's. How do you feel right now? Because you look like shit."

"Gee thanks, honey," I said bitterly, patting his arm for extra sarcastic effect. For all his talk about my stupidity, had he really said something so careless? But I could answer that for myself, and that word was yes. He was probably more exhausted than me right now and not thinking before he spoke. "You really should just go back to bed before we get into an argument, before you say something thoughtless. Oops." I lolled my head to the side harshly. "Too late." I gave him a sideways glare while pushing back in toward the mirror, giving my under-eye makeup just one more try.

"There's no way I'm allowing you to go to the kitchen."

"I'm sorry?" I pivoted to face him, slamming my cover-up onto the counter in emphasis. "Did you just say *allow* me?"

"Yes. Is there a problem with my word selection?"

"Not if this were still nineteen fifty."

For once, unbelievably, my sarcasm seemed to resonate with him. In a strange rush, all the tension wilted from his massive frame. He hung his head and rubbed the space between his eyes with his thumb and forefinger.

"Jesus, Abbi. Please don't fight me on this. You aren't well enough to stand on your feet all morning in Inglewood and then haul around a damn delivery cart in the noontime heat." When he raised his head again, utter exhaustion distorted his handsome face. "You know you're not."

"But I can't stay cooped up in this house all day either." Just speaking the words had my throat cracking and my eyes tearing. But I kept my stance resolute in the span of one sentence. I was being a little stubborn and likely a lot stupid, but I needed to do this. For once, I needed to hold my ground.

"Abbig—"

"Sebastian." I dug my nails into his sinewy forearm. "Please."

He dropped his head again. Then shook it. Once.

"I said no, Abbigail. That's the end of it."

He left the bathroom without another word.

For a few long moments, I simply stood there, staring at the open doorway. Feet swaying. Mind reeling. *What just happened?*

I didn't know if I had a definitive answer. There was a large part of me that knew he had a point. But an even larger part needed to make mine, too. And if I caved on day one, what would that mean for day two? And every other day after that?

That was when the answer hit. Like an anvil to my solar plexus.

It was simple. It meant that I was still a prisoner. I had a new cell and a new warden, but I hadn't been exonerated. My sentence hadn't even been reduced! I was as much a captive in this mansion as I'd been at the one in the desert.

My stomach lurched. Suddenly and violently. Oh God, I was thankful to already be in the bathroom. I rushed to the toilet and dropped down in front of it, getting to work on what my body ordered me to do. But I didn't have time to close the door, meaning Sebastian heard everything from the start. Seemingly at once, he was back by my side. He pulled my sweaty hair back from my face and started soothing my nape. I batted at his hands—I couldn't take even that contact, my skin was so sensitive—but he didn't get the point, and I was too weak to expound on it beyond that.

After spilling the contents of my stomach, my tears started tumbling. I was frustrated and furious and fed up. I didn't know if I could keep doing this, but the brochures Dr. Landon had given me about this condition said I was in for months of it. Most expectant mothers with hyperemesis gravidarum had symptoms well into their second trimester. The tiff with my man hadn't helped matters. I was supposed to stay calm and emotionally even, as much as I possibly could.

"Baby," Sebastian pleaded. "What can I do?" He rubbed my back while I hovered over the toilet, making sure I was done. But I didn't want to be touched. His well-meaning gesture felt like electric shocks.

"Stop touching me," I moaned. "My skin hurts." I flushed the toilet and tried to wobble to my feet. Bas stayed right there, struggling to steady me, ignoring my request to keep his hands off. I shrugged out of his hold and gripped the counter for balance.

"I'm fine." I sniffled. "Or I will be in a couple of minutes. My skin is overly sensitive, so it doesn't feel good to be touched."

"Okay. Okay." He held his hands up. "Sorry. I'm still learning all of the details." He shook his head, "Christ. I really am sorry. I should've been there for you from the beginning. You shouldn't have been going through this alone, Abbigail."

"It's fine," I insisted. "Come on, Bas. Seriously. I'm not the first pregnant woman in history to have morning sickness."

"Fuck. Why can't you understand?" He just stared at me, waiting for me to look at him.

"What?"

"I want to be here for you, damn it. I want to be a part of every single minute of this."

I splashed cool water on my face, thankful I hadn't done my makeup beyond the little bit of cover-up. I quickly brushed my teeth, and even before I looked back in the mirror, I could feel Sebastian's stare on me, pensive and watchful. I bit the inside of my cheek to hold back from screaming. Right now, his scrutiny was making my pores prickle worse than his fingers.

"Do you... maybe... want to lie down for a little bit?" he finally offered. "But just for a little bit. Maybe, after that,

I can drive you into the kitchen when I go to the office. You can spend an hour or two there, and I'll have Joel swing by at lunchtime to bring you home."

I jerked my head up. Bit down on my lip yet again, this time to hold back fresh tears. Holy crap. Was Sebastian Shark really extending a compromise to me?

Part of me still didn't believe it. I continued fussing with the hand towel, not sure I'd accurately heard what he'd just said. "Really?"

He smiled. The warmth climbed all the way to his eyes. "Yes. Really." He steered me out of the bathroom, down the hall, and back toward the master suite. When we stepped back into our space, he turned and scooped my hands into his. "Abbigail, I'm honestly not trying to keep you from your business." A sound between a grunt and a laugh escaped him. "Who would understand the need to oversee the daily operations of their business better than me?"

I scooted up to my tiptoes and rubbed an affectionate kiss into his stubble. "Thank you," I whispered. "That means the world to me. Truly."

He dipped his head to nuzzle his lips against mine. "Come on." And then tugged on my fingertips. "We both need some more sleep."

Our big, comfortable bed looked too inviting to resist. I climbed in, and he packed extra pillows around my body before pulling the covers up to my chin. When he finished, he slid his fingers up to the side of my face. Our gazes met. In the gray light of early dawn, his eyes were shadows of cobalt and slate. The etched planes of his handsome face were mellowed and mesmerizing.

"We'll work this out, Red. I promise. We'll come up with a

plan that we both agree on."

I turned my head and pressed my lips to his broad palm. "I know. I do. Thank you for wanting to meet me halfway on this."

"We'll call your doctor too," he said. "I'm sure she has some good advice about smart working hours for you right now."

Exhaustion crashed over me, worse than the anvil. Still I managed to mumble back to him, "He."

"He . . . what?"

"I said 'he.' My doctor is a man." My words were thick with sleep, and so were my eyes. I barely comprehended the sight of Bas as he froze in place, his limbs newly stiff and his gaze five shades darker.

"Well," he growled. "I guess we'll be looking for a new doctor, then, too."

★ ★ ★

When I woke up, the sun was streaming in the high windows above the lower-level ones in our bedroom. The bed beside me was empty. But as I searched my nightstand for my phone, preparing to rain hellfire texts on Bas if he'd gone off to the city without me, Dori popped her head in the doorway.

"Hey there," she murmured. "I'm so happy you slept so well. And someone else"—she gave a dramatic eye roll—"is going to be too."

I sat up a little straighter, shifting one of my pillows to cushion my head. "Oh, dear," I giggled out. "He's gotten to you already, hmmm?"

The woman heeded my hand motion to come and sit next to me on the bed. Her steps were as careful as the tone she used for her reply. "He's a very, umm . . . intense man, yes?"

"You are very diplomatic, Dori." I flashed a sardonic smile.

"Well, it's clear that the man cares for you," she defended. "Very deeply."

"You know, he's a little like a cared-for pit bull." I widened my grin. "Very scary when you walk by but a big lover inside." I canted my head. "Now if I could just housebreak him a little better . . ." We shared a long bout of giggles over that until she unexpectedly sobered.

"He and I talked a little this morning," she conveyed. "And he told me how you were sick again this morning. I could tell he felt responsible for whatever happened."

I pulled in a long breath. Tried a tentative smile once again. "You . . . could?"

"Definitely." Her declaration was forthright, and my chest reacted with a surge of comforting warmth. "I told him about a few blogs I've been reading, so hopefully, he will direct some of his intensity toward them."

"Oh, Dori . . . Dori, Dori, Dori." I patted her thigh while chanting the chide. "That's like asking a leopard to change its spots. And strangely, it's part of what I love about him. Now the overwhelming need to control me . . . that I could definitely do without."

"I had a boyfriend like that once," she said thoughtfully.

"Yeah? How did you handle it?"

"Well, notice I said 'had,' right?" She winked and then changed the subject. "Something to drink? Tea?"

"That sounds great, but I can go downstairs and get it."

"Why don't we try this? Just see what you think. While we're here at the house, you stay resting. Either here, or on a sofa, or wherever." She waved her hand around, indicating she literally meant any spot in the house. "But when you're here, you let me do things for you. As in, everything."

I scrunched my face up, already hating the plan, but she put her hands up in defense.

"Just hear me out and give it a try for a few days? Or does stubbornness come along with the Shark name?"

"Oh, we aren't married. Plus, I don't know if I'll change my name."

Shit. Where did that thought come from?

"Good luck with that…" She rolled her eyes playfully, but it was interesting how well she had already caught on to Sebastian's temperament—though most of the time, the man did wear it like a neon billboard.

"I think if you rest as much as possible while we're home, you will have more stamina when we go out," Dori persisted. "It will be better for everything, if you want to go to your office, run errands, or whatever. Does that make sense?"

I couldn't help but break out a bigger grin in reply. This woman definitely had a servant's heart and was quickly worming her way into mine. "All right," I conceded at last. "You do have a good point…"

"But?" She spoke the word I was already implying.

"But it's just so hard for me to lounge around so much," I confessed. "I get so restless… and bored! I'm used to being very independent, and this has been a hard change for me. I don't think Sebastian understands that."

"I can only imagine. Then maybe you walk around from room to room? I mean, this house is enormous. I just don't want to see you out back pulling weeds!"

We both laughed, but once more, she was the first to turn serious. "Maybe… you need to tell him all of this?"

I crunched a frown. "Tell him what?"

"That this change, from being so independent to being waited on, has been a hard adjustment for you."

I thought about it for a few beats. "You're very smart for a girl so young. Has anyone ever told you that?"

"Pfft. I'm probably older than you, Abbi. Just blessed with good skin genes. My mama was a very wise woman. I learned a lot from her."

"How would Sebastian not know that about me already? I mean, he knows me inside and out. He knows me better than I know myself half the time. Why wouldn't he know this is hard for me?"

"Men are often simple creatures. They see things in black and white. Sometimes they need to just be told things you think they should know, especially when it comes to how you're feeling." She patted my leg, which was still covered by all the blankets. "Now, I'm going to get you some tea, and then we'll see about going to the office. I think Mr. Shark said his driver is at our disposal, and we just need to give him a call when we are ready for him to get us."

"I have a perfectly fine vehicle outside. I don't need to be driven around town."

She tilted her head. "Mmm, well, you do when you're still getting dizzy with no warning and vomiting at the drop of a pin. Do you want that to happen to you—or your unborn child or me—in the fast lane on the 405?" She gave me a saucy wink while popping back to her feet. "Didn't think so. Now let me go get you some tea."

Well . . . wow. I was totally in love with my new friend. I made a mental note to thank Bas for asking Dori to come back to LA with us. This was the kind of person I needed around me while I endured this house arrest. Though I adored my sister-in-law, even thinking about Rio and her fireball intensity right now was an exhausting task.

But the thing was, I did think about her. A lot.

Rio had been my lifesaver. The pinch hitter to see Abstract through one of our biggest growth spurts yet. Even if that was the case, I'd have to break mine and Bas's "announcement" to her and Sean with care and delicacy—and sooner rather than later. But first I needed to talk to Sebastian and make sure he was on board with sharing our news. Not because I needed his permission, but because this was his story, too. It was only considerate to involve him in the decision as to when we made the information public.

A text message came in from my man as if he could sense that I was up and moving around.

I'm happy you slept so long, Red.

Okay, scratch the cosmic dribble. Dori must have let him know I was awake. But just like a modern-day fairy godmother, she appeared now too. She was carrying a cup of tea and dry toast, all artfully arranged on a tray. Despite her beautiful offering, she had the grace to look contrite when she saw the expression on my face and the phone in my hand.

"I'm sorry." She lifted a sheepish grin. "He wanted me to let him know when you were awake. And his orders still trump yours."

"I know, I know." I looked to the ceiling as if asking heaven for enlightenment. "Because he signs the paychecks and all."

"Because I want the best for that little baby," she rebutted. "Whoever's being the least stubborn and thinking with that child's best interest at the moment, that's where you shall find my loyalty."

I lowered my head into an approving nod.

"Now drink this while it's warm."

She set the tray down on the bed where I could easily reach it. "I brought the toast in case you were feeling adventurous." She took a few steps back from the bed before looking around the room. "Do you want me to let some daylight in here?"

Are you not speaking to me?

Sorry. Dori just brought me some tea. Thank you for bringing her back with us. I love her.

She is pretty great.

I'm sorry about this morning, Bas.

You stole my line.

What are your thoughts about telling Rio about the baby? I'm going to have to explain why I'm missing so much work.

Up to you.

I'll make sure she doesn't tell anyone else except Sean.

Wouldn't you rather tell your family yourself though?

You have a point.

Of course I do.

"Ugh." I tossed my phone into the covers. I knew he was joking, but even this was complicated. With Sebastian being a high-profile person in the city, announcing the fact that he was about to become a father—unwed to the mother, at that—came with a mile-long list of complications.

"What's wrong?" Dori queried after opening the shutters and walking back across the room. "The tea not agreeing with you?"

"No," I replied at once. "No; it's not that. This is great, Dori. Really."

"Which is why you still look like the bed's about to become quicksand?"

She'd picked a pretty perfect metaphor. I attempted a smile, fighting the feeling that I was sinking faster than I could fight, and stated, "I . . . I just didn't think all of this through yet."

"All of what?"

I rolled my shoulders. "It's not a big deal. Listen; I'll get ready, and then we can head to my work kitchen. Is that a good plan?"

"Okay. But if you want to talk something through, just know that I'm here, okay?"

"I appreciate that. But this is definitely one I need to work out with my baby daddy." I laughed at the terminology while scooting out of bed and heading to my closet.

★ ★ ★

I finally saw the wisdom of Dori's words about driving, and we had Joel drive us to Abstract's Inglewood prep kitchen. We walked in to a scene that seemed more like the three-minute warning on a timed Food Network show, with activity happening everywhere—all generated by just two people. Rio was barking orders like Gordon Ramsay turned into a badass goddess, with Grant Twombley as her fast-moving minion. But after just a few minutes, I realized the man could hold his own around my sister-in-law, giving just as good as he got from her smart mouth and short-fused temper.

"This is oddly entertaining," Dori remarked in a discreet whisper. She slid in to serve as cover while I snapped a few surreptitious pictures of Bas's tall friend, decked out in a full apron decorated with the Gumby and Pokey cartoon characters. Sebastian would beg me for copies of the pics to use as blackmail with his bestie.

Cartoon apron and sarcastic shouts aside, I noticed that the pair were, strangely, functioning as a finely tuned creation machine. They already had the lunch orders done and were frantically finishing an emergency add-on for one of our more prominent downtown clients. I glanced at the order sheet, breathing an instant sigh of relief that said client wasn't Viktor Blake. While Bas and Elijah had carefully kept me removed from the gritty details of their ongoing investigation, I'd heard remnants of Viktor's name enough to know a wide berth from the man was a wise idea these days.

And that was more than enough brain space surrendered to that mess today. Instead, I focused on the main attraction in front of me, walking over to peek at what was simmering in the pots and pans atop all three of the industrial stoves. "You guys could give a girl an inferiority complex," I said to Rio, dipping the back of a spoon into the sauce she was working on.

"You, my love, will never be replaced by that tree. Don't even go there." She snorted Grant's way with the first sentence and then hip-bumped me with the second.

Across the kitchen, Grant answered with a scathing laugh of his own. "What did I tell you about calling me that, Blaze?"

"Something similar to what I told you about calling me that," she fired back, adding a careless shrug.

"Hey." I returned my sister-in-law's hip nudge, though with gentler force. "Can we talk for a minute, Rio?"

"Sure, sweetie." She bustled from the stove to the counter and then back again. "What's up?"

"I . . . umm . . . kind of need your undivided attention. Are you at a place where you can step away?" I motioned to the stove, letting her know I was aware of her predicament. I knew what it was like to be in the middle of getting an order together at the eleventh hour.

"Oh, of course. Grant, can you deal with this?" She nodded back to me and explained, "This is sauce for tomorrow's lunch. It just needs to simmer." Dashing back a last look at Grant, she dictated, "Don't let it stick to the bottom."

"Got it!" The big guy flashed a grin while ducking into the walk-in, putting ingredients away.

Rio wiped her hands on a towel, and we moved over to the closet-sized office in which we did our paperwork. We both took seats next to the desk, and she folded her hands in her lap while raking her stare across my face. "So what's up, honey? You okay?" She looked me over carefully as only Rio could do. I was surprised she hadn't already guessed the news I was about to share with her. "You look a little green . . ."

"I have to tell you something. But it has to stay right here between us. Well, you can tell Sean, of course."

"Ooohhh-kaaayy. But I'm not going to lie; you're freaking me out a little bit. I mean, first you get taken to the desert for weeks and barely called from there. The whole time, everyone around here"—she thumbed over her shoulder toward Grant—"acted like you were some huge state secret. And then I saw the stuff on the news about one of Shark's freighters being boarded by pirates, and some of the crew being taken hostage."

I sighed and made sure she saw it. "Yeah, things have really been a mess. Luckily they are negotiating now, as far I understand. Bas doesn't tell me a whole lot. But I'm really sorry about all the secrecy while I was gone. The guys thought it was best for everyone." I followed that statement up with a significant eye roll, letting my sister-in-law know exactly what I thought of that action plan.

"I get it." She held up her hand to stop me. "I know there's been a lot going on that's been out of your control. Just tell me one thing right now." She gulped hard, suddenly looking almost panic-stricken. "Are you . . . closing the business?"

"What?" My exclamation knocked me back in my seat. "No!"

She poured out a huge breath. "Oh, thank God."

"No," I repeated. "It's not that. Not at all. I would never do that. Shit. After how hard we've worked for all of this? Are you kidding?"

"I was hoping I was." She laugh-sighed. "And yeah, that's good. Because you're right. We've come way too far to just close the doors. But what the hell is going on? Seriously, you look like you've lost weight, and your color is paler than usual." She reached out to touch my forehead, testing for fever the old-fashioned way.

"I'm . . ." I scooted forward again, nervously kneading my fingers together. "Well, I'm pregnant."

Rio clapped her hands in front of her mouth to stifle her wail. Three seconds later, she shot up and slammed me with a full-body hug.

"Wait!" She suddenly drew back. "You're happy, right? I mean, I just assume everyone is happy when they say the words. But just because I want to say them so badly, doesn't mean—"

"Oh, Rio. I'm sorry." I gripped her shoulders. "I didn't mean to be insensitive. I know you and Sean have been trying so hard."

She slid her hands into mine. "Stop!" she ordered. "Stop that right now. I'm happy for you. I'm over-the-moon happy for you! And I'm over that phase where I hate every woman who gets pregnant when I don't; honestly. I'm truly so happy for you, honey." Again, she baldly studied my face for a few beats. "You doing okay, though? You must have morning sickness. Is that why you've been staying at home?"

"Well, we did just get back into town yesterday, so the whole desert-villa banishment hasn't been a lie." I held up my hands in swear-on-a-Bible mode. "But the morning sickness thing isn't a fib either. And it's at the extreme level, sister."

There were times when the woman's vitality was a welcome thing. Right now, watching her dropped jaw and distressed gaze, was one of them. While I wouldn't wish this bullshit on anyone, this was the closest thing to commiseration I'd had all week—and it was nice.

"It's called hyperemesis gravidarum," I went on, sounding out the words in distinct syllables, because Christ, it was a mouthful. "I've had to have IV fluids and the whole nine yards.

Unpleasant barely scratches the surface when describing it."

"Oh, you poor thing. I've read about that. Kate Middleton had it with her pregnancies." She smirked when I snort-laughed at her. The woman was a notorious royals watcher. "Anyway... why haven't you told me sooner? How far along are you?"

"Still early; only six weeks or so. But that's why I'm asking you to keep this under wraps for now. Sebastian and I can't have this getting out to the public until I'm further along. But being so sick certainly hasn't eased our stress. It's so hard to do anything. And I mean... anything. I spend most of the day in bed."

On cue, Dori walked over and set a bottle of water on the desk. "Have you met Dori yet?" I asked Rio. "I'm sorry I didn't introduce you when I first got here. You and the big guy were in the middle of a sparring match."

Rio narrowed her gaze at me but converted to a smile while shaking Dori's hand. "It's a pleasure to meet you. Are you the new lady in waiting?" She gave her a dramatic wink.

"I am. And loving every minute of it!" My new friend reached over and pushed the bottle of water closer to me, silently hinting that I needed to drink. But then she went back across the kitchen and got busy helping Grant.

Rio swung her gaze to me, bugging her eyes out in a *what the hell?* sort of way.

"She was one of the staff at the house in Twentynine Palms. We got along well, so Bas asked her to come back with us." I shrugged because it had all really happened that easily.

"Your life has changed so dramatically in such a short time, Abbigail. Just don't forget who you are inside here." She reached forward and touched my sternum.

"Never. Promise." I stood up but apparently too quickly, because stars danced in my vision and I had to grab on to the desk to steady myself.

I heard Dori's voice from across the kitchen. "Drink the water."

I felt for the bottle, but Rio was already handing the uncapped container to me, mumbling, "She's a miniature Shark. No wonder he liked her."

The comment made me spray the water I just drank all over my sister-in-law's face and chest, and then I burst out laughing even harder. Quickly, I found a towel and blotted frantically at Rio's face and shirt.

"You did that to yourself!" I was still chuckling.

"I did, I did." She joined my laughter.

We hugged each other for a full minute before Dori and I left, making one pit stop on the way home.

"What are we stopping for?" Dori asked as we got out of the back of the car. I still wasn't used to pulling up to places in a limousine. It wasn't uncommon in Los Angeles, and while people didn't gawk as much as they would in a smaller town, they still looked to see who was "arriving."

"I just need a few things," I said, heading toward the front entrance of the store.

"Abbigail, I can do these errands for you. I don't want you to overdo it."

"Dori." I came to a full stop while turning to face her. "I haven't been inside a Target in months. Please don't deny me my fix."

Just then, my phone signaled an incoming text from Sebastian.

Get back in the car.

I screwed up my face while I stared at my phone. I looked at Dori with an accusatory glare next. "Did you tell him we were here? When did you have time to text him? This has to stop!" I went to stand in the shade of the building's overhanging architecture.

She held her hands up in innocence. "Wasn't me this time."

Joel!

No. Can I get you anything while I'm here?

I would address this new stalking problem when he came home later.

That's what Dori is for. I'm serious. Go home.

No.

Red.

The exact color I see right now.

CHAPTER TEN

SEBASTIAN

Ten weeks later...

"Are you nervous?" I asked Abbigail while we waited for the ultrasound technician to come into the little room.

"Nope. I'm ready." Sitting on the exam table, she swung her dangling legs back and forth to the beat of her drumming fingers. "Are you nervous?"

"Of course not."

"Liar."

I chuckled, though didn't surrender the assessing steeple of my fingers—as I battled the rising bulge in my pants. Christ. Even in a flimsy medical gown with her hair in a messy bun, the woman of my heart inspired a raging fire in my balls.

At least focusing on my erection helped with distraction from the nerves she'd accurately called me on. That and getting to my feet again. I moved forward, making room for myself between her kicking legs, basically putting my own safety at risk. With her hands in mine, I looked into her stunning green eyes. Would I ever get over this woman's beauty? Did I even want to?

"So. You still want to find out, right?" I queried while brushing some loose tendrils out of her eyes. I only asked because the way her body was vibrating, she certainly appeared agitated. "It's not too late to change your mind, Red. They can just do all the measurements and record all the other stuff and not tell us if it's a boy or a girl."

"No way. I totally want to find out." She unleashed an impish grin. "We have a bet, remember? And you are definitely going to lose."

"Not a chance," I drawled. "But do we have to do one of those ridiculous staged gender reveals on social media? God, it makes my skin crawl just thinking about being a part of something so pedestrian."

She giggled. Loud. "Did you just say 'pedestrian' in a full sentence?"

I flared my gaze. "Well, it is!"

"Well, your PR team still thinks it's the best way to break the news to the public at large."

"Remind me to fire the PR team."

"Oh, come on, Bas. It's kind of cute. Soon, everyone will know that a baby Shark is about to make its way into the great wide ocean . . ."

I cut her off with a groan. "One quick email can put an end to that nonsense. And with the way you've started showing all of a sudden, the information will be viral as soon as one paparazzo gets cunning with their lens."

And the news outlets were circling like—well—sharks, for every morsel of news they could get about me these days now that the South Pacific hostage situation had come to the best conclusion we could've hoped for. The pirates had been appeased without any loss of life. The crew had all returned to their families unharmed, and most of the cargo was recovered and delivered to its intended destinations.

What had begun as a media nightmare was flipped into a happy ending that worked out in our favor. I was proud of the Shark Enterprises logistics team, who had worked day and night to pool resources from every corner of the globe and connect them to the right branches of the local government. Everyone had been tireless about ensuring the crew was treated fairly while the negotiations took place. Better yet, the freight we were responsible for finally found its way to its final ports of call.

The message behind the capture was still unclear, at least in the public's eye. But I had received a few private messages that I had shared only with Grant and Elijah. Troubling information to worry about another day.

Today, I had only happiness filling my thoughts and heart—exactly what I was reminded of as Abbi spoke again.

"Well, the sooner the better." She leaned back and rubbed her stomach. "I'm excited about not having to hide my fat stomach anymore."

"You're not fat." I gave the moment the somberness it deserved. Then said, kissing her eyelids and nose between each singular word, "You. Are. Stunning." Before she could issue a peep of protest, I leaned in and lovingly kissed her lips. There was even a chance to sweep in and taste her, so full of luscious sugar and spice at the same time, before she dipped back and shot me a wary glare.

"Don't you dare go further than that sweet talk either, buddy. Do not, if you value your balls, say I'm *glowing*. I swear, if you think it, I will throat punch you." She shifted her weight and grimaced, having surpassed the I-gotta-pee-like-a race-horse phase about three minutes ago. "Whoever came up with that dumb saying was confusing the oily, sweaty state of a pregnant woman with something else altogether."

"Or maybe it was a husband threatened to be throat punched for saying his wife looked oily?"

As I raised my brows, Abbi burst out laughing. At the same time, there was an efficient knock on the door. The technician strolled in, apparently deciding we were finally worthy enough for her presence.

"Hi," the girl asked brightly. "And how are we doing today?"

"Good, good," Abbi answered before I could growl about being kept waiting longer than we should've been.

"Great. Are we ready to get started? Did we drink lots of water? It helps if the bladder is full. We get better pictures that way. So now go ahead and lie back, Mrs. Shark. I'll just get everything set up here."

"It's Gibson," Abbi said at once.

"Hmmm?" the girl asked sweetly while going about her routine.

"I said it's Gibson. Abbigail Gibson." Abbi made sure the girl was watching as she pointed to her name on her chart. Though the technician nodded and smiled, not an iota unnerved, I sure as hell was. The sensation was foreign—and not fun—but it was there, pressing at the back ends of my skull like a Vulcan squeeze. Compelling the truth from me, even if I was only confessing it to myself.

I didn't want her to correct the technician.

I hated the fact that she had.

Would she do the same thing when they asked her what name to put on the baby's birth certificate?

Abbigail was mine, damn it.

And so was our child.

The conflict raged through my head as the technician entered a bunch of information into the machine. I must have gotten obvious about it, because Abbigail squeezed my hand and gave me a definite "settle down" look. Since she'd shot it my way before during these appointments, she obviously thought I was pulling my typical "impatient patient" routine. In many ways, she had a point. I had to concentrate on what mattered here, damn it. Her and our baby.

After the technician asked me to dim the lights in the room via the switch by the door, she squirted a liberal amount of gel on Abbi's growing belly. When she swirled the wand around in the goo and then pressed the device in, an image came to life on the screen.

The air stopped in my throat. Abbi's breath hitched, as well.

We had seen the baby a bunch of times now, but every occasion was amazing. The little person was getting bigger and was starting to look less like an alien. Abbi was sixteen weeks pregnant now, and all things were going along as expected. Because of the severe morning sickness, she had barely gained weight, but the baby was growing right along the standard growth curve. Thank fuck.

The ultrasound technician prattled on about the measurements she was taking, pressing the wand in at different places, tapping away at the screen to measure "long bones," as she called them, as well as the baby's length, position, and so on.

Through the whole process, Abbi kept up her tough grip on my hand. A few times, I had to remind her to breathe, because it seemed like she wasn't. The tech would ask her to turn a certain way, or reposition her arm, but for the most part, we were both just observers.

Finally, the tech posed her last—and biggest—question.

"Were we wanting to know the sex? You're at sixteen weeks. It's early, but I think we can all plainly see. Did we already see? I mean, it's pretty obvious."

The woman gave a condescending chuckle. I glowered. Luckily, Abbi was feeling more gracious.

"We would like to know, yes," she answered.

"Well..." The woman slid the wand over Abbi's belly, positioning it so the image became clear right between our baby's legs. "You have a very cooperative little man here today." She placed an arrow graphic on the screen and froze the picture so the end was right at a little penis.

"Oh, my God," Abbi sobbed.

"Definitely a boy!" the technician chirped.

"A boy..." No way could I hold back the wonder and love in my voice. I was gutted. Transfixed. Awestruck.

"I'll go log in and make sure all the images are emailed to you. Congratulations! You can get cleaned up, Ms. Gibson, and I'll be right back."

As Abbigail sat up again, she found my gaze with her tear-filled stare. "So... are you happy?" There was a heartfelt glitch in her voice. Though the room was still dim, I watched her chin wobble. "You thought it would be a girl. Was that because you really wanted one more than a boy? I mean, are you still good with—"

"Are you kidding?" My voice cracked with the emotion flooding my entire body. My hands shook as I cupped her cheeks. My lips sought hers for a fervent, velvet kiss. "I'm over the fucking moon, baby. He's healthy and right on track. Thank you." I kissed her again. "Thank you."

She laughed while forming her fingers atop my own. "Well, you're welcome—but news flash, my love… You helped."

"Jesus Christ. I'm having a son." As she started getting dressed again, I spun around and stabbed my hands through my hair. I tugged on the ends in a desperate motion. More tears choked me. I could barely move oxygen into my lungs. "A son…"

Abbi stood up. The paper drape fell to the floor, and her little dress dropped over her body. I swept her into a tight, trembling hold. We held each other for long moments, racked by feelings we didn't know how to express. Was this how it was for everyone? The disbelief. The euphoria. The excitement.

And the love.

Holy shit. So much love.

Finally, I leaned back. I had to see Abbi's face again, to confirm she comprehended even half the storm that was overtaking me. Elation swelled through me, erupting in a laugh, when I witnessed her amazed smile, joyous flush, and joy-sparkled stare.

"You knew from the very beginning," I murmured to her. "You kept saying it was a boy."

"Welll…" She gave me an adorable shrug. "I just had a feeling—and about two thousand visits to the porcelain god." She rolled her eyes and snickered softly. "He's already a force of nature."

"Like his mama," I husked, tears rolling down my cheeks.

"Like his daddy," she said, wiping them away as hers flowed freely.

"We're having a boy!" I bent low and grabbed her hips. As I hoisted her up and twirled her around, a giddy squeal spilled from her. "Can you believe it?"

"Oh, I think I can." She laughed again as I settled her back on her feet.

After we checked out from the OB office, paperwork and a few ultrasound prints in hand, we were feeling energetic enough to walk to where Joel was parked with the town car, instead of calling for a pickup in front of the building. The security detail nearly had an instant meltdown, but I was the boss, damn it, and I was feeling unstoppable, indestructible.

It wasn't a high I had often these days, but I relished being able to truly savor its certainty—at least for a few minutes. With Terryn gone—God rest that bizarre woman's soul—a good part of the daily crazy was out of my life. I hadn't realized how tense the lady was really making me until she was no longer around. HR had quickly replaced her, but I was having trouble "meshing" with the right person as of yet. Surprise fucking surprise.

Another shocker, this one more legitimate: the LAPD had wrapped up the investigation into Terryn's death with eye-popping speed. It was strange but not shocking, considering the rest of the "popping" they'd discovered during the autopsy. The exam exposed high levels of several prescription drugs in the woman's system. When combined, the chemicals caused psychosis. Well, shit. That explained a hell of a lot.

The pain in my ass—errr, the detective assigned to the case—hadn't even bothered to call about the resolution on the case. There was a short email to my attorney, forwarded at once to me. After reading the summation of the case, as well as learning Terryn had no family connections we could contact for forwarding her personal effects from her desk, I'd felt a twinge of sorrow for the woman.

A twinge.

Period.

Which was all I gave the matter now, as well.

"Hey." Abbi's silken summons brought me back to the moment, where I looked up in surprise. We were already downtown, just a few blocks from where Joel was dropping me before shuttling her back to Calabasas. "You've been so quiet," she commented. "What are you thinking about? Work?"

"Actually . . ." I chuffed out a laugh. "I was thinking about Terryn, of all people."

Abbi startled a little—enough to ensure I saw every inch of her newly probing stare. "Okay, who are you and what have you done with Sebastian Shark?"

"Oh, he's still right here." I leaned in and gave her lips a playful peck. "I've just been making sure he's not a caveman asshole when I'm with you. For your sake and the baby's. Our son." That giddy grin took over my whole mouth again. "I'm glad the effort hasn't been for naught, though. That it's noticeable. It's not always easy to curb my behavior. I've been this way my whole life, you know? It's hard to choose different actions. To be consciously different."

"I have noticed." She caught my hand in hers and lifted my knuckles to her sugar-pink lips. "But I don't expect you to change completely, Bas. I fell in love with you exactly the way you are. I love the demanding, commanding, insistent, expectant, respectable man you are. I adore that man, as a matter of fact."

"Yeah?" I deliberately rumbled it out. "Maybe you can show me how much you adore me when I get home tonight?" And then guided her fingers to the prominent swell in my slacks.

"Oh, I like that idea, Mr. Shark." She stretched her beautiful fingers across the hump of my cock and deliberately squeezed.

My eyes widened before I could control them. "Jesus." The bold move was so unlike my Little Red.

"Nah." As she kept stroking me, she flashed a saucy grin. "Just me."

"Just you who?" I volleyed. "I'm the one to gets to say it now: who are you, and what have you done with my virginal Abbigail?"

"Oh, honey," she purred. "I'm no virgin anymore." And kept rubbing, up and down, my entire throbbing length. "And have you read, in your endless pregnancy research, what happens to a woman's hormones around this time in the pregnancy?" She waggled her brows at me and gave me a wolfish grin.

Oh, yes. My girl. A wolfish grin.

"Hormones or not, turnabout is fair play," I told her then. "So don't you ever forget that woman I fell in love with when I met you, as well. I was obsessed with—and still am—with that innocent, pure, kind-hearted, gentle, loving, giving, completely perfect woman. I love you just the way you are. You don't have to change a single thing for me."

I showed her exactly that with a thorough kiss. I had every intention of making it slow, tender, and adoring. We'd always remember this fantastic day; however we'd had so many days go by without indulging ourselves physically. For that reason alone, the heat burst between us like pine needles on a campfire. With her hand still caressing my crotch, I was ready to kick that fire ring and start a damn forest fire.

"Baby?" I said, still between kisses because I couldn't give up the high of touching her.

"Yeah?" she panted.

"If you keep doing that to my cock, I'm going to come right here and now."

Her lips, now swollen from my kisses, parted in an adorable smile. "You think we have time?"

I swallowed hard—because all I could think of now was sliding myself in and out of those plush, succulent cushions . . .

"Okay, Mr. Shark," Joel called from the front seat. "Here we are."

Abbi and I jolted apart as the car came to a full stop in front of the Shark Enterprises building. I looked up at the chrome and glass structure, attempting to summon the usual spike of anticipation that hit whenever I arrived here. But right now, it wasn't the building spiking anything in me.

I arched a brow at Abbigail. She pouted her bottom lip, inviting me to lean in and steal a greedy nip at that luscious pinkness.

"Mmmm. Later," she rasped and scratched her fingertips over the edge of my jaw. "It's sooooo on, Daddy."

My eyes looked like four-alarm blazes. Yeah, I knew that for a fact. She had me so aroused, the gleam in my own gaze reflected back at me from Abbi's brilliant greens. "Trying to decide if I like hearing you call me that because it's fucking hot or because we're having a baby. But I think it's the first one when you say it in that raspy, sexy voice and with that goddamn needy look all over your entire body." I felt a tremble pass over my entire body from head to toe. "Fuck, you're sexy."

"Mr. Shark? Damn, I'm sorry; I'm going to get a ticket if I stall at this curb much longer. You know how the meter monitors get around here. If you need more time, I can pull—"

"I'm going. Shit!"

One last, frantic kiss and I was out of the car. Joel pulled away from the curb before I could even get up on the sidewalk.

Buttoning my suit jacket didn't do much to hide the erection throbbing between my legs. Luckily, no one was in the elevator when I got in. I reached into my waistband to adjust things, attempting to make the monster a little less visible. If I had to, I could deal with the problem when I got into my office but hoped to hold out for the real deal tonight. Likely, the minute I got to my desk, I'd be swamped with work. That would take care of all thoughts of my hot lady until I got home.

Fortunately, it did—until a few hours flew by, and I was jerking up my head when Grant's knock sounded on my office door.

He and Elijah strode in before I could even answer his announcement.

"How did it go? Did you find out what you're having? Banks and I have a bet going, and the stakes are very, very high."

I looked back and forth between my two best friends—and their expectant stares. I debated how to respond—for all of three seconds.

"We've . . . uh . . . decided not to find out, after all."

I almost gave myself away by cracking a proud smirk. Sometimes, life as an asshole really was so sweet. The chance to mess with my best friends was too damn good to pass up.

"You've got to be kidding me," Elijah exclaimed. "Ohhh, wait. Or was it just that they couldn't tell? And you don't want to admit failure on a test. That would be more like you."

"For that comment, I'm definitely not telling you." I pointed at him while getting up from behind my desk. The guy's impatient irritation was so worth the price of going there. I gave in to a secret smile while striding over to my usual spot in front of the floor-to-ceiling windows. My buddies joined me, one on either side.

"Fuck it," Grant muttered. "I'll just text Rio. She probably already knows."

But as soon as the asshole pulled out his phone, I plucked the device from his hand. I was fast as a—well, a shark—about it, so he didn't have time to react and defend his property.

"Bastard," he snarled.

With a careless shrug, I said, "I've been called worse."

"Probably today alone," Elijah said.

"The bigger concept we have here," I mused, "is why you feel okay about whipping out your . . . device . . . for casually communicating with Rio Gibson." I lobbed the phone over my shoulder, knowing it would land safely on the big couch a few feet away. I did it all the time with my cell too. "Is this a normal, daily occurrence, Mr. Twombley?"

"No," fumed Grant.

"Yes!" refuted Elijah.

Grant leaned back to dagger Banks with a glare, but his effort wasn't necessary. I was already shifting out of the way, turning to lean against the windowpane. If the thing ever broke, I'd plummet to my death—but that didn't stop Elijah from mirroring my pose one pane over. The effect was more officious than I intended, with us facing down Grant as if he were a defendant and we his prosecutors, but for now, it was working. The guy was definitely squirming.

"Come on, Twombley." I stuffed my hands in my pockets, trying to appear relaxed. "What gives, man? And don't think of bullshitting me."

"Us," Elijah corrected.

"Nothing 'gives,'" Grant retorted while stomping to the

sofa and seizing back his phone. "Just drop it, for fuck's sake!"

"Damn, Twombley. That's a lot of bluster for nothing going on."

"It's not what it looks like!" Grant spread his arms, turning his long index fingers into a matched pair of pointing desperation.

"Nooooo!" As Elijah and I moaned it together, we also twisted off the windows in opposite directions, moving like synchronized swimmers in the middle of a routine.

"You two can fuck off," Grant leveled. "Seriously. Rio and I have been working together in that damn hell-hole kitchen for weeks. We've just gotten to know each other. She spends most of her days there. Did you know that? Shit. She's probably there more time than she's at home."

He mumbled that last sentence, but I heard him. One glance at Elijah, and I knew he had too. "Uh-oh," Banks drawled beneath his breath. "I think I know what this is." He folded his arms. "LVS," he stated. "Totally clear-cut case."

"What the hell?" I demanded. "LV what?"

"Lonely vagina syndrome," Elijah explained.

Grant barked out a laugh. "Her vagina isn't lonely, asshole."

"Because you're the one keeping it company?" I rejoined.

"I have not. Fucked. Her. Now stop."

"But you want to."

I grabbed the chance to add my own censuring finger at Elijah. "Not helping." As I lowered my arm, I turned back to Grant. "At the risk of being glaringly obvious, the woman is married, man. To Abbigail's brother. That's a no-fly zone."

"Jesus," Grant spat. "Don't you think I already know—"

"Just making sure," I countered. "Shit! You could have any

woman in this city. Move on, okay? Call LuLu. Do something else. Do *someone* else. Just not Rio Gibson!"

"I'm not an idiot, Bas."

"At the risk of repeating myself... just making sure."

"I wouldn't do that. She wouldn't do that. She's in love with her husband." He rolled his eyes. "He's all she ever talks about. Trust me, my ears practically bleed from hearing about the guy all the time. You guys are so far off base, it's comical."

"But you're not laughing."

I hated admitting Elijah was completely right about that, but it didn't negate the point. Grant looked as far away from "laughing this off" as a basketball player who'd just snapped his ankle.

"Can we just change the goddamned subject?" the guy finally bit out.

I pulled in a long breath. Upon letting it out, I blurted, "It's a boy."

Both my friends froze completely.

Then stared.

Then broke into wide, joyous grins.

I mirrored their stares. "I'm going to have a son," I said at last, rubbing the back of my head. "Can you fucking believe it?"

Grant was the first to react, tackling me with his hug. His arms were around me before I could dodge him. Elijah surged up from the side, making it impossible to escape the group affection. Disgusting. Messy. That was what I should have thought but was too happy to care. We all laughed at the ridiculousness of it. The scene itself—but best of all, the reason for it.

"Congratulations, man!" Grant smacked my back with hearty gusto. "Tell Abbigail we said so, too."

"And everything looks good?" Elijah's query clearly came from his soul, since he'd been through this before. "All the measurements and weights . . . the crazy stuff they check?"

"Yeah." I clapped him on the shoulder and pinned him with a meaningful stare. "Everything is just as it should be for the boy's gestational age." I smiled. "All systems go."

"Do you guys have names picked out yet?"

"No. We haven't even begun that string of arguments yet." I laughed, knowing Abbi would want some family name I would hate, and then I'd cave . . . and so it would go.

As if reading that exact thought in my mind, both men laughed as we all settled in across the sofas.

"So, let's actually talk about business, yes?" I proposed. "As in, how we're dealing with these goddamned maritime pirates. Where are we with the whole mess?"

"Dude." Grant sent over a look as if I'd just asked them to help me pick out new underwear, not a plan for dealing with the scumbags who kept taking our shipments hostage. "I've been making marinara sauce and pesto pinwheels for the past five weeks. Ask me how to chiffonade basil, and I got you covered." He sprawled his hands along the tops of his thighs. "But these modern-day Bluebeards have definitely taken a back seat to babysitting your pyromaniac sister-in-law."

"Wait . . . what?" I countered, staring at him in complete disbelief. "What did you just say?" I demanded. "Explain."

"*Chiffonade*. You take the leaves of basil, or really any leafy green veg, and then you—"

"Twombley!" I shouted to bring him back to fucking earth.

"What?" He honestly looked like he didn't know why I was redirecting him.

"Pyromaniac?" Elijah and I said in tandem.

"You knew that." He pointed at Elijah accusatorily.

"Yeah, but I didn't." I turned to Elijah. "And you did? What the fuck, Banks?"

He released a resigned sigh. "She has priors." Then attempted to dismiss the whole tangent—which wasn't one—with a similar shrug.

"What?" I whipped a shocked glare between them both. "How is this the first time I'm hearing about this?"

"Dude. Chill," Grant flung. "She's not an actual threat. It's . . . well, it's more of a mental health problem. Well, not a problem—more of an issue, really . . ."

"Stop." I stabbed a hand up like a crossing guard. "Just stop." Only he wasn't some schoolkid, and Rio Gibson wasn't just the "weird girl" he was defending. Christ, he was really defending her. And the fact that she'd been arrested on pyromania charges.

"She's just working out some stuff, okay?" Grant growled.

"Exxaaaccctttlllyy. Isn't every pyro?" Elijah muttered.

"What I'm saying is that she's not out there, like, blazing on a daily basis . . ."

"Oh, that makes everything better," I deadpanned.

"She struggles with it, damn it. She's got some demons."

"Again. Don't we all?"

"Exactly." Grant looked over, actually thinking Elijah's quip had been on the level, which hammered me with an undeniable truth. Grant Twombley had it bad for Rio Gibson. God help us all.

"It's just that the way she deals with hers can lead to a felony arrest. She needs to be in treatment, but even her husband doesn't know about the problem. No one in that perfect little family she married into does—so she's been struggling alone."

"Until you came along?" I asked.

"Something like that." He shrugged, but the gesture looked awkward on his broad, usually dominant frame. Grant Twombley didn't fucking shrug.

"So who could use a bottle of water? Or something even stiffer?"

"Jesus Christ," I muttered. "It's like herding cats around here."

"Yeah, I'm afraid I'm not going to have much more to offer." Elijah handed us both bottles of water before sitting on the arm of the sofa. "I'd like to wrap up the investigation with the keychain and then dig more into the pirate mess. I know public relations has been all over it while we've been away, so check in with them."

My friends both stood to leave.

"Congrats again, man," Elijah said one last time, and then they both left.

After the guys left, I got back to work with a vengeance. In the after-hours stillness of the building, I was able to work efficiently. I cleared my email inbox and worked on a spreadsheet of projected expenses for the Edge's construction until my eyes began to cross. When I looked at the clock on the wall, I realized it was closing in on seven o'clock, and I was more than satisfied with the day I'd put in. I texted Joel that I was ready to head home, and since I'd worked late, we should avoid a good amount of rush hour traffic. Then I sent a text to Abbigail to see if she needed anything before I headed out of downtown.

Leaving the office. Do you need

me to stop anywhere?

Nope. Dori's been great.

See you soon. Wear something blue tonight.

★ ★ ★

When I got home, I went straight to our bedroom—but my woman was nowhere to be found. The bathroom was empty too.

"Abbigail?" I called her name and then again at louder volume, but she didn't respond.

I changed out of my suit, putting on some lounge pants and a T-shirt. The whole time, I told myself nothing was wrong. Abbi had simply gone downstairs for a snack or was out back in the casita with Dori. I chuckled to myself, knowing I'd look there first. Offering Dori that eye-popping raise was the best decision I'd made in a long time. The woman was rapidly becoming Abbi's friend as much as assistant and had brought some much-needed laughter back to my girl's face.

Which was why the sound of Abbigail's tears had me stopping in place.

At first, I even dismissed it as an aberration of the wind or a strange-sounding bird. But as I came out of my walk-in closet, I heard it again. Louder now. A stab straight to my gut.

Because it was definitely weeping.

And it was absolutely coming from somewhere in this room.

Abbi's closet?

"Abbi?" I called again. Still no reply. But when I listened closer, I heard sniffles. Her sniffles. I knew that as fact—deep in my belly.

Heeding that same inner instinct, I pushed at her closet door.

Sure enough, she was inside the grand enclosure. Curled up on the floor. Crying her eyes out.

"Baby?" I managed to croak, despite the panic surging me. "What's wrong? Abbi, are you okay? Is it the baby?" I dropped to my knees in front of her and frantically scanned her from head to toe. It had been a few days since she'd thrown up, and we were both hopeful we were coming out of the worst of the hyperemesis gravidarum. "Did you throw up?" Though I could usually tell if she had with a glance at her pallor and posture. "Do you need to get to the toilet?"

"No. No, I'm fine. The baby's fine." She hiccupped and clutched my arms as I helped her stand. Her round belly looked so beautiful, naked beneath her open robe.

"So what's wrong?" Continued panic pushed it out again, making me sound like a bull with a freight train up its ass. Couldn't be helped. I was terrified, and this was my default. "Why are you crying? Abbi, please talk to me."

Christ, these fluctuating hormonal mood swings were going to be the death of me. Although she'd always been a crier, the bouts had gotten worse with the pregnancy. She clung to me like polyester clothing charged with static electricity.

"Baby." I pulled back, trying to see her face under the red curtain of her hair. I stroked the strands away from her tear-soaked cheeks. "Tell me what's going on."

I scooped her up with my arm beneath her knees, carried her out to our bed, and laid her down with her head on the pile of pillows.

"You have to tell me what you need, Red, so I can give it to you. We've been through this before." Her green eyes finally showed some response. Thank God. My dominant tone usually did the trick on jarring her, no matter what sort of funk she'd worked herself into.

She tilted her head a little higher.

And with that look, gave me exactly what I'd asked for.

I knew what she wanted now, all right.

Even through the tears, her sexual need was thick and heavy and palpable. My libido responded at once. My heartrate doubled. My cock jerked in my thin pants. A low growl worked up and then out of my throat.

I climbed onto the bed with her. I didn't waste time on tender foreplay. Right away, I straddled her hips but settled most of my weight back on my bent legs.

"What can I do for you, Abbigail?" A wide swath of creamy skin was exposed between the open halves of her robe, her round belly and lower half covered still. I ran my fingers across her chest and along her collarbones, from one shoulder to the other. Her breath caught in her throat. When she exhaled again, her crying transformed into a needy moan.

"Sssshhh, baby. We'll get there." I kept touching her. Needing the contact of my skin against hers. "But first, tell me why you were crying."

"Oh, God," she rasped. "Just . . . just touch me, Bas. More. Everywhere."

"The truth first," I said. "I don't like finding you crying when I come home, my love. Did something happen with Dori?"

"No. No, I love her," she insisted.

"Good. I'm glad." I ran my fingers across her collarbones

again, this time scratching my nails along her skin too. Abbi's eyes fluttered closed. She tossed her face against the pillows.

"So good," she mewled. "Oh, Bas. That's so . . . good . . ."

"Look at me," I dictated. As soon as she complied, I repeated, "Tell me, Red."

She swallowed hard. "I . . . I wanted to . . ." She hiccupped again.

"Ssshhh. Settle down."

"I . . . I wanted to wear something blue. Like you said."

"Okay. But that's not something to cry about. You're stunning in blue." I took a second to finger some of her long red curls, fanned like some fantasy goddess across the pillows. "Your hair looks beautiful with every shade of blue."

"I . . . I like blue too," she stammered back. "You know that. I have a lot of pretty pieces in blue. The color itself isn't the issue."

"Okay, baby. Then what?"

"I went to find something to wear for you. Something sexy and . . . and . . ."

"And what?"

"I tried on everything," she explained. "And none of it fit. Nothing fits me anymore, Bas. Nothing." Tears began welling in her eyes again.

"Oh, sweetie." I leaned forward and kissed her swollen lips. I'd always loved when she cried because her mouth plumped and became even more kissable. The same was true now—except she didn't let me continue with my adoration.

"How can you say that?" she sobbed as soon as she ripped away. "My body . . . this isn't me. I've been taken over by another creature and—"

Well, that did it. Time for another kiss, one I didn't mind

throwing some deeper demand into. It was the right call, but I already knew that. The urgency in Abbi's response grew with each touch of our mouths. She started rising up to meet me, clinging hard around my nape and skull. But I resisted the urge to simply fuck the silliness out of her. I pressed her shoulders back into the mattress, making her wait for what I gave her.

"Abbigail." I ghosted my lips across her forehead and then her eyelids, cherishing the lingering salt from her tears. "You could wear a paper sack, and it would be more beautiful than the finest designer gown. If you want new lingerie, we can buy you things that fit—or not. Silk and satin don't make you beautiful to me. They only enhance the gorgeous girl I already see. None of the jewelry or finery really matters to me, all right?"

Of course she popped her mouth open again to argue, but I started to have this drill down. I dipped in again, silencing her with a full, open-mouthed kiss. As soon as she opened for me, I stabbed my tongue in with deep demand, refusing to relent until she gripped my forearms, digging her nails into the exposed skin there.

When I released her, we were both panting. My chest was thundering. My dick was thumping so hard, I swore the thing had its own pulse point. While I was certain I'd have to repeat my speech to her post-coitus, physical needs—mine and hers—were becoming difficult to ignore.

"I need to fuck you so badly, woman. My cock needs to be inside you more than anything else right now."

She sketched out a swift nod. "Yes. Oh God, Bas. Yesss."

I stretched my body over hers. Nudged her legs apart with my knees so I could distribute my weight onto the bed and position my thighs between hers. I buried my face in her neck and kissed her smooth skin, licking and nibbling up and down the length of the slender column. Then I burrowed into that space with my nose and inhaled the delicious scent of her spicy arousal. Her chemistry had changed since she'd been carrying our son, but it spoke to me even louder now. All but shouted to me to claim her again and again until she screamed the walls down with my name on her lips.

Abbigail reached between us, and I leaned back to see what she was doing. She'd untied the belt on her robe and now fully bared her body to me.

She was breathtaking. Mesmerizing.

A fucking miracle.

I couldn't think of a better way to qualify what I gazed at, full of unblinking wonder. So many changes, all happening before my eyes. So much gratitude in my heart, threatening to stretch my own damn skin now.

I couldn't help but reach out and cover the swell of her stomach with my large hand. He was still so small. I could spread my fingers over her tummy and protect him. If I used both hands, I could shield him completely. I mentally swore I would guard him every day for the rest of my life.

Both of them.

It was time to symbolize that in one of the best ways I knew.

I pushed away from her long enough to take my pants off and toss them aside. I stroked my erection while kneeling tall over her. Abbi's fixed stare jacked my need even higher.

"Which position is most comfortable for you, Abs?"

"Your dick inside me."

She punctuated that with a cheeky grin. Instead of working up an answering expression, I leaned down and took her nipple between my teeth without any sort of warning. My nip wasn't hard, but I knew both her swells were agonizingly sensitive and the bite would be more intense than usual.

Her astonished keen was like music to my ears. Her lusty wriggles were like electric zaps to my limbs. And when she arched her back, she thrust her swollen breast against my face.

Abbigail yanked my face away from her chest by fistfuls of my hair, and I chuckled. "That smart mouth of yours gets you in trouble, Little Red."

"Mmm, God, my nipples are so sensitive," she said, reaching up to rub the one I'd bitten.

At once, I pushed her hand away. "Mine," I grunted before licking the bruised tip.

"Oh, shit. Shit. That feels so good. Oh, Bas, that's so good."

"Yeah?" She'd never been able to come from nipple stimulation, but maybe today was a new day. The sensitivity was heightened from the pregnancy, and I'd read some women became so sensitive that they could . . .

Ohhh, yeah. Challenge accepted.

I went to work on her breast while fingering between her legs. Her moaning and squirming told me she was all over my new plan too. "Feel good, Abbi?"

"Sooo good." She arched her back more, pushing her tit into my mouth.

"Can you come for me like a good girl?" I taunted.

"Yes! Don't stop, Bas. It's right there. Right there. Fuck, yes!"

She reached between her legs with desperation, but I smacked her hand away from her clit too. "Also mine," I said and sucked exceptionally hard, dragging her entire areola into my mouth. Alarmingly, a drop or two of sweet fluid hit my tongue, and my eyes popped open. Too deep in the moment and already aware of what it was thanks to my obsession with pregnancy research, I continued stimulating Abbi. I circled her clit faster with my wet fingers and sucked on her nipple. Over and over, I repeated the treatment until she cried out, scrabbling her fingers into the bedding for some sort of grounding through her climax.

"Sebastian! Oh, my God." She panted hard. "Jesus!" Her breathing was harsh, and her eyes squeezed shut as I kissed my way up her chest, neck, and then finally to her slightly parted lips.

With a twisted face, she asked, "What is that? That taste on you?"

"Future midnight snack for Junior, I do believe." I grinned wider at the alarmed look that broadcast across her face then as she shot to her feet beside the bed.

"What?" she cried. "And you didn't say anything? You didn't stop?"

"Why would I?" I couldn't help but laugh. "I told you, I want to be a part of all of this. Now come back here and get on my dick." I held up my straining cock for her to mount.

"Ride me, Little Red. Now."

Playfully, she slumped her shoulders and let her head lull back, trudging to the bed like she was headed to the gallows. "Ugh. If I have to." But she couldn't hold the act and started giggling as she crawled onto the bed and straddled me. Her pussy was so wet from her own release; it only took a swipe or two through her folds, and I sank all the way into her lush body.

"Oh, sweet mother of God." My eyes rolled back in my head. Her vise of a pussy gripped my shaft and made me see stars, even without any movement. With my hands splayed across her hips, I held her in place, planted my feet flat on the mattress, and fucked up into her. "Fuck, yes, baby. Your hot cunt feels so good on my cock."

"It's yours," Abbi promised between her husky, heavy breaths. "Every inch of me, Sebastian. I'm all yours . . ."

I scooted back toward the headboard and then bent my legs, like a mountain. "Bring your feet up here," I instructed, patting the areas next to my shoulders. "Now lean back on my thighs."

She flashed a saucy grin. "My very own hunky lounge chair."

I smirked in return. "Something like that." I paused, hissing, as I secured her feet against the headboard, ensuring she had leverage for moving up and down if she wished. "Damn," I gritted out. "Oh, fuck!" I was buried so deep inside her pussy, and it felt so blissfully good. So completely right. And sitting this way, there was no strain on her abdomen either.

We fucked that way for a few minutes before I got frustrated with not getting enough friction on my dick. Bending my legs back in a "W" allowed me to lie her down on the bed and pound my way home in the traditional missionary position. The orgasm that haunted me most of the day finally pulsed up my shaft and jetted from my tip in one epic jerk after another. Fucking hell. I felt like a little piece of me died and was reborn a better man, every time I came inside this woman.

My woman. My Abbigail.

I flopped off to her side and pulled her into my arms. "Damn, woman, I love you. Thank you for that." I settled my breathing and fought the need to sleep, wanting to just bask in her glow a little longer.

"I love you, too," she said and then interrupted herself

with a yawn. Didn't stop her from scoffing, "I can't believe you tasted that and didn't say anything."

I frowned against her neck. "Why?"

"Mmmph." She was already drifting off to sleep. "Animal."

"I want every part of you." I nuzzled into her hair. "Every part. For every day. Forever, Abbigail."

"I like the sound of that, Mr. Shark," she said dreamily.

"You got yourself a deal." I kissed her forehead and then added, almost to myself as she drifted off entirely, "Mrs. Shark."

I had never been more sure about something in my life. I needed to lock this woman down. Marry her. The sooner the better. I just needed to come up with an offer she couldn't refuse.

CHAPTER ELEVEN

ABBIGAIL

"Is that really my cousin?" With hands on either side of my stomach, Vela looked up at me in wonder.

"That's really him." I beamed as my baby boy fussed around beneath my ribs. "He's strong, isn't he?"

"Does that hurt you? Is he really kicking you right now? With his little legs? Maybe he wants to play soccer like I do!"

"Maybe." I laughed. "It doesn't really hurt, though. Sometimes it's uncomfortable if he gets in the wrong place and does it. Or if I eat something he doesn't like."

Vela thought for a moment. But just one. "He tastes the food you eat? My mom said he doesn't need to eat food while he's in your belly. I'm so confused!" She put her little hands on either side of her head like it may explode from informational overload.

I laughed again. Vela had as many funny comments as she did questions. "He doesn't eat the food, exactly. My body reacts to the food, and then he feels that, and that's what seems to make him unhappy. Is that less confusing?" I looked to Sebastian, who was thumbing through a magazine, to assist with the explanation. He just put his hands up helplessly, like he had no idea what to say either.

Dori to the rescue. "Vela, have you ever eaten too much

ice cream? Or something else that makes your belly hurt?"

The little girl nodded vigorously. "One time, I ate twenty-three chocolate chip cookies my mom baked for a work Christmas party. I couldn't help it! They were so yummy right when they came out of the oven!"

I laughed. Couldn't be helped. This beautiful little human was so animated with every story she told.

Dori was equally cute when she matched her excitement to the child's. "I know what you mean!" she exclaimed and clutched her stomach dramatically. "But then you feel really, really bad later on." She grimaced, and Vela did the same.

"Oh, it was the worst. I had the worst stomachache that night. I thought I would never eat another chocolate chip cookie for the rest of my life!" She playfully fell over to the side and rolled on the floor.

But Dori continued with her lesson. "So, if Abbi did that, the baby would really move around a lot, because Abbi's belly would already be hurting in the same way. It would make the baby unhappy."

"Oooohhh. Yeah, that makes sense. Because he has to live in there." She twisted her face up, thinking of the turmoil in an upset stomach. She came back over to where I was stretched out on the sofa. "Aunt Abbi, I don't think you should have chocolate chip cookies until my cousin comes out of your belly. I'm really sorry about that." She patted my hand and then skipped out of the room, calling over her shoulder, "I'm going to play on the computer until my mom gets here."

"Okay, Star," Bas called back, chuckling at the scene that had just played out.

"What a character," I said.

"She's absolutely precious. Do you need anything? Either

of you?" Dori asked.

"All good here," I said, rubbing my itchy stomach.

"No, thank you, Dori," Bas answered.

"Have you used the shea butter today?" She motioned to where I was still scratching.

"No, I'll do it when we go up to bed. I don't want to get up." I frowned at the thought of going all the way upstairs.

"Then I'm going to turn in. We have a big day tomorrow with the party planning. What time is Rio getting here?" Dori asked.

"After the lunch deliveries are loaded and she drives up from Inglewood. So hopefully by noon. I'm so excited. I still can't believe we landed this event. It's easily the biggest contract in Abstract Catering's history. I have a million ideas."

About a month ago, Rio caught wind of one of Hollywood's most influential power couple's annual extravaganza almost going belly up because they parted ways with their long-time trusted caterer. We discussed submitting a proposal and threw caution to the wind and went for it. The party was known throughout socialite circles as the "party to be seen at" for the movers and shakers in Los Angeles, and it had the potential to take our business to the next level if we could get our foot in the door.

"Have you been putting them in the Dropbox so Rio can review them? Remember she asked you to do that."

"Thank you. I knew my pregnant brain was forgetting something! Woman, I don't know what I would do without you."

"All right. Good night." She smiled and gave me a quick hug on her way out. One of the security guys walked her out to the pool house and made sure she was safely inside before coming back in through the slider in the kitchen.

"What time did Pia think she'd be home from this date?" I asked Sebastian.

"It's not a date," he was quick to remind me.

"It's totally a date." I grinned. "But Vela should just spend the night so Pia doesn't have to rush home."

"I told my sister she was welcome to spend the night, but she has school in the morning, and Pia wants her to sleep in her own bed."

"Dori could've gotten her off to school, I'm sure. The woman is capable of just about anything, it would seem."

"Abbi, I told her all of that. But there is no convincing Cassiopeia when she has her mind made up. Don't stress yourself over it, babe."

"Okay. Okay." I put my hand up in surrender. "Then, on to more fun things. Do you have your list ready? Are we going to end this tonight?" We hadn't come to an agreement on a name for our little boy so had come up with a less conventional way to choose.

Of course, Sebastian wasn't happy with that either. "Are you sure this is how you want to do this? Leaving our son's name to random chance?"

"It's not random chance," I defended. "If we can't agree on one together, and these are all names we love equally, then we should still be happy with any of them that are picked."

"I don't know. I'm not sure it feels right."

"What if we say we each get one veto?" I offered as a second-level solution.

"Explain."

"Well, if one person isn't completely enamored with the name that's drawn, we pick again. We each get one chance for a redraw."

"Fair enough. Let's do this," he said, standing and rubbing his hands together.

Bas went to the kitchen and got a small container for the slips of paper. We each had three and folded them the exact same way, per his instructions. We called Vela back into the room and let her have the honor of choosing the piece from the bin.

"Really? This is going to be my baby's name?" she asked, hopping from one foot to the other.

It was adorable the way she had taken to calling our son her baby, and we just stopped correcting her about a month into the habit. No matter how many times we did so, she just kept doing it. Stubborn Shark genes were not to be reckoned with. Bas just rolled his eyes every time, and I giggled harder.

Vela reached her little hand into the bowl and swirled the papers around. She pulled one out and handed it to her uncle. He unfolded it, eyes fixed on me the entire time.

"Are you ready for this?" he asked, taking a big breath in. This was really working him over. Surprisingly so.

"Yes! What does it say?" I asked, as impatient as Vela now.

His gaze shot down to the paper and then back to me. I couldn't tell if he was happy or not though, and he came striding across the room to where I was still lounging on the sofa and pulled me to my feet.

"It's Kaisan. Our son will be Kaisan Albert Shark."

"I love it." As soon as the whisper spilled from me, tears did the same out of my eyes—of course.

"So do I," he said against my lips before rolling his head and deepening the kiss. At once, my pulse sped and my blood heated—but Vela's whooping reminded us to keep the passion somewhat under control.

"I picked a great name!" She skipped around the room, still excitedly yelling, as Bas and I kept a tight embrace on each other, savoring the special moment.

We finally loosened our hold when one of the night security guards led Pia into the room. "Well, goodness!" she exclaimed, shrugging out of the cute jacket she wore over a trendy, lightweight blouse. "What did I walk in on?" She bent lower to receive an affectionate hello from her daughter.

"I picked the name for my baby!" Vela announced. "It's Kaisan! Isn't that a great name for him?"

"That's a beautiful name! Congratulations to the actual mama and papa!" Pia winked at us over her daughter's head. A few tendrils escaped the messy bun into which she'd pulled her dark waves for the evening.

"So how was your date?" I asked with an answering wink. Sebastian squeezed me a bit harder, but I didn't care. A date was a date, and I didn't understand what the big deal was. Pia deserved a little male company in her life, a man other than her brother to affirm she was beautiful, talented, and admired. Vela was nine years old now. That was more than enough time for her mother to forego physical... outlets... of any kind. I almost laughed as my brain autocorrected to the tactful version of that, but the underlying truth remained the same. It was time for a little rainstorm over Pia's dry spell—which, according to her confessions during our few personal conversations, was seriously closing in on its ten-year anniversary.

"Well, things weren't so bad." Pia laughed lightly and smiled coyly. "It was nice to get out and do something not soccer or work-related. And the movie was pretty good. Not sure I'll be looking for the sequel, but it was kind of nice to be out among the living."

Vela was still too busy dancing, and Bas too much her devoted audience, that neither of them noticed the woman giving up her mirth to a distinctly painful expression. I'd seen the look on Pia's face before and had been tempted to ask about it, especially because it happened more frequently as Kaisan's arrival drew near. But I also noticed how she always tried to hide it from Bas, so the timing had to be right. And this moment definitely wasn't one of those times.

"All right, kiddo," the woman declared, stowing her sorrow as swiftly as she'd exposed it. "Let's get out of your aunt's and uncle's hair. I'm sure they want some time alone. Use your best manners, please."

At once, Vela tamed the jumping beans in her blood long enough to pivot and face Sebastian and me. "Thank you for having me—and for letting me help pick my cousin's name. I appreciate being part of your history." She gave us both hugs and kisses and then turned to Pia, ready to leave. Her mother stood with her hand covering her mouth, tears filling her eyes. Pride radiated off her in waves so strong, I could feel them across the room. And very rightly so. She had an extraordinary child on her hands.

"Vela?" I called as the girl skipped toward the front door.

"Yes, Aunt Abbigail?"

"Come over anytime, okay? Even if your mom doesn't need a babysitter. We love having you here."

She came running back to hug me again. "Love you," she said.

"I love you too, little lady. Next time we'll make brownies, okay?"

"Deal!" She held her hand up for a high-five, and I couldn't leave her hanging. "Brownies!" she yelled as we smacked hard.

"Yay!" She gave Sebastian another quick hug, and they were off.

"Wow. I'm beginning to really see why you adore that child so much," I said to him.

He chuckled into my hair. "She's one of a kind."

"Pia is doing an amazing job with her." I winced, fighting a pang of stress in the middle of my chest. "I hope I'm as good of a mother."

Bas wrapped his arms back around me. He pulled me in and kissed me softly. "You're going to be the absolute best, baby—because you're one of a kind too." Another kiss now, with a little sweep of his tongue and nudge of his hips. "Are you ready for bed?"

I smiled and nipped at the stubble along his chin. "Is that a rhetorical question?"

"Depends on how you answer it."

"Well, do you mean bed, like let's go lie on pillows and go comatose for the night, or bed, like let's get naked and fuck until I'm crying in ecstasy?"

"Is that before or after I lick your cunt until you scream your way through your third orgasm?"

A long, low moan left me. "Ohh . . . Mr. Shark."

Bas scraped his teeth down the column of my neck . . . and then lower. "Hmmm; yes, Ms. Gibson?"

"I'm absolutely ready for bed."

★ ★ ★

The next day, Rio was propped in the overstuffed chair in my bedroom by lunchtime. We finished the light meal Dori had fixed for us—an outstanding Mexican soup recipe she promised to share—and now it was time to get down to business. The rain had finally let up outside the windows, and my little man was kicking up a storm from the warm broth I just sent his way.

I stretched back on the bed. "Oh, someone likes pozole too," I said while rubbing my growing middle. Dori grinned wider at the comment, but my sister-in-law's reaction was markedly different. Rio seemed to shrink into the safety of the corner, and she got very quiet.

I didn't push her for an explanation. She didn't owe me one. I knew what I needed to and accepted her even with all the default baggage she brought to this situation. It had to be a hard combination of feelings for her to handle, despite the brave face she put on most of the time. And though she and Sean were starting regular visits to a fertility specialist, the doctor's recommended medication wasn't covered by the insurance policy at Sean's current job. Of course, I offered to pay for the drugs, but she and my brother shut me down before the words were even finished. And while Rio and I were fifty-fifty business partners, we'd just started to see a sliver of black on the P and L statements—enough breathing room for us until another piece of equipment broke, or the van needed new tires, or any one of a hundred possible business emergencies.

Contingencies we might not have to stress about in another month if the news Rio had just laid on me was totally on the level.

"So . . . we're really going to be stepping up to the big kids' table." I sat back up and directed my twentieth gawk of the day at the event contract in my hand. A document I almost never thought I'd see. That, in many ways, I still couldn't believe I was looking at. "It's so surreal. Practically impossible to believe."

Changing the subject—necessary on a bunch of levels—worked the right magic for yanking Rio back out of her shell. "Well, believe it, sister. And enjoy it." The confident fire returned to her dark-honey gaze. "We've worked hard for this."

"I still think I owe you my left eye for it."

"No giving up eyeballs until you've signed on the dotted line." Pushing her spikey hair up off her forehead, she added, "On second thought, just keep your eyeballs to yourself. You'll need them both to race after your little Speedy Gonzales." She nodded toward Kaisan's continuing sprints across my belly. "Plus, I'm going to be an upstanding citizen here. The get on this gig wasn't all me."

I frowned. "What do you mean?"

"That I think I had some behind-the-scenes help—though our fairy godfather refuses to admit it."

"Now I really don't know what you're talking about."

"Grant."

"What about him?"

"I mean that I'm talking about him. I think he pulled some strings. Not sure who he knows or from where . . ." She trailed off for a moment that lingered a few seconds too long. "But all I can say is that the contract was messengered over within hours after I mentioned that the client mysteriously dropped Sparkle City Catering for their party. Just seems a little too coincidental."

"Interesting," I said. "Well, I'm going to go on believing it was the amazing food samples you prepared for their whole staff that closed the deal. Not to mention your amazing salesmanship."

"I agree with Abbigail." Dori made the statement as she settled onto the bed next to me and took out her trusty smart pad. "Everyone at the tasting was posting pictures of your beautiful trays as fast as they could, Rio. You made them feel special and important."

Rio whisked a semi-bashful grin at us both. "And that's how we want everyone at the party to feel, too. Right?"

"Exactly." Dori beamed and tapped in her passcode, preparing to take careful notes of our first—and only—event-planning meeting. She had quickly picked up the ins and outs of my catering business too—thank God. The woman was amazing. Bas kept joking he was going to steal her to be his own assistant at Shark Enterprises, but Craig was filling in that job more regularly since Dori was handling more responsibilities in Calabasas. So far, it was all working out great.

"Okay, so scoot your asses over. I want to sit here too." Rio laughed while nudging her way onto the bed. "We should all be looking at the same set of notes here. Because of course, the most important event of our career is also going to be a last-minute whirl." She rolled her eyes. "Aren't we the lucky ones, hmmm? Can you believe the size of the venue?"

I groaned aloud thinking of the property we toured a few days prior. The Greystone Mansion was a massive Tudor Revival in Beverly Hills, built in 1928. The clients planned on transforming the venue into a "Storybook Fantasy" for their guests and we were developing the menu accordingly.

Dori tapped a finger on the air before reciting, "'Luck is what happens when preparation meets opportunity.'"

"Ohhh." Rio dashed a glance back at me. "We need that on the bulletin board at the kitchen."

"So I think we've nailed down most of the menu, right? Except for the third dessert, because there's an issue with the macadamia nut supplier. So what's left?"

"Except everything?" I was glad to have my head resting against the headboard. The size and scope of this job was making my brain swim.

Thank God, yet again, for Dori and her capable game face. "Don't worry, ladies. We've got this. But first and foremost, we really need to start with a complete supplies and shopping list. I have to start placing orders ASAP. Since it was so close to the holidays, the prime produce and meat vendors are already getting slammed. Every caterer in town already wants plenty of the more exotic ingredients."

"Got it," Rio said.

"Definitely," I chimed at the same time.

"I kind of started, but I need a little help from you both. The recipes are vague in some parts." Dori shuffled the stack of papers and recipe cards she had in her binder marked "Biggest Party Ever" in large, gold letters. "It looks like you ladies are like my mom and cook half by recipe and half by your hearts. You need to tell me what's missing from these ingredients lists so I can be sure to place the proper orders for everything."

"Okay, let's start there," I agreed, pointing to my checklist. "After we get that done, we can start marking off the other items on this to-do list." I heaved in a long breath, despite Kaisan fighting me about the effort. "I need to feel some accomplishment today."

We ran through the recipes, dictating item after item that was missing from the written instructions. But after the tenth recipe, as well as my third bathroom break, I was exhausted.

"All right," Dori abruptly announced and closed both her binder and smart pad. "Naptime for Mommy Shark. No arguments." She wagged a finger. "If Mr. Shark thinks you are overworking, he will put the kibosh on you being involved in this event."

Rio arched a brow. "Okay, none of us wants Daddy throwing down that hammer. Besides, I need to get on the freeway before traffic gets too crazy. Sean and I both start so early in the morning. If I don't see him when he gets home at night, I don't see him at all."

"I'll walk you out," Dori said. "Sleep well, Abbigail."

They left the room quietly, and I was out before I even heard the door click closed behind them.

I woke up with the need to pee so badly, it was a wonder I made it to the bathroom. But the physical relief was swiftly replaced by inner frustration. The clock on the marble counter revealed that I'd been out for two hours. That was a hundred and twenty minutes I seriously couldn't afford. There were still so many things on the action list for the upcoming event.

In the back of my mind—or maybe not so far to the back—I hoped we hadn't taken on more than we could handle. If I were functioning with my normal full charge, the last-minute pace wouldn't seem so daunting. I'd just suck it up, do whatever it took for knocking out the list, and get shit done. But with constant exhaustion pulling me under, I wasn't sure there'd be enough hours in the days we had left. I couldn't keep depending on Rio to take up the slack either. It wasn't fair. Our business was a partnership. While she wouldn't outwardly take the credit for it, we both knew she'd landed the deal while I was fighting morning sickness.

I made my way downstairs just as Sebastian arrived home. He'd worked a little later than usual but would've just been sitting in traffic anyway, so the difference was the same.

"Hey, my sweet Little Red." With a delicious groan, he pulled me in and kissed me with sexy languor. "How was your day?" he asked tenderly. "What did you do today? I want to hear everything, but tell me in the kitchen. I'm starving."

I let him lead me across the foyer's grand expanse and then through the formal dining room, until we were in the kitchen and he was heating up a big bowl of Dori's soup. "The day was good," I said. "Rio came over, and we worked on finalizing the event menu. Dori got together a full shopping list, and we double-checked her order form. Just basic stuff like that. All boring to the business mogul man that you are."

I kissed the top of his head before taking a seat at the table with him. My stomach was still full from lunch, but I wanted to keep him company while he ate. But as I watched him, something seemed . . . off. But not with him . . .

"Oh, wait!" The recognition zapped me at once. "You need the fixings for your pozole, baby."

"Huh?" Bas mumbled around a mouthful of Dori's delicious soup.

"All the great stuff that goes on top of the broth," I explained. "That's what makes the whole thing. Hold on. I'll get it out of the fridge for you."

I scrambled up from my chair, since I was only a couple of steps from the refrigerator—but apparently I had two left feet tonight. Maybe three. At once, my ankle got caught on one of my chair's legs. I stumbled out but caught myself. Still, I felt like I'd tripped over a hairline crack.

"What the hell?" I muttered. "Clumsy elephant in the house—unless I really just learned to walk lately?"

I was just as unsure about Bas's reaction. I was already bracing for his hysterics in all their blustering glory, but this time the man merely shrugged. "It's the increased blood supply," he said offhandedly. Him and his damn pregnancy books.

"What?" I laughed, walking more carefully to the refrigerator to get the shredded cabbage, radishes, onion, and cilantro that Dori had prepared in little ramekins.

"The reason you are tripping on your own two feet," he went on. "Increased blood supply makes it so you have less feeling in your extremities. Almost like you are numb without the tingly pins and needles."

I set the tray in front of him. "It's freaking me out that those are possibly the sexiest words I've ever heard you say."

"Hmmm?" He glanced at me, openly perplexed, while piling his bowl high with the fresh veggies and herbs. "Why?"

Damn good question. I didn't know if I had a clear answer. I couldn't decide if he was sexy because of his endless quest for knowledge or because the knowledge he sought was explicitly about my changing body and our developing child. Right now, I wasn't sure the clarity even mattered. The only thing that seemed important was the message I did decide to vocalize at that moment.

"I love you, Sebastian Shark. I love you so damn much it hurts."

He dropped his spoon so suddenly, the silverware clattered against the table. He stood just as abruptly, and the look he drove into me said everything.

He didn't care about any other answer either.

With two sweeping stalks, he covered the short distance around the table and right into my personal space. I still just sat there, mooning like a schoolgirl over her first crush. Desperately hoping...

That he'd lean over, exactly as he did.

That he'd smash his mouth on mine, exactly as he did.

That he wouldn't relent either—exactly as he did.

That he'd keep pulling and sucking and kissing, until every molecule of oxygen had been stolen from the room. Until he left me dizzy and hot and swoony with desire.

All so true... until the man sat back down and started eating his dinner again.

Grinning about it.

Oh, this man.

"But you didn't overdo it today, did you?" he finally asked.

After clearing my throat, not trusting what it would sound like after what he just subjected me to, I answered, "No. I even had a nice long nap. This rainy weather and that pozole..." I motioned to the bowl in front of him. "Little man loved that stuff. He was Kung-Fu Fighting after I had a bowl."

"Good. It is delicious. Dori's spoiling us something terrible. But I have to say, Craig's been equally invaluable at the office. I think it's a better fit for him. It's funny how things fall into place, isn't it?"

"Yes, it can be."

He set down his spoon again, this time with calmer intention. "What's up?" he probed, his brows knitting. "That was a very wistful answer."

I kneaded my lips nervously. "Don't miss a thing, do you?"

"Not where you're concerned, Red. But you know that part already." He moved back around the table, sliding into the chair next to mine. "What's going on?" He slipped his hand into mine. "Everything still good with Dori?"

"Oh, God, yes. She's even teaching herself about all the Abstract stuff. I think she may be a robot or something. How can one person be that good at so many things?"

"That's still not an answer to my question."

"I know."

More working my lips together. At this rate, I was going to rub off all the flesh. Not a good thing when I was hoping for more soul-searing kisses from the man tonight.

"It's . . . well, it's Rio," I finally confessed.

"What about her?" he queried.

"Ever since we told them we were expecting, there's been this extra bit of tension with her . . ." I stroked the crease of his thumb and forefinger with the pad of mine. "I don't know if I imagine it or if it's really there."

"Yeah. You said you sensed that before." He used his free hand to push some hair off of my forehead. "Have you tried talking to her about it?"

I pushed out a soft sigh. "I don't know if now's the right time." The sound became a full moan when he leaned back, pulled one of my feet into his lap, and began rubbing in all the right places. "I mean, she's barely had a chance to even see Sean lately, with all the party prep on top of maintaining day-to-day operations . . ." Despite the nirvana of his treatment to my swollen arches and toes, I grimaced. "I'm really feeling like I'm not pulling my weight on things—and that's even before this little dude came along for the ride." As I stroked my stomach, I went on. "I keep thinking that between Dori and me, we should be able to accomplish the equivalent of one person, but it's clear Rio's still doing mostly everything. And I feel terrible."

"Okay . . . this one is easy." Sebastian paused his hand, ensuring he'd get my full attention for his assessment. "This is your guilty conscience talking, baby—but you have to let it go." His stare was dark as midnight and solid as granite. "To be clear, I'm insisting on it."

"Hmmm." I made a play for cute and coy, in hopes of filing down some of his newly sprouted ire. "You're kind of hot when you get insistent."

"And you're not changing the subject by way of my cock," he volleyed. "This is for your health and our baby's. You promised when you bid that contract that you wouldn't overwork yourself. You gave me your word, Abbigail."

"And I haven't been." I raised both hands. "I promise, Sebastian."

"All right. I'm just reminding you."

And that was that. The decree had been issued. The matter was clear. This wasn't a topic I'd be able to talk out with Sebastian. No matter what I said, he would beat the same drum of resistance. But I wasn't about to leave Rio hanging in the wind. Every word she spoke this afternoon was right. We'd worked too damn hard to achieve this success.

I was just going to have to work through this problem myself. To alleviate my own guilt and get the job done.

It was that simple.

★ ★ ★

The next couple of weeks went by in a blur. We'd seen the doctor again, and our little Kaisan was still checking out great. The baby was growing right on track, and my due date held steady. We scheduled our birthing class with a private birthing coach who would come to the house with the option of a small group class with two or three other couples in one of our homes as well. Sebastian compromised on the class concept for me, initially not wanting to do it at all.

When I explained I was feeling the need to have the comradery of other expectant mothers in the same situation around me right now, he understood a little better. Thank God for his countless pregnancy books, because apparently this nesting and need for tribal support were mentioned in several of them.

The big party night finally arrived, and I had worked more hours that week alone than I had in the past two months combined. Or at least my body felt as though I had. I knew I was pushing myself to the limit, and despite Dori's constant nagging, even she couldn't deny the amount of work that needed to get done was insurmountable unless we all pitched in. At that point, we were fully committed to making the shindig a raging success, and things needed to be done in a specific order and everything with absolute attention to detail. Abstract Catering's reputation was on the line, and we had the potential of landing so much future business from this singular event.

Swollen feet, an aching back, and a nauseated stomach all combined to make me as miserable as I had been in Twentynine Palms.

Dori paced in the ladies' room while I swiped a second coat of concealer under my eyes, trying to hide the dark circles. The cover stick, along with everything else in my makeup bag, had become a good friend these last few days—filed under the heading of "How to hide exhaustion from a man who knows every mole on your body."

"Hey, Dori?" I queried. "Can you zip this? Or at least try to." I turned my back to Dori so she could secure my maternity cocktail dress. Until I'd had to shop for this party, I didn't even know they had formalwear at maternity stores. "If this thing doesn't fit, I don't know what I'm going to do. I swear, this kid's popping out more and more every time I look in the mirror."

For the fifth time this hour alone, my assistant asked, "Are you absolutely sure you are okay? You look pale, Abbi."

I huffed and confronted her gaze via the mirror. Her expression hadn't altered much; she'd been transparent about her concern since we'd begun the day, back at six a.m. In the twelve hours since, she'd insisted I put my feet up at least once an hour, but as go time for the party neared, I'd started to ignore her.

Like right now.

As soon as she opened her mouth and drew breath to speak, I cut her off with a determined gaze and a high-set chin, both delivered via the mirror. "Dori, we're going to plow through this, damn it. Afterward, I promise I'll lie down until my due date."

She folded her arms. Clearly, she wasn't buying my front. I would've fought back with a defiant glare, if only the middle of my body didn't pick that exact moment to erupt in sharp pain. I gasped just as violently before bending forward and grabbing the counter for balance.

"Abbi, please!" Dori gripped me from behind like she'd become a human tong and I was a burning mini quiche. "Just sit down for longer than five minutes! Let us do the rest!"

The girl didn't know that this quiche was getting pissed off. "Sweetie," I gritted out. "Let. Me. Go."

"I'll take you to the kitchen," she persisted. "You can supervise from there. Everything's nearly done. The early arrival guests will be here in an hour. We can handle setting up the rest."

"No!" Though my voice remained a rasp, my glower was warrior fierce. The expression took effort. A lot of it. My elbows shook. My breaths came in fast, frantic puffs. "We're this close. I'm not bailing out now. It's just a little cramp. I need to drink more water, that's all. I'm just a little dehydrated."

"Mr. Shark will have my head on a platter if something happens to you or that child. For God's sake, you're scaring me. Pleeeaaassse." As she begged it, she moved in and squeezed my hand.

"Compromise?" I persisted. "Tell you what. I'll sit down right now, and while you braid my hair, I'll drink a whole bottle of water. Then I'll be right as rain, like my mom always used to say. You'll see."

Dori was still plainly skeptical, but she helped me over to a comfortable padded chair in the adjoining lounge area of the ladies' room. I fought the urge to just curl up in the thing and sleep like the corpse I felt, especially after Dori brought me some water and started brushing my hair. Heaven. This was damn near close to heaven. If my baby boy stopped playing darts against my abdominal wall, I'd likely change that assessment to a solid nirvana.

I'd foregone having a professional stylist do my hair and makeup, knowing I'd feel more comfortable with Dori's assistance. We'd agreed on a single French braid down the middle, just to keep it out of my way while we made sure the food was ready on the ornate gold serving trays, the DJ was ready to pump trendy tunes, and the bars were fully set. After guests had traversed the elaborate entrance the hostess was obsessed with most, they'd have a stunning event to enjoy all night.

I couldn't wait for them all to see it. Just like I couldn't wait for it all to be over.

I was still busy mental rallying myself when Rio burst through the door of the restroom.

My sister-in-law looked like a badass goddess in a black

leather midi dress. Her jet-black hair was slicked back on the sides and spiked on end on top, giving the illusion of a mohawk. Fierce ankle boots finished the look, and she was a force to be reckoned with.

"Holy. Shit." Dori and I blurted it in tandem, but barely. Rio was already pumping a fist, her jubilance like a blare of trumpets on the air.

"Partner of mine!" She whooped. "We're almost there. We rocked this shit like the fire starters we are, baby!"

Compelled by her contagious excitement, I jumped to my feet and gripped her in a heartfelt hug. Dori's whoops joined our giddy laughs, despite how she'd have to restart my braid.

"Yes, we did!" I cried out, just before tears pooled in my eyes. I leaned back to see Rio caught in the same emotional vise. "Oh, my dear hell. Ohhh, Rio. Girl, you're stunning tonight."

"Right back at you, mama." She winked. "This gown is gorgeous!"

"I can't thank you enough for all of this. You really pulled out all the stops tonight. I really do owe you so much for this. For all you've do— Unhhh!"

My groan was raw and sudden, sounding like I'd just hoisted myself to the top of a thousand-foot cliff. Which was exactly the height to which my pain just jumped. As a bigger flood of the stuff hit, I doubled over. I was pretty positive I was white-knuckling the chair arms by now, but I was past being horrified or guilty about it. Way past. All I could think about was the band of awful sensation through my middle.

"Abbi? Abs? Shit. Shit!" My sister-in-law looked around the lounge frantically before fixing her stare onto my assistant. "Dori. What the hell do we do?"

I attempted to breathe through the next brutal spike. No use. At all. "Ohhh, God," I moaned out. "Shit. This kid's mad now."

"I knew it," Dori exclaimed. "Ohhh, no! I knew this was going to happen."

I chose to ignore her. No, that wasn't right. I simply couldn't give her any attention right now because Kaisan was demanding all of it. And I gave it. Willingly. Desperately. "Okay, little man," I muttered. "Ssshhh. We're going home, okay? Settle down, big boy. It's all right."

But there was the damn joke. On me.

Deep inside, I didn't know if it would really be all right.

I rubbed my belly, trying to ease the agony, but couldn't really reach where the pain knifed me. My vagina was the apex of the torture, with the agony shooting straight up into where the baby was.

"Fuck!" I yelled. "Oh fuck. It rea . . . lly . . . hurts." Yikes. The stabs were starting to take my breath away.

"Can you get something to put her feet up on?" Dori asked Rio.

"What about the stepstool over there in the corner? Looks like a cleaning crew left it in here."

"That's fine," Dori said. "Anything. Make her comfortable. I'm calling 9-1-1."

"No!" It was my loudest shriek of the night. "Just no, no! Sebastian will lose his mind. Please, Dori. Let's just stop and think ab—" I cut in on myself with a new wince, tightening with every shallow breath I could get in. "Uhhh, okay . . . about that. Fuck! Oh, fuck, fuck! Fine, go ahead and call!" The pain was getting worse. I was getting shaky. It was way too early to go into labor.

Way. Too. Early.

What the hell had I done?

"Hello. Yes, I have a pregnant woman going into premature labor."

Dori's voice was ridiculously calm as soon as the emergency operator picked up. Actually, she'd been shockingly calm since this horror started.

"Yes, at the Greystone Mansion in Beverly Hills." She listened for another moment. "She's just over eighteen weeks. Yes, otherwise normal pregnancy." Pause. "Yes, I will call her obstetrician just as soon as we hang up." To me, she asked, "Abbigail, are you bleeding? Or did your water break?"

"I— I don't know." I gasped.

"Can you check, honey? Please."

"Lemme see." Rio pushed my thighs apart like she was going to shove stuffing up a turkey. And I let her. I just sat there, dazed and scared...

Who was I kidding? I wasn't scared. I was terrified.

And furious. With myself. For the selfish and cavalier way I'd treated my body the last few weeks. For how I'd even entertained the thought that any of it belonged to me anymore. For how I'd figured Kaisan would just be up for any adventure I subjected him to. He was half Sebastian, after all. The man who tackled every day as if it were his last on earth...

Oh, God. Please don't let this be my little boy's last day on earth.

Rio bent down in front of me to have a peek and then looked back up to Dori at once. I didn't see her expression but definitely noticed how Dori lowered her voice when speaking to the operator again.

The next volley of questions was also indiscernible to

me, though my senses were thundering with so much fear that I might not have heard an elephant stampede outside the door. Rio ducked in near me and crooned in my ear, insisting everything was going to be all right. Just when I thought her leadership about the event was going to top my list of gratitude points about the woman tonight.

"An ambulance is on the way," she told me. "Not long now, honey. Hang on."

"H-H-Hang on? To wh-wh-what?" I stammered.

"The hospital isn't far from here, so we should be to the emergency room in no time," Dori interjected. "I'm going to call Dr. Julie now, okay? How are you doing, Abbi?"

"Okay. I'm okay . . . I th-th-think." The pain started to subside, making room for overwhelming exhaustion. "Oh . . . shit. I'm so . . . tired. I just want to . . . sleep." I closed my eyes, longing to shut everything out. The trendy bright lights. The cold sterile bathroom. Having to talk. Having to think.

It wasn't my lucky night.

Another wave of cramps took hold, and I doubled over again. "Shit! Shit! Shiiit!"

"Hi, Dr. Julie. This is Dori Sanchez, Abbigail Gibson's assistant. We are heading into the ER at Cedars via ambulance. I think she is in premature labor, possibly. We are hoping you can meet us there. Please call me at 760-555-4833. Thank you."

Dori looked at me with fearful eyes. "I think I hear the sirens. I'm going to go out front and meet them, okay?"

"I'll stay with her," Rio offered.

"Thank you. I'm going to call Mr. Shark as well. He can meet us there."

She impaled me with a firm look. I couldn't recall Dori

ever appearing that strict. She definitely wasn't taking no for an answer on the matter. It was written all over her face. When I looked up to my sister-in-law, I saw a similar expression on Rio's face.

"Let her call him, honey," Rio said softly. "You and the baby will both need him . . . now more than ever."

CHAPTER TWELVE

SEBASTIAN

"Where is she?" I bellowed the moment I walked through the sliding glass doors of Cedars-Sinai's emergency department.

All heads swung in my direction as I kept stomping through. My voice bounced back at me from every gleaming surface in the place.

Elijah and Grant, who literally had my back, clamped my forearms with mutterings about being calm and levelheaded. The moment I could, I planned on shedding them like a molted skin.

Still, Grant tried again. He stepped right in front of me, blocking my path to the desk, where a doe-eyed nurse awaited my incoming detonation. "Bring your shit down about twenty. Right now, motherfucker—or they will have your ass outside while your woman and your son need you."

As much as I wanted to rip his head from his body . . . he was right. I stopped and grabbed my hair until the sharp pain grounded me. "I'm good," I seethed. "I'm fine! Get the fuck out of my way, Twombley."

He finally let go of my arms, raising his hands in surrender.

"Mr. Shark." The greeting came from Abbi's obstetrician, who'd just appeared through a set of wide double doors. "We've been expecting you. If you'll come with me, I can take you back to Miss Gibson."

The woman nodded as if we were in a restaurant and she was simply showing me to my reserved table. That shit wasn't going to fly any more than my buddies' efforts at restraint. I stopped her with an urgent hand to her elbow.

"Dr. Julie," I pleaded. "Help me out here. Nobody's told me anything—only that she was brought in via ambulance. Can you tell me what's going on?"

"We can talk in front of Abbigail, Mr. Shark," the efficient brunette answered. "She's aware of the whole situation already, and maybe it's best that we talk as a team."

I nodded. At least I thought I did. Beneath my breath, I repeated the doctor's last sentence. It was oddly calming, so I did it again—

Until she pushed the door open.

I was all but knocked off my feet when I saw Abbigail. Why did these places always reduce the person in the bed to a helpless, sickly looking stranger?

I didn't want to know that answer. I was too focused on gulping down the rising panic in my throat, the prickling fear along my neck. I clawed at myself there, but it didn't help in restoring my control. I couldn't breathe. Couldn't move air into my lungs and form words with my lips and tongue.

"Is . . . is she sleeping?" I whispered.

"Mmm. Maybe. We gave her a mild sedative." The doctor placed her hand on my arm, already predicting the questions I was about to cut free. "Something that's safe for the baby at this stage; don't worry."

"Hey, I'm awake," Abbi said quietly. "Just resting." A wan smile hitched at the edges of her lips. "Hi, Papa."

I rushed over but halted hard when I got to the side of the bed. I didn't want to hurt her, and there were wires and monitors and tubes everywhere. She even had an oxygen cannula under her nose.

"Red. Baby. What is all this?" I turned back to Dr. Sanford, impaling her with my stare. Answers. I needed answers. Five minutes ago.

"The oxygen is just to put less strain on Abbigail right now. She was significantly stressed when they brought her in. The cramping can be painful, and pain does some crazy things to all parts of the body." The woman walked up to the other side of the bed while she spoke. "So right now, mostly everything you see here is just for comfort and to get our mama feeling better. When she feels better, the little one will relax and settle down. All the drama tonight was his way of letting Abbi know he wasn't happy with the strain she was putting on her body."

Fuck.

I managed to hold the oath in, though not my stern look at Abbigail. But her eyes were closed, so she didn't get the benefit of my frustration.

But she would. Oh, how she would.

"We've already had a long talk about why Abbi won't be doing that again and what it could mean for the baby if she does." The doctor's smile was gentle. Abbi also smiled but kept her eyes closed. The little sneak knew what she was doing. More accurately, she likely knew what I was doing—and how to avoid the fallout from it. "If I were you, I'd consider this the one and only warning he was probably willing to give," Sanford went on. "Next time, he will pack his bags and move out. And we all know it's just too early for that. We want to keep him a happy tenant for now."

The woman was beyond tactful about her rebuke, perhaps because she sensed mine wouldn't be.

"Are you hearing her?" I broke in at once. My voice was three times the decibel level of Sanford's, layered with the same ratio of fury. "Abbigail? Are you seriously listening to Dr. Julie right now?"

Her gaze flew open. Her greens were gleaming with emotion, though for the first time in a long time, I couldn't decipher the exact source of it. She wasn't completely contrite, but she wasn't full of sorrow either.

Or maybe she was.

To the point it had transformed into something else, as well.

"Yes, Sebastian." Her voice was just as impossible to figure out. The tremor beneath it didn't help. Was she mad? Sad? Scared? Frustrated? Confused? All of the above? Because I sure as hell was. "I know the drill. I've already talked about all of this with the doctor before you got here."

"Gee, thanks. That's completely reassuring." I spat it out, and so many parts of my brain ordered me to take it back. But I was floundering for self-control here, and that path always took one path. Right through my temper. "So sorry I wasn't here for the full debriefing. My apologies. I was in fucking parking lot traffic on the 101 for a damn hour, thinking someone had actually listened to me and was taking it easy on herself at the party she insisted on planning. I was ready to get out and run down the side of the freeway, thinking I'd arrive just in time to hear her say I'd missed all the important shit. I was losing my goddamned mind—"

"Okay." Julie Sanford clapped a hand over my right bicep with three times the force of Twombley and Banks combined.

"Mr. Shark? Yelling at Abbigail now isn't going to change a thing, all right? We've talked, and she understands what she did that caused the cramping and the spotti—"

I sliced her short when snapping back toward Abbi. "You were bleeding?" I demanded. "No one said you were spotting! Why wasn't I told?"

"Bas!" Though the last of her rebuke was a raging hiss, her eyes shined with iridescent moisture. "If you'd calm down long enough, I could—"

"I am calm!"

"Mr. Shark!" Dr. Sanford's scold was so brutal, I wondered if we shared some distant Shark DNA. "Lower your voice. Now look at your wife's face. Look. At. Her. Is your yelling making her feel better or worse?"

"We're not married." Abbigail rasped it with even wider eyes. Her unshed tears filled every space inside those bright green orbs. Why she zeroed in on that specific fact was beyond me. Of all the things happening...

"I'm sorry, dear." The obstetrician rubbed Abbi's arm. "That was habit. I know the situation, and I misspoke." The doctor looked at me, disappointment etching her frown lines into deeper grooves around her mouth and eyes. "And look at how easy that was for me to do," she bit out, as if telling me to eat my peas or go to bed hungry.

"How... easy... what?" I finally uttered. Couldn't the woman just spit this shit out? What was I missing here?

"Can I speak to you out in the hall, please?"

I blinked some more but not in any more bafflement. Now the real panic was setting in. Holy shit. What was really going on here? I loathed the thought of leaving Abbi's side, but the insistent look on Julie's face made it clear we were going to have a little chat. In the corridor. Right now, dammit.

"Baby, we'll be right outside the door." I fumbled around her bed, looking for the nurse call button, and then jammed it into her delicate hand like a maniac. "If you need anything, just press that and someone will come. Okay? Abbi? Okay?"

"Sebastian!" Abbigail's plaintive tone pulled me up short. "Stop! Go with Dr. Julie."

"Mr. Shark?" The doctor stood at the door, nodding toward the hall beyond the heavy panel she had propped open. Once I followed her out, she led the way through an unmarked door not far away. The small room on the other side had just a round table with four upholstered chairs arranged around it, as well as a water cooler with a stack of paper cups perched on top.

"Let's sit down, shall we? My feet are killing me. Breaking in some new tennis shoes, and it hasn't been going well." She smiled halfheartedly, but at least she didn't launch right into the lecture.

And I knew I was in for one. Likely deserved it, too.

No. Fuck that!

I had every right to be pissed right now. And to make myself heard about why. "You know," I said, "I told her not to overdo it. Did Abbigail tell you that part of the story? That I had every right to be scared out of my mind about her health, after what happened during her first trimester? That I warned her that she was taking on too much with that damn party? Not just any party either. Those were the most demanding clients on the planet, and she was so insistent on being involved up to the last detail."

"I know," the doctor said, folding her hands atop the table. "And I'm sure that you did." She reached under the table and rubbed one of her ankles. "Damn. That feels good."

"A month ago, when they were planning and planning, I could tell this event was going to be too much for her to be dealing with. I asked her to get more help for the night of the party."

"Ughhh." Sanford looked down at her feet again. "Honestly, I think I'm going to have blisters."

Is she even listening to me?

"I told Abbigail not to push herself, not to endanger the baby or herself—"

"Maybe I should've gotten the next bigger size . . ."

"Dr. Sanford. Are you hearing a word I'm saying?"

She narrowed her eyes.

And I knew, in the blink of mine, that she had heard me. "You make it impossible not to, Mr. Shark."

I shuttled my head back between my shoulders. Pressed my fingertips into the tabletop. "What the hell are you—"

"You talk endlessly. About the same thing. Over and over. To be honest with you, Mr. Shark, my feet don't even hurt. I've been doing this for years. I know better than to break in new sneakers while I'm on rotation." Julie got up, strode to the water cooler, and filled a cup for herself as well me. As she shoved the Styrofoam at me, she went on. "But I pulled this ridiculous mental game to prove a point to you. Except you're so obsessed with proving yours, which of course, is how right you are and continue to be, that you couldn't even realize how obnoxious I was being until it got so far out of hand."

I let the cup of water sit there. I wasn't sure if she was actually being nice about the drink or was about to pull a Yoda and order me to stand on one foot with the thing balanced atop my head. "All right. I'm a little lost here."

"Of course you are." The doctor sat back down again and looked at me for a long moment. "This is Abbigail's first pregnancy, and you nagging her endlessly about what she should be doing and not doing—none of which is actually going to make her do it, by the way—isn't helping. How do you not see that?"

A new expression took over her face. Remarkably, I was able to identify it. I knew disapproval when I saw it. My father had always made damn sure of that—with his belt, his bottle, or the back of his hand.

"You've been so worried about being right about everything that you didn't see what was important to her. And whether you understood why that party's success was important to her or not, you missed what she needed from you. Even though it was right in front of your face, man." She took a sip of water while her words sank in. "You need to plug into your woman and her needs. Right now. Stop being so damn focused on yourself."

I huffed. Screw that. I went ahead and growled. "I have no idea what—"

"Of course you don't," she quipped and took a brisk sip of her water. "But I have news for you. A baby is coming. Your baby. And that little human is going to change your life in ways you can't even imagine."

She touched my arm. It wasn't her death grip of before, but it burned in with the same force—so deeply that I could only stare at where she'd made contact. "You, Mr. Shark, are about to not be the center of the universe anymore. For anyone in your household."

She retracted her touch. Sat back. Gave me a simple shrug, her expression full of gentle challenge. She almost seemed smug, as if she were waiting for me to hoist my jaw off the ground and say something.

"That's not—"

She tilted her head to one side, already silently calling my bullshit.

"I don't—"

She let her head flop to the other side, still calling me on my crap.

"You don't—"

She put her hand up. "Cut the crap, man. For now, please go spend time with your woman. If everything looks good after twenty-four hours, you can take her home. I'll see you in my office in three days."

Dr. Julie patted my shoulder as she walked by on her way out the door. When I looked down, I noticed, for the first time, the woman didn't even have tennis shoes on. She was wearing black leather pumps.

Fuck me.

I really did have my head up my ass.

For the next five minutes, all I did was sit there and cradle that stupid head in my hands. That five minutes stretched to ten. Then to fifteen.

Sanford's words sank in long. And deep.

To the point that they started to ache. Then hurt.

"What the hell?" I muttered. Then several more times. The laminate table wasn't much help for advice anymore. I was on my own for this deduction, and it was a lonely goddamned valley in which to be.

But an abyss only I could traverse.

How had I fucked all this up so badly? Normally, I was the man on top of the heap. The king of the hill. Top of the list.

The guy everyone else wanted to be. It had always been my nature to control whatever situation I found myself in. From childhood on, controlling everything from start to finish was the surest way to manage the outcome.

Then the universe had given me Abbigail.

And better than that . . . the promise of our baby.

But that new life had changed everything. Had sent me running toward the security of my old ways to avoid the terror I was feeling. The utter uncertainty. My control had been slipping, and I went into default mode. Buckled down and took back the reins. Despite everything Abbi had made clear, from early on, I went back to trying to control her through indirect ways.

And now, my behavior was putting her and our son's health at risk. I was driving her to defiance, to act out just to prove she could.

But now what?

I'd figured out only part of the tough stuff. Answered only one of the questions here.

I needed to give her what she needed...not what I thought she did or what my version of "best for her" was. But what was that?

I was giving all I could—but there were factors in our world that I couldn't control. A hidden maniac—no; maniacs—were still out there, ready to threaten us again. Shark Enterprises needed my leadership. The Edge was still an architectural infant.

I didn't believe Abbigail was trying to get in the way of any of that. Just the opposite. She supported my dreams. Believed in them. Wanted to be a vital part of them.

But was I doing the same for her?

How did we find the perfect balance? Other people managed this shit all the time; I was sure of it—but I had no examples to draw from in my personal life. Despite my joke about Doc Sanford and her Yoda spiel, I possessed no mentors.

Maybe I had to figure this out on my own. Come up with a new plan on my own.

That didn't involve trying to control everyone and everything.

I pulled in a long, labored breath. Surged to my feet. Sat again. Stood once more.

And battled like fuck not to drop to my ass once more.

"A new plan," I finally mumbled. "A new plan. A new plan."

And just like the mantra into which I'd made them, the words brought yet another epiphany.

A new plan meant I needed a new me.

But maybe . . . that was what I already had. What the woman in that bed across the hall had already given me.

A new version of Sebastian Shark. A guy I kind of . . .

Liked.

Maybe . . . I just had to believe it now too.

When I went back into Abbigail's room, she was sleeping soundly. I pulled a chair up to the side of her bed and lay my head on the mattress at her hip. I closed my eyes too. I had told Grant and Elijah to go on home. We had to stay at least twenty-four hours, and as long as everything went well, we'd be able to go home after that. They had drawn some blood earlier, and the preliminary lab work looked good so far. The hormone levels in Abbi's blood didn't show signs of labor, so Dr. Julie was confident the cramping wasn't actual preterm labor. My Little Red was just exhausted and dehydrated.

Nevertheless, this had been a real shot across the bow.

A wakeup call for Abbigail and me. A call to action—and to connection. Not just about the little stuff.

We had some big things to talk about now.

Just as I was drifting off, I felt her fingers sifting through my hair. I enjoyed the attention for a few minutes, being still and silent with her in that moment... knowing now that we had to make these kinds of times important. More importantly, I wasn't sure how to address the mess I'd made. Not just this immediate one. So many of them... even after I'd promised the woman I'd change. I had done no such thing. I'd just found a way to be sneakier about my control.

Unacceptable.

I had to work on this. Had to figure it all out, even if it meant going to some uncomfortable emotional places. Yeah, even worse than the ones I'd already been.

Maybe I could talk to Mr. Gibson, the patriarch of the Gibson clan. The figurehead and emotional leader of the family could lead me through the tough times and help guide me into the next phase of my life's journey with his daughter. Okay, yeah. Now that was a keeper of an idea. It all made perfect sense, and I wasn't sure why I hadn't considered the option before.

I turned my face on the mattress but still left my head lying on the thin, plastic-coated pad beside Abbigail. I pressed my lips into her palm and held her hand to my cheek afterward. She returned my stare with openly adoring eyes.

"Will you forgive me?" I whispered. "Jesus, Abbi. Will the two of you ever forgive me?"

Her brows knitted. "Oh my God, Sebastian. For what?"

"He's not even here, and I'm already fucking him up." Still a whisper. I didn't trust my voice to come out steadily. "World's worst father, and the infant hasn't even been born. Is that a thing?" Lifting my head, the water that had collected in my eyes ran down each cheek, and I quickly dashed it away with frustrated fists.

"Sebastian," she pleaded in a matching rasp. "Sebastian. Shark. Stop. Right now."

I complied, of course—but instead of saying anything else, I stood up. I began busying myself with her blankets. "How do you feel, my love? Can I get you anything? How about something to drink? They brought in some"—I looked in the cup and then took a quick sniff—"apple juice. Do you even like apple juice?" I grimaced. "Fuck! I don't even know if you like apple juice!" I threw my hands up and then raked them back through my hair.

"No, I don't like apple juice." She giggled but reached for me at the same time, an open gesture of reassurance. "I don't usually drink juice at all. Of any kind." Her features sobered. "But I'd love it if you would lie with me. Please?"

I tilted my head, letting her sleepy little smile wrap tighter around my heart. Still, I replied, "Will we both fit? That bed is pretty small."

"Can we try?" Out came her sweet little pout. Christ... Even on a mild sedative, she knew how to work me. If we were in any other circumstances than this, I'd be seriously turned on—and willing to cling to enough of my asshole side to do something about it. "Baby?" Abbigail persisted. "Please? I'd love to be in your arms right now... that is, if you aren't still angry with me..."

So screw the damn juice. I slammed the cup down to the bedside stand on my way to sweeping my whole upper body down and then cupping her face to kiss her fiercely. "Baby,"

I husked when we drew away by just inches, our breaths still mingling and our stares still locked. "I'm not angry with you." I pressed my forehead to hers, praying my thoughts would seep into her brain by osmosis. "I was never, ever angry with you."

"You're so full of shit." She giggled again but without so much conviction. "Oh, Bas. Come on. You were furious when you first got here."

"Abbi, I was scared," I confessed. "Scratch that." This was the new me. I could do this emotional exposure thing, even if it felt like having my heart carved out of my chest, valve by fucking valve. "I was terrified. And confused. And out of my mind with worry." I tucked in and took her lips with lingering adoration. "I had no idea if you were even dead or alive. They wouldn't even tell me that much."

Her lips shifted against mine, lifting into a gorgeous little grin. "Well, here I am. Very much alive. But you can do a quality assurance check if you'd like . . ."

Though she tilted higher, eyes glazed with longing and lips opening in invitation, I let her have just a brief taste before whispering, "Woman . . . I was damn near out of my mind."

"Hmmm. I can tell. You know, Mr. Shark . . . you're kind of sexy when in your scared-out-of-your-mind mode."

"Yeah?" I teethed her top lip and snarled just loud enough to make her shiver and sigh. "Well, don't get used to it."

She pushed up again, grabbing me by the collar. She still smelled like kitchen spices and expensive perfume. She was glowing and gorgeous, her aroused nipples outlined beneath the thin hospital gown. "Then give me something else to think about," she rasped. "Like your body stretched out next to mine."

"Well . . ." I smiled and stroked her cheek. "Whatever my

sweet fertility goddess wants . . ."

Surprisingly, we managed to arrange ourselves in her small bed, my large frame molded behind her small one, with all of her cords and tubes on top of the covers so the night nurse could access whatever she needed when she came in during rounds. Hopefully the staff would just go away when they saw us sleeping, but a man could dream.

For the longest time, I just ran my fingers through her hair. Every minute or so, I rubbed my face in the silky strands. Being pressed up against her sweet body was torture for my swollen dick, but this was a moment for other things. More important things. But first, the most important thing of all.

"You still all right, babe? Is it too much with me here? Do you want me to get up?"

"No." She laughed it out while securing my arm tighter around her, splaying my fingers across the miraculous swell of her middle. She pressed her soft fingers over mine. As she lightly scraped the hairs on my knuckles with her cute pink fingernails, only one thought filled my mind.

This is the best damn moment of my life.

I had no idea how any other conflux of time was going to best this. Ever. I wanted to handcuff her to me and never let her out of my sight again. Not for a single second.

I kissed the back of her head. "Try to sleep. I'm not going anywhere. Ever."

"Promise?" she asked sleepily.

"Yes. I promise with my entire heart and soul. For whatever those black things are worth."

"Don't say that." She squeezed my hand. "I love every part of you, Sebastian Albert Shark."

"Abbigail Eileen Gibson, I love every part of you, too."

One beat passed by. Another.

No. Better. Moment.

But as soon as the thought dominated my mind, another took its place. A concept that was altogether exhilarating, numbing, heart-stopping, and mind-boggling. In the middle of this damn hospital room, I felt like I stood at the lip of an airplane, ready to jump—with nothing but cardboard wings on my back.

Perhaps this really would be the best moment ever...

Unless I gave Abbi and me a new one.

Unless I rose beyond myself—and all my fears, limitations, issues, and challenges.

Unless I took a chance on something I couldn't control. Something I never thought I'd do, as long as I walked this earth.

Which was maybe why it felt so damn right.

"Hey. Woman of mine?"

"Hmmm?" Abbigail murmured.

"Will you marry me?"

Another beat of silence. Then two. As the third loomed in on us, I tried not to envision her tears from earlier, when she'd told Dr. Sanford we weren't married. Had I misinterpreted the frustration beneath them?

Give her what she needs...

But what if my name and my ring weren't what she needed? What if I was back to pulling all my old shit, attempting to control her in yet another roundabout way? But that wasn't it at all. I didn't want to control her. I wanted to set her free. To shower her in my devotion, worship her with my body, honor her for the rest of my life. I wanted to grow old with her. To fly on cardboard wings with her. But only if she wanted it too.

Only if she said—

"Wh-What?"

Not exactly that.

"You . . . uhhh . . . you don't want to?" I stammered.

"I didn't say that."

She tried to turn in my arms, but I stopped her. "No, stay there. It's okay. We're situated in here too perfectly. We can redo this all for the Instagram story again later. Right here, right now, is just for us. For our hearts. For our son and for the family we're making. Will you be my wife? And make me the proudest man and father ever? Let's do this the way it's meant to be done."

"Yes."

I could tell she was crying. I could feel her body's slight tremble, and when she lifted my hand to her lips, her sweet mouth was warm and wet with tears. "I love you so much," she rasped. "I love you more with every day that passes. With every day your son grows bigger inside my body, I feel my heart swell with the love and the joy that you bring and will bring into my life. I would be honored to be your wife, Sebastian. Yes! Yes! Yes!"

She pulled me in, cinching me tighter. And damn, did I let her—because no way in hell could anyone see the drops seeping from behind my own eyes. Her fragrant, soft hair was a perfect place to let them fall. As they mingled into her brilliant red locks, I could finally clear my throat and tell her, "As soon as you're home, I promise I'll do this the right way, my love."

Abbigail spurted with a cute laugh. "Wait. That wasn't the right way?"

"I'm going to call your father and ask him," I asserted. "Then I'm going to get down on one knee, with a ring in my hand the size of—"

"Bas," she chided. "None of that matters. I would marry you right here in this room, in this sexy hospital gown with my ass sticking out."

I growled at the mention of her ass being exposed in this damn flimsy gown, because at the moment, that perfect backside was pressed so tightly against me, if I just opened the fly on my slacks, I could be inside her, celebrating our new commitment to one another in all the right ways.

But the moment was already right.

Already perfect.

Already so complete in all the ways that mattered.

I had the love of my life in my arms. A love I never thought I'd be lucky enough to find or brave enough to deserve. A woman who was willing to accept me for everything I was and elevate me to everything I could be. A human who had shown me how to rise beyond myself . . . into the glory of her love.

Into the joy of our beautiful new life.

ALSO FROM
ANGEL PAYNE & VICTORIA BLUE

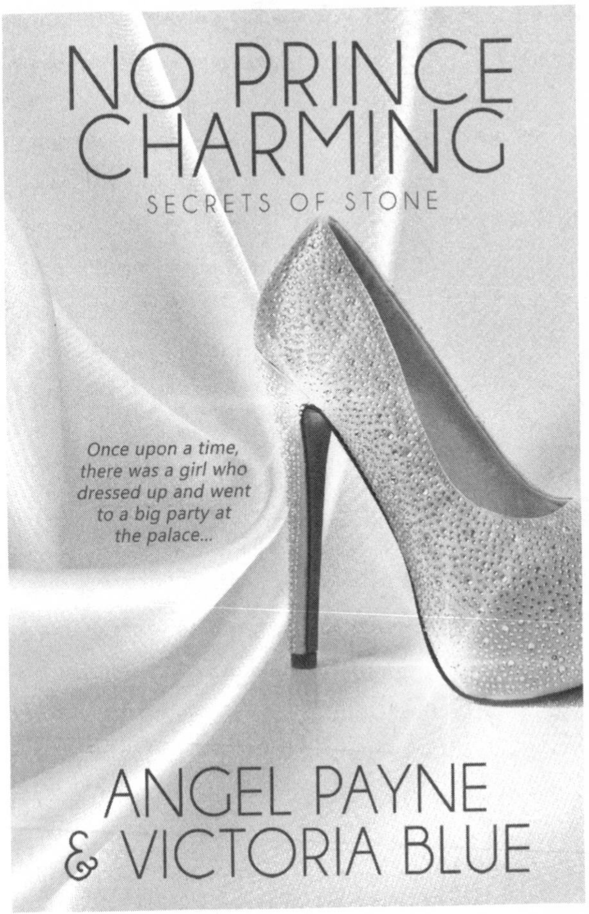

Keep reading for an excerpt!

EXCERPT FROM *NO PRINCE CHARMING*

BOOK ONE IN THE SECRETS OF STONE SERIES

Oh my God.

The words sprinted through my head, over and over, as I prodded at my lips in assurance I wasn't dreaming. Or hopping dimensions. Or remembering the last half hour in a *really* crazy way. Or had hours passed, instead? I didn't know anymore. Time was suddenly contorted.

Oh. My. God.

What the hell had just happened?

Forget my lips. My whole mouth felt like I'd just had dental work done, tingling in all the places his lips had touched moments ago—which had been everywhere.

My mind raced, trying to match the erratic beat of my heart. "Christ," I whispered. My voice shook like a damn teenager's, so I repeated myself. Because *that* helped, right?

Wrong. So wrong.

It was all because of that man. That dictatorial, demanding…

Nerve-numbing, bone-melting…

Man.

Who really knew how to deliver a kiss.

Hell. That kiss.

Okay, by this age, I'd been kissed before. I'd been *everything* before. But after what we'd just done, I'd be awake for long hours tonight. *Long* hours. Shaking with need... Shivering with fear.

I pressed the Call button for the elevator with trembling fingers. Turning back to face the door I'd just emerged from, I reconsidered pushing the buzzer next to it instead. The black lacquer panel around the button was still smudged by the angry fingerprints I'd left when arriving here not more than thirty minutes ago—answering his damn summons.

Yeah. He'd summoned me. And, like a breathless backstage groupie, I'd dropped everything and come. Why? He was my hemlock. He could be nothing else.

I was even more pissed now. At him. At me. At the thoughts that wouldn't leave me alone now, all in answer to one tormenting question.

If Killian Stone kissed like that, what could he do to the rest of my body?

No. That kind of thinking was dangerous. The tiny hairs on the back of my neck stood up as if the air conditioner just kicked on at full power.

It had been a while since I'd been with a man. At least like... that.

Okay, it had been a long while.

For the last three years, career had come before all else. After the disaster I simply called the Nick Years, Dad had fought hard to help rebuild my spirit, including the doors he'd finagled open for me. Wasting those opportunities in favor of relationships wasn't an option. My focus had paid off, leading to a coveted position at Asher and Associates PR, where I'd quickly advanced to the elite field team for Andrea Asher herself. The six of us, including Andrea and her daughter, Margaux, were called corporate America's PR dream team. We were brought in when the blemishes were too big and horrid for in-house specialists, hired on a project-by-project basis for our thoroughness and objectivity. That also meant the assignments were intense, ruthless, and very temporary.

The gig at Stone Global was exactly such a job. And things were going well. Better than well. People were cooperating. The press was moving on to new prey. The job was actually ahead of schedule, and thank God for that. Soon, I'd be back in my rightful place at the home office in San Diego and what had just happened in Killian Stone's penthouse would remain no more than a blip in my memory. A very secret blip.

I shook my head in defiance. What was wrong with having lived a little? At twenty-six, I was due for at least one heart-stopping kiss with a man who looked like dark sin, was built like a navy SEAL, and kissed like a fantasy. *Sweet God, what a fantasy.*

"You didn't do anything wrong," I muttered. "You didn't break any rules . . . technically. He consented. And you sure as *hell* consented. So you're—"

Having an argument with yourself in the middle of a hallway in the Lincoln Park 2550 building, waiting on the world's slowest damn elevator.

I leaned on the Call button again.

While *still* trying to talk myself out of pouncing on Killian's buzzer too. Or perhaps back into it. If I could concoct an excuse to ring his doorbell before the elevator arrived . . .

No. This is dangerous, remember? He's *dangerous. You know all the sordid reasons why, his* and *yours.*

Maybe I could just say I accidentally left my purse inside.

And that'll fly... how? One glance down at my oversize Michael Kors clutch had me cursing the fashion-trend gods, along with their penchant for large handbags.

I leaned against the wall, closing my eyes and hoping for a lightbulb. I was bombarded with Killian's smell instead. Armani Code. The cologne was still strong in my head, its rich bergamot and lemon mingling with the spice of his shampoo and the Scotch on his breath, like he'd scent-marked me through the intimacy of our skin...

My fingers roamed to my cheek, tracing the abrasion where he'd rubbed me with his stubble. My head fell back at the impact of the recollection.

In an instant, my mind conjured an image of him again, standing in front of me. Commanding. Looming. Hot... and hard. I felt his breath on my face again as he yanked me close. The press of his wool pants against my legs. The metallic scrape of his cufflinks on the wood of his desk as he shoved everything away to make room for our bodies. Then the wild throb of my heart as he tangled his hands in my hair, lifted my face toward his, and...

Yes.

This story continues in

No Prince Charming: ***Secrets of Stone Book One*****!**

ALSO BY
ANGEL PAYNE & VICTORIA BLUE

Shark's Edge Series:
Shark's Edge
Shark's Pride
Shark's Rise

Secrets of Stone Series:
No Prince Charming
No More Masquerade
No Perfect Princess
No Magic Moment
No Lucky Number
No Simple Sacrifice
No Broken Bond
No White Knight
No Longer Lost

ALSO BY ANGEL PAYNE

The Bolt Saga:
Bolt
Ignite
Pulse
Fuse
Surge
Light

Misadventures:
Misadventures with a Time Traveler

Honor Bound:

Saved

Cuffed

Seduced

Wild

Wet

Hot

Masked

Mastered

Conquered

Ruled

Cimarron Series:

Into His Dark

Into His Command

Into Her Fantasies

Temptation Court:

Naughty Little Gift

Pretty Perfect Toy

Bold Beautiful Love

Suited for Sin:

Sing

Sigh

Submit

Lords of Sin:

Trade Winds

Promised Touch

Redemption

A Fire in Heaven

Surrender to the Dawn

ALSO BY VICTORIA BLUE

Misadventures:
Misadventures with a Book Boyfriend
Misadventures at City Hall

For a full list of Angel's & Victoria's other titles, visit them at AngelPayne.com & VictoriaBlue.com

ACKNOWLEDGMENTS

An independent note of gratitude to Scott Saunders: Not only do you have an amazing gift for storytelling and instinctively know how to make my words better, you do it with a level of grace and professionalism that is unmatched. You've made me a better writer and a more patient responder in conversation, and I appreciate those gifts. Being able to learn new things, especially life skills at this stage in the game, is a precious treasure, and I'm grateful beyond words. —VB

And lastly, welcome into my world, Megan Ashley! Already, I don't know how I survived before you pulled your chair up next to mine. But damn, girl! I'm so glad you did! XOXO VB

—Victoria

Victoria: you are amazing, astounding, and so damn talented. I am so grateful for you and for getting to share this special journey with you. Thank you for being in my life.

Speaking of special people: the care and feeding of a writer is never an easy task—and those who dare to be there as friends for one are special creatures sent by the heavens. I am beyond grateful for the individuals who have helped me become more aware, more human, more self-forgiving, and more grateful. "Thank you" hardly seems the way to encompass my gratitude for you...Shayla Black, Rebekah Ganiere, Meredith Wild, Nelle L'Amour, Carey

Sabala, Jillian Stein, Liz Berry, Jodi Drake, and Sierra Cartwright. You goddesses mean so much to me. Your humor, light, and love are pure, spun gold.

A special shout to the crew at Requiem Anaheim: Gabriel, Kris, and team, you keep me supplied in so much love...and lattes! I am forever grateful to have found you and the special, safe place you've created for my soul. I hope to be writing in the tree with you for years!

—Angel

Our Shark world continues to grow with the support of the most remarkable team at Waterhouse Press, guiding and encouraging our efforts along the way. Thank you to those who have given their time, commitment, and individual talents to help make our story the best it can be: Meredith Wild, Jon McInerney, Robyn Lee, Haley Byrd, Keli Jo Nida, Jennifer Becker, Yvonne Ellis, Kurt Vachon, Jesse Kench, Amber Maxwell, Dana Bridges, and Scott Saunders.

We're also thankful to the Waterhouse proofing, copyediting, and formatting teams. Thank you for making the finished product sparkle!

Thank you to Martha Frantz for keeping our fan groups organized and running smoothly. To every single member of Victoria's Book Secrets and Payne Passion: Our words are for you, and because of you! Enjoy them with your whole hearts!

A special thank you to the beta readers who made sure we were on the right track: Amy Bourne and Martha Frantz. We love you two so much!

—Victoria and Angel

ABOUT ANGEL PAYNE

USA Today bestselling romance author Angel Payne loves to focus on high-heat romance starring memorable alpha men and the women who love them. She has numerous book series to her credit, including the action-packed Bolt Saga and Honor Bound series, Secrets of Stone series (with Victoria Blue), the intertwined Cimarron and Temptation Court series, the Suited for Sin series, and the Lords of Sin historicals, as well as several standalone titles.

Angel is a native Southern Californian, leading to her love of being in the outdoors, where she often reads and writes. She still lives in Southern California with her soul-mate husband and beautiful daughter, to whom she is a proud cosplay/culture con mom. Her passions also include whisky tasting, shoe shopping, and travel.

Visit her at AngelPayne.com

ABOUT VICTORIA BLUE

International bestselling author Victoria Blue lives in her own portion of the galaxy known as Southern California. There, she finds the love and life-sustaining power of one amazing sun, two unique and awe-inspiring planets, and four indifferent yet comforting moons. Life is fantastic and challenging and every day brings new adventures to be discovered. She looks forward to seeing what's next!

Visit her at VictoriaBlue.com